# A TIME TO DANCE

# A TIME TO DANCE

a novel by

# WALTER SULLIVAN

LOUISIANA STATE UNIVERSITY PRESS   Baton Rouge
and
London

1995

Copyright © 1995 by Walter Sullivan
All rights reserved
Manufactured in the United States of America
First printing
04  03  02  01  00  99  98  97  96  95    5  4  3  2  1

Designer: Amanda McDonald Key
Typeface: Sabon
Typesetter: Moran Printing
Printer and binder: Thomson–Shore, Inc.

Library of Congress Cataloging-in-Publication Data
Sullivan, Walter,  1924–
    A time to dance  :  a novel  /  by Walter Sullivan.
        p.    cm.
    ISBN 0–8071–1985–7    (alk. paper)
    I. Title.
    PS3569.U3593T56    1995
    813' .54—dc20                                                    94-37394
                                                                          CIP

The paper in this book meets the guidelines for permanence and durability of the
Committee on Production Guidelines for Book Longevity of the Council on Library
Resources. ⊚

Publication of this book has been supported by a grant from the National Endowment
for the Arts in Washington, D.C., a federal agency.

A time to weep, and a time to laugh;
a time to mourn, and a time to dance.

*Once more for Jane*

# A TIME TO DANCE

# 1

When Bunnie had her first stroke, she and Max were alone at their house in the country, and Max didn't know what to do. He had come to her room to say goodnight, and there she was, naked on the floor, her head on an upstretched arm, one leg pulled up as if she were posing for a not-very-decorous painting. At first, Max couldn't believe what he was seeing. In the old days he and Bunnie had indulged in a good deal of what Max presently considered misbehavior, but Max was almost ninety now and Bunnie was eighty-six, and there was no excuse that Max could think of for Bunnie to be lying on the floor without any clothes on. He was ready to reprimand her and may have said something; he couldn't remember. After he had spoken, if he had spoken, he saw that her eyes were closed, and though he still couldn't explain why she was where she was, he assumed that she was asleep.

Max poked her hip gently with the toe of his shoe. Nothing happened. He knelt beside her and gave her a slap on the behind, but Bunnie remained unconscious. Well, now, Max thought, well. Max was a wiry little man, limber and sound of joint for one of his maturity. He didn't mind kneeling beside Bunnie while he considered what to do, but no useful ideas came to him. It was true, he remembered, that he and Bunnie had had a few drinks before dinner. If recollection served—which in his case was anything but certain—they had had one or two after. But this was what they did every night, and though Bunnie often dozed in her chair—doubtless had done so this evening—usually she could be awakened easily enough, and always before, she had stayed awake long enough to put on her nightgown and slide between the covers.

Max was a man of broad experience. He had been a newspaper reporter, chief-of-staff to a senator, speechwriter for governors, novelist, sometime literary critic. In his best years, he had been capable of dealing with emergencies, but recently he had depended increasingly on Bunnie. When he forgot names, she furnished them. When he forgot appointments, she reminded him. When the roof leaked or a tire went flat, she was ready with suggestions. She would certainly know what to do now, but since her deep slumber was the problem, she could hardly be asked for advice. Call somebody, Max thought, but he couldn't decide whom to call. He and Bunnie had many friends in Nashville, but it was 11:30—Max didn't know where the time had gone; he wasn't aware that he and Bunnie had stayed up longer than usual—and he was reluctant to call them so late at night.

He shook Bunnie. She didn't awaken, but Max noticed that her arm felt chilly. Here was something Max could deal with. He took the comforter off the foot of her bed and spread it over her. He got a pillow, moved her arm, and put the pillow under her head. He knelt beside her again, but his knees, well preserved though they were, were beginning to weaken. Max took a chair. Sitting felt so good, he removed his shoes and was inspired to lie on Bunnie's bed and put his own head on the remaining pillow. This, Max concluded, was more like it. He crossed his hands on his breast, put one ankle over the other. All he needed was a suit of armor and a dog at his feet to look like the effigy on an ancient knight's sarcophagus. And a more generous mustache. Max kept his mustache short and neatly trimmed. He thought of his English ancestors, of dimly lit cathedrals where some of them were interred. Death again, Max thought. The nearer he got to the end of his life, the more frequently he seemed to think about dying, and this was discomfiting. Sometimes it was better to sleep than to think. Max sighed and allowed himself to drift into slumber—not to awaken until Mrs. Pakenham, who kept house for them, arrived and found Bunnie.

Of course there was hell to pay, more hell than necessary, Max thought, considering the circumstances. Mrs. Pakenham's shriek woke Max, who was astonished to find that he was lying on Bunnie's bed, surprised that he still had his clothes on. Then he heard Mrs. Pakenham's frantic voice saying, "Mrs. Howard, Mrs. Howard, are you all right? Are you awake? What happened, Mrs. Howard?" When Bunnie didn't reply, Mrs. Pakenham turned to Max what he thought was an unaccountably angry face and asked questions to which Max did not know the answers. He didn't know why Bunnie was on the floor. He couldn't say why she hadn't put on her nightgown. He didn't remember why he hadn't called an ambulance, though it seemed like a good idea now that Mrs. Pakenham mentioned it.

"I'll do that right now," Max said, but Mrs. Pakenham was already gripping the phone, punching in the numbers, talking to the dispatcher. Mrs. Pakenham suggested that they lift Bunnie onto the bed, but though they tugged at her, they weren't up to it. They tried first with Max at Bunnie's head and Mrs. Pakenham at her feet, but Max couldn't get Bunnie's shoulders off the carpet. When they switched places, Max was able to lift Bunnie's ankles, but he couldn't make her buttocks clear the floor. Max did the best he could, but his failure seemed to increase Mrs. Pakenham's outrage. She glared at Max with her pinched little face and said, "I never, Mr. Howard. I never."

To Max's mild surprise, he became the victim of considerable opprobrium. Like Mrs. Pakenham, the paramedics who came with the ambulance thought it curious that Max had not called them earlier. Tommy Harper, who had been Max's and Bunnie's doctor for fifty years, was miffed that Max hadn't got Bunnie to the hospital sooner. Susan, Bunnie's niece and closest living relative, came from Virginia and said, "I can't believe you did this, Max. I can't believe you let this happen."

"Well," Max said, "it was late, you know."

Susan said something that Max didn't catch. They were in Bunnie's hospital room and were constrained to speak softly. Bunnie was still unconscious or asleep, whichever it was. She had an IV and wore a blood-pressure cuff. Her hair needed combing and her mouth was sunken—someone had deprived her of her teeth—but it seemed to Max that she was resting comfortably. Now that nobody was telling him how badly he'd behaved, Max began to feel guilty. He told himself that he hadn't meant to go to sleep, which was true, but he knew that he shouldn't have lain down on Bunnie's bed in the first place. The longer he sat beside her now, holding her hand, brushing her hair back off her forehead, the worse he felt. If she . . . Max couldn't bring himself to think the word . . . if something happened to her, he would always wonder how things might have turned out if he had called an ambulance. He put his lips close to her ear. In a quivering voice, he told her that he loved her.

In a week, Bunnie was out of the hospital, having suffered no noticeable damage, Max thought, except to her disposition. She said that one of her legs was weak, but she could walk and talk and, insofar as Max could tell, do all the things she had been able to do before she went to the hospital. Susan returned with them to Nineveh, making it clear that she didn't trust Max to perform well in case of another emergency. Having Susan in the house stirred up memories of more than thirty years ago that Max refused to dwell on. Max knew he might be imagining it, but it seemed to him that when Bunnie wasn't present, Susan eyed him warily. Susan didn't seem to have aged. She was past fifty, but she had taken care of herself. Doubtless, she dyed her hair, keeping it the same brown it had always been, but her legs were as firm and tenderly curved as they had been on the morning that Max had made his indecent proposal.

Bunnie fussed, which was not like the old Bunnie, who had lost her temper from time to time but had not been continually furious. Surely, Max thought, Bunnie didn't know that he had let her lie on the floor all night without calling for help. Surely no one had told her about that. Still, she blamed whatever displeased her, and that was just about everything, on Max. It was true that Max turned the sound too far up on the television and sometimes forgot what he had gone for when Bunnie asked him to bring her a cup of coffee or her cigarettes or a book, but he didn't like being held responsible when the orange juice was too sour for Bunnie's taste or Mrs. Pakenham neglected to dust the mantel in the library. Though Susan brought her medicine and made her take it, Bunnie abused Max because it made her nervous.

This was hard to deal with, and Susan made things worse by insisting that Bunnie and Max move to Nashville to be closer to Bunnie's doctors. "It's not like you're leaving Nineveh," she said, but in Max's view, that was exactly what they were doing. "You can come back on weekends," Susan said. "Anytime you want to, you can spend the day here." Max tried to tell her that he and Bunnie could stay at Nineveh and go to Nashville when Bunnie had an appointment with her doctor, but his failure to call the ambulance had cost him his credibility. Susan found an apartment, packed Bunnie's clothes, discontinued the newspaper. Movers came and loaded enough furniture to fill the apartment. Susan put Bunnie in her car and set out. Max had no option but to follow.

It wasn't as bad, Max had to admit, as it might have been. Though the apartment had three bedrooms, it was small, about half the size of the downstairs at Nineveh. There was no wet bar, but the kitchen was close to the living room where Bunnie and Max spent most of their time, and there were visitors. Almost every afternoon friends called: old friends, new friends, people who went as far back as Max's days on the newspaper, students Bunnie had taught before she retired, younger men and women with political and literary aspirations. It was nice, Max thought, to have so many people to drink with. Nice, he thought too, not to have to walk upstairs to his bedroom. There was a pool where Max could swim, there were walks on which the recuperating Bunnie could get her exercise. Mrs. Pakenham came from Nineveh to keep the apartment in order.

Susan went back to Virginia, and Julien came to live with Max and Bunnie. Julien was Susan's son who had gone to France after he graduated from college and stayed longer than he should have. He had changed the way he spelled his name while he was living in Paris. Bunnie had always been fond of Julien. She had sent him money during what Max inappropriately referred to as "Julien's exile." Now that he had come to his senses and come home, she was paying his tuition to business school at Vanderbilt. He was tall with the same brown hair and deep blue eyes as his mother. Max was glad to have him. He wasn't home much, but when he was, Max enjoyed his company. When Bunnie had her second stroke, Max was particularly grateful for Julien.

Once more, Max found Bunnie in her bedroom, this time wearing a robe, thank God. After Bunnie's first stroke, both Mrs. Pakenham and Susan had hinted that they thought Max had done too little to cover Bunnie's nakedness—another injustice, Max believed, since, as much as Bunnie outweighed him, he could hardly have dressed her. It seemed to Max—a passing thought at this time of urgency—that Bunnie had gained weight since they had come from Nineveh. Once more she had fallen on her side. Her robe looked like a red tent where it had settled over her expansive hip. No time to dwell on this. Max knew that he had to call somebody immediately. All he had to do was remember who.

Here was where Julien came in handy. Just as Max began to rack his brain and to curse his mutinous memory, Julien arrived, made the call, dealt with the paramedics, drove Max to the hospital. Julien talked to the emergency room staff, gave the secretary the information she needed about Bunnie, spoke briefly with Tommy Harper as Tommy passed through the lounge on his way to the treatment rooms. Max sat in a corner in a chair that was too big for him and felt not so much helpless as detached. He wondered if he too had had a stroke. He saw Julien and Tommy coming toward him. He recognized them, knew their names, but when Tommy greeted him, he didn't respond. Tommy spoke of Bunnie in a gloomy voice. Max caught Tommy's tone, and his fear increased, but the words Tommy spoke passed through Max's brain. He couldn't decipher them.

The next day, Bunnie was in a room, still in a coma, but still alive. Max's mind began to work again: he could comprehend the words that were spoken to him; he could speak. He held Bunnie's hand. He kissed her cheek. "Talk to her," Tommy Harper said. "She may be able to hear you, Max. Encourage her." Encourage her? Max wondered. To get well, he supposed. He told her that he loved her. He called her endearing names. Longing himself for the peaceful days of the past, he promised her that when she left the hospital, he would take her back to Nineveh.

Bunnie got better. Two days after her stroke, she opened her eyes. The next day she said a word or two. The day after that, she was able to sit in a chair and look out the window. Good, Max thought. Wonderful. Thank God, he wasn't going to lose her. For a few minutes, he was elated. Then Bunnie spoke and drew Max into her own world of confusion. "Maxie," Bunnie said, her words as clear and neatly articulated as they had always been, "can you see the park?"

Sure enough, Max could. It lay below Bunnie's window complete with flower beds, a small pond, a pavilion.

"Isn't it nice?" Bunnie said. "For the people, I mean. In case they forget their watches."

"Well," Max replied, not understanding this at all, "well." He searched the landscape. Was there a sundial? All Max saw were benches and people and a couple of ducks on the placid water. Maybe he was missing something. He didn't want to answer too quickly and feel stupid afterward.

"Maxie," Bunnie said, "where are you looking?"

"At the park," Max replied. "You said the park."

"You don't see it, do you?"

There was a note of condescension in Bunnie's voice that Max didn't like. "See what?" he demanded. "I see the park. What else am I supposed to see?"

Bunnie sighed as if her patience were being tested. "The clock, Max. How else could people tell the time when they've forgotten their watches?"

Max looked. He searched the park from end to end. He started to take off his glasses and clean them, but remembered that the earpieces were too short. He had to clamp them onto his head just right to make them stay there. He examined the park again. There was no clock. He needed to get Bunnie straight about this, but when he started to speak, Julien interrupted.

"It's all right, Max," Julien said. When Julien's classes were over, he visited Bunnie, then drove Max back to the apartment. "Bunnie sees what she sees, don't you, Bunnie?"

"Damn it," Max said, his thin voice rising, "if it's there, why can't I see it?"

"Hah," Bunnie said, "Julien's just acting smart. It's there all right. A big white clock with black numbers. But don't worry, Maxie. Julien can't see it either."

In a way, Max was relieved. If Julien didn't see the clock, then surely it wasn't there, but Julien didn't say whether he saw the clock or not. He patted Bunnie's hand and gave her a conspiratorial smile as if he and Bunnie knew things of which Max was ignorant.

"Listen," Max said, "if there's a clock out there, why in the hell can't we see it?"

"It's all right, Max," Julien said again, which was no explanation.

Max was uncertain. Probably Julien was humoring Bunnie, but Max couldn't be sure. He was tempted to ask Bunnie what time the clock said, but if she gave the right time, his confusion would be compounded. Maybe he and Bunnie really were one flesh, Max thought. Maybe this was more than just a saying. Maybe if two people lived together long enough, loved each other and endured each other for almost sixty years, they did become connected in a mysterious way, so that what happened to one somehow happened to the other. Max didn't fully believe this. He knew that it was Bunnie who had had the stroke, not he. He knew that Bunnie was Bunnie and he was Max, but his confusion seemed to answer hers as if out of a sympathy bred through all their years together.

It seemed to Max that the hospital made Julien restless. Before Bunnie's stroke, Julien had served the dinner Mrs. Pakenham cooked, loaded the dishwasher afterward, and spent the rest of the night in his room studying. At the hospital, Julien didn't appear to be able to concentrate. Of course, he looked up from his book when Bunnie said something about the clock in the park or called Julien Henry, which was his father's name, but increasingly, Julien spent less time in Bunnie's room and more time at the nurses' station. Concerned as he was about Bunnie and mystified as he was by some of the things she said, Max didn't immediately perceive that Julien had fallen for one of the nurses. Apparently, Julien had an eye for women. If Max remembered properly, while Julien lingered in Paris, he had lived with a French woman. An older woman, Max believed, but that didn't mean much to him. Except for Bunnie and a few of their ancient friends, to Max all women were young and fresh and beautiful, though some were more beautiful than others.

It took Max a day or two to decide which nurse Julien had fallen for. There was a slender little brunette with pouty lips and high cheekbones who struck Max's fancy, but she worked the morning shift, so she couldn't be the one Julien was after. Max also liked a redhead. He liked her strong, freckled arms and her solid, round hips that stretched the cloth of her uniform. She was tall, too big for Max, of course, but not for Julien. She wasn't the one, either. If Julien were in the room when she entered, Julien spoke to her pleasantly enough, but then looked back at whatever book he was holding.

The nurse Julien liked—you could see it in his eyes, deduce it from the way he followed her out of the room and walked with her to wherever she was going—struck Max as unexceptional. She was average height, average weight, average everything, Max thought, though her eyes were a shade of deep green that he didn't recall having seen before. She would look better, Max decided, if she tried harder. If she wore any makeup, Max couldn't detect it. Her not-quite-blond hair seemed always on the verge of coming loose from its bun and falling around her shoulders. But she moved well, Max had to give her that. She would have been a knockout in the days of hoopskirts when women were supposed to glide across the floor as if by magic. Maybe, Max thought, this gracefulness that made her ordinary body seem mysterious was what had attracted Julien.

She was good at her job, too, for which Max was thankful. Once she talked to Bunnie about the clock in the park with such conviction that Max took another look out the window to see if he had somehow missed it. One day when Bunnie claimed to have been to a party the previous evening, the nurse asked whom she had danced with and what she'd had to eat and drink. There was always something, and Shannon Marsh—Max finally got in the right position to read her nametag through his canted glasses—could handle whatever came up. When Bunnie convinced Max that she had been put in the wrong room and that she needed to move before the proper occupant arrived, Shannon came to the rescue.

In the middle of a calm afternoon, on a day when all of Bunnie's previous conversation had been rational, Bunnie said, "Maxie, this is very embarrassing. I'm in the wrong room. We have to get out of here before somebody finds us."

Max looked around for Julien. He was gone, out chasing Shannon no doubt. Could Bunnie be right? She had been in this room for more than a week, but Max knew that things could get mixed up in hospitals. He remembered cases when surgery was performed on the wrong people. Babies had been sent home with the wrong parents. As illogical as it seemed, maybe Bunnie was supposed to go home today. Maybe Tommy Harper had said so when he made his morning rounds and Max, sitting across the room from where he was examining Bunnie, had failed to hear him. On the other hand, much that Bunnie said didn't bear on reality.

"Are you sure?" Max asked.

"Of course I'm sure," Bunnie said. "Why would I make up something like that? All the nurses have mentioned it."

"Did Tommy—"

"Max," Bunnie said, her voice rising, "there's not much time, you know. I've let us stay here as long as we could so I could enjoy the view, but we have to leave now."

"Where?"

"Another room, I suppose," Bunnie said. "Or home. We could always go there. We wouldn't even have to ask the nurses."

Max needed Julien. He started to go in search of him but the urgency in Bunnie's voice stopped him.

"Look at the bed, Max. We can't leave it that way."

The bed didn't look so bad to Max. After Shannon had got Bunnie out of it and into her chair, Shannon had straightened the covers, but you could tell Bunnie had been lying in it. The sheets and the pillowcase were wrinkled. The spread was folded at the foot.

"Make up the bed, Max. When the new person comes, it'll be better if she doesn't know I've been lying there."

"Wait a minute," Max said, "wait a minute."

"We don't have a minute. Make up the bed, Max."

Bed making was not Max's forte. His own bed was made by Mrs. Pakenham. On the days she didn't come, his bed didn't get made, which in Max's view didn't make sleeping in it any less comfortable. "Let's call the nurse," Max said. "Maybe she'll want to change the sheets."

"I've already told you there's no time for that," Bunnie said. "Hurry now. I don't want to be embarrassed."

Damn, Max thought, this was harder than he had expected. When he smoothed the sheet in one place, it wrinkled in another. He walked around the bed, trying to get the bottom sheet tight, but there was a trick to this business that he hadn't fathomed. It occurred to him that if he could get the top sheet straight, it would hide the wrinkles on the bottom sheet. Before he could do this, he would have to remove the spread—it was a coarse-weave blanket really, but Max wasn't concerned with fine distinctions. The blanket was tucked under the mattress. Max tugged at it and tugged again. Finally it came loose, and the top sheet came loose with it. Max gathered the blanket in his arms, a great ball of cloth that drooped toward the floor, one corner dragging. What now? Max thought. He looked around to see where he might put the blanket. Discovering that Shannon was in the room, he handed it to her.

"Mr. Howard," Shannon said. "Max. What are you doing?"

There was no tone of accusation in Shannon's voice. Her lips turned up in a tight smile that was almost a smirk, though Max could detect no malice in it. Still, Max was mortified to have been caught with a blanket in his arms. He was mad at Bunnie for having put him in that position and mad at the hospital if it were true that Bunnie had to vacate this room and go to another. "I was making up the bed," Max replied with what he hoped was dignity. "Bunnie says we're moving."

"Moving?" Shannon said. "I don't think you're going to have to move today. What is this, Bunnie?"

"Well," Bunnie said, "it's all a mistake, you see. I'm supposed to be in another room. The person who ought to be here is going to arrive any minute."

"Oh, dear," Shannon said, "that is a problem."

Wait a minute, Max thought. Wait a minute, he started to say, but neither woman was paying any attention to him.

"Yes," Bunnie said. "I thought if we could make up the bed, Max could make it up, that is, the new patient wouldn't know I'd been here."

"I don't think that's going to work," Shannon said. She glanced at the bed where the blanket she had taken from Max lay in an untidy pile on top of the loose and wrinkled sheets.

"No," Bunnie said, "Max was the only boy in a family of girls. They never taught him about housework."

This was too much. "Listen," Max said, his voice climbing to a higher pitch, "don't bring my family into this. When I was a boy, no men did housework."

"Yes," Bunnie said, "and he's too old to learn even if he wanted to."

"I *don't* want to learn!" Max said, his anger rising.

"I'll tell you what," Shannon said, "let's see if we can work a swap. We'll take the new patient to the room you were supposed to be in and pretend that was where she was supposed to be all along. Then you can stay here. How about that, Bunnie?"

"Will it work?" Bunnie asked.

"Of course it will," Shannon replied. "I'm the nurse. They'll have to believe what I tell them."

Shannon remade the bed, tucked in the sheets Max had pulled loose, fixed the blanket. Max watched the fluid motions of her arms, the perfect articulation of her limbs as they seemed to flow from one side of the bed to the other. She was beautiful to watch. He could see why Julien was attracted to her. Max's anger began to subside, though he remained disgusted with himself for having believed Bunnie. How could he have allowed her to make such a fool of him? How could he have made such a fool of himself? I'm too old for this, Max thought. He and Bunnie were both too old. The accumulation of years brought confusion enough. They hadn't needed Bunnie's stroke to compound it. He wished Bunnie were well. He prayed that she would get well soon. He thought of how Bunnie had looked when they had lived in Washington, how beautiful she had been, how much he had loved her. He started to remind Bunnie of those days, but he could get no words past the tightness of his throat. Max blinked and leaned back in his chair. He looked at Bunnie. Bunnie looked at him. Max felt at peace in the silence.

# II

It seemed to Max that he spent half his time asking himself where he was and what was going on and what the people around him were talking about. When he woke up in the morning, he was never sure of his location. Was he in the house at Nineveh? The apartment in Nashville? Sometimes he believed for a moment or two that he was back in Washington, working for the senator, and once he thought he was in Alaska, though he had never been to Alaska, and beyond his window flowers bloomed and birds sang. Recently, he had begun to wonder if he were still alive. He knew that he was not in hell or heaven: the bed was too comfortable for hell and the aches and pains of old age were too sharp for heaven. But why not purgatory? Couldn't purgatory be a place where you were forced to lie in bed for the next decade or century or ten thousand years, remembering the bad things you did and the good things you failed to do until your soul was cleansed? Well, it could be, so far as Max knew, but almost as soon as the thought of death came to him, he was certain that he was still alive and there was another day before him.

Now that Bunnie was in the hospital and he went to see her every morning and afternoon, he was able to get himself oriented more quickly than usual. He had decided a while back that the best thing to do in the morning was to get up. If he tried to wait until he was sure where he was, his mind would start flopping around as it did when he awakened in the middle of the night, going from one subject to another, jumbling the past and the present, until there was nothing but a confusion of images in his brain. On good days, once he got himself upright and was sitting on the side of the bed, he would begin to recognize the furniture or the color of the walls or the height of the ceilings. Finding his way to the bathroom helped, and by the time he got to the kitchen he would be sure enough of where he was to turn his attention to what he had done yesterday and what he would likely do today. For Max, this kind of remembering took the form of a dialogue. He asked questions, and Bunnie, when she was there, answered, and at least temporarily some of the gaps in his memory were filled. It was all a damned nuisance, but the pain of it began to ease around the middle of the morning when he had his first drink.

Now, shortly after he awakened, he would think of something he wanted to ask Bunnie; then he would remember that she was in the hospital, and since the hospital was in Nashville, he would know where he was. He would go to visit her, but when? With whom? It was best to begin with the fundamentals. What time was it? What day was it? He knew the year, all right. He knew how old he was: as he liked to tell people, he had been "born with the century." It was March, he thought, and having achieved a sitting position, he found his watch and saw that the time was 6:00—A.M., surely. It was Saturday, the eighteenth. The routine of his days had been so similar recently that he was able to perform the next feat of recollection. He would go to the hospital twice, both times with Julien since on Saturday Julien had no classes. But there was something else, too—Max felt it at the edge of his memory—something that did not fit with what he already remembered.

He showered, shaved, dressed; went to the kitchen and made coffee, cooked bacon and eggs, the first not left in the frying pan long enough, the second slightly scorched, but both palatable to Max, who had a good appetite.

"Bunnie," he said. He was going to ask her to jog his memory, and then what he was trying to remember came to him. Bunnie couldn't be in the hospital, because last night they had had dinner with the Carlyles. Some of the details were vague in his mind. Had he been drunk? This seemed probable, since he and Bunnie and Simmons and Vera Carlyle drank a lot anyway and were likely to drink more when they were together, but the vagueness Max encountered came at the beginning, not at the end of the evening. He was almost sure that he had been in Bunnie's hospital room when she told him about their dinner engagement. What happened then? Julien had been coming and going. Had the nurse been in the room? Bunnie had said she needed to go home and get ready, and this was the part that totally escaped him. His mind leaped from the hospital to the drive out to the Carlyles' farm, though why Simmons insisted on living in the country was a mystery to Max. It was foolishness that Simmons thought he couldn't paint in the city.

But they had gone; Max was sure of that. He and Bunnie had bounced along the country roads in his worn-out '39 Ford, which he could not replace because with the war just over you had to bribe the dealer to get a new car. Always, when they took the last curve before the Simmons' driveway, the Ford slid into ruts and bottomed out, threatening muffler and oil pan and gas tank. It had done so last night. As always, Max had God-damned the county road commissioner and Simmons and Simmons' friends for consenting to come out here to see him, and tonight there were a good many who had consented. He and Bunnie had not, Max recollected, been responding to a simple invitation to dinner. This was a big party in honor of Edith and John Ross, who were down from New York. The Rosses were old and dear friends of Max and Bunnie. They were both writers, John a novelist and a good one, and Edith a poet who was said to be good, too. Max couldn't tell much about modern poetry.

He could, however, tell charm and beauty when he saw them, and that other quality that he had never been able to name—to call it sex appeal was to make it less powerful than it was. Edith was small like Bunnie; small like Max; for that matter, small like John. They were all well suited to each other and to the fulfillment of what they all thought about a good deal of the time. And . . . oh, my God! the remembering Max said to himself when the big event of the night came to him. How many drinks had he had? How many had Edith had? In his case, not so many, because when he had kissed Edith pretty much in the way you were supposed to kiss the wives of your friends, he had decided that he was going to try to make love to her that night, take her away from the crowd to a convenient and he hoped private place, and he wanted to be at his best, if he should succeed. He propositioned her when they were standing at the bar. Earlier in the evening he had patted her behind and later rubbed his thigh against hers. Now they faced each other. His hand was on her hip once more. He wanted to kiss her, but there were people all around them. He looked at her face—how did she make her skin so white?—and at her dark wide eyes that regarded him without blinking. There was a mist of perspiration at her hairline. Her lips were slightly parted.

Max had made love to Edith before, and the memory of that event, brought to consummation ten years ago in a locked bedroom of the house in Nineveh, enflamed Max's passion. She was forty now. Would she be as willing? As eager? He leaned closer to her and whispered,

"We've got to get out of here."

"There's nowhere to go," she said, her tone as soft as his and strained, uneven.

"We'll find a place," Max said.

"Where?"

"Simmons' studio."

"All right," she replied. "You go ahead. We can't walk out together."

Max made an agonizingly slow progress across the room, waiting for people to move out of his path, escaping from those who wanted to engage him in conversation. In the shadowy studio, where a little light from outside penetrated the undraped windows, he had to wait for Edith. Then she was there, in his arms, trembling, clinging to him.

"Oh, my God," she said. "My God, Max, there's not even a lock on the door."

He kissed her, got his hand under her skirt, felt the top of her stocking, her bare thigh. Then came the pleasure of a great surprise: she was wearing no panties.

"They're in my purse," she said. "I didn't want to risk leaving them here."

She was lunging against him and quivering when he touched her. "Hurry," she said. "For Christ's sake, hurry, Max."

He wanted to, but he didn't want to let go of her. He backed her slowly across the floor until they were stopped by a table. He was trying to guide her to a daybed on the other side of Simmons' easel.

"Hurry," Edith said again, an edge of impatience in her voice. "Put it on. What the hell are you waiting for?"

"What?"

"Your condom. Put it on."

"We don't need that," Max said.

"You don't, you mean. Put it on!"

"Be reasonable," Max said. He almost told her that at her age she didn't need to worry anymore, but he had sense enough to stop himself. "I never thought we'd need one. I don't have one."

She turned quickly out of his arms, a stumbling motion that made her grope at the table for balance and knock something clattering to the floor. In the dimness, he did not see her hand move. There was a sharp smacking sound close to his left ear, then the burning of his cheek where she had slapped him.

"You bastard!" she said. "You son of a bitch!"

He tried to take her back in his arms. She slapped him again, ran around the table and out the door while he peered stupidly after her, his fists clenched, his fly still open.

He touched his cheek, and his hand came away sticky. Was he bleeding? There was something dark on his fingers, of what color he could not tell, but it seemed too thick for blood. He scrubbed his still-tingling cheek with his handkerchief, straightened his clothes, and went back toward the noise of the party, the crowd around the bar.

Now, in the light of morning, in the kitchen of his apartment in Nashville, it came to him: paint. A streak of deep, sick-looking yellow—Max had always thought Simmons' colors were hideous—that he hadn't been able to wipe off. He hadn't known at once why his friends smiled when they saw him, but Bunnie had not smiled. When she was angry, her brown eyes seemed to darken, her features grew heavier. Even so, Max thought she was still very pretty, and his passion unrelieved, he began to think of how he might make up with her on the way home. She turned away, and he followed her to the corner of the room.

"You'd better go fix your face," she said, her voice tight and thin. "Edith had paint on her hand when she slapped you."

Later, when they were in the car, she called him a bastard and a son of a bitch, just as Edith had.

My God, he thought now, had he got all the paint off? He left his soggy bacon and brown-tinged eggs and went shuffling down the hall to his bathroom. He put his face close to the mirror and felt what he would have called in one of his own novels a riot of emotions. The face he saw was not the face he had expected. He was old, old. His hair was thin and white, the skin on his neck sagged, the flesh around his eyes was wrinkled. He had lost his grip on time. He reached for and found his familiar landmark. He was eighty-nine; he had been born with the century; what he had been remembering had happened over forty years ago. But where was Bunnie now? Had he imagined that she was in the hospital? Had the idea that they were going to the Carlyles' for dinner been a trick of his own mind?

It occurred to him that he should go and look. Investigate. He had been a reporter sixty years ago. He had known then how to get at the facts. He went to Bunnie's room and found no Bunnie. He went to Julien's room and shouted, "Julien! Julien! Get up! Get up!"

Julien's body jerked under the cover, and he rose quickly to a sitting position. His eyes snapped open.

"Wake up!" Max said. "Bunnie's in the hospital."

"God almighty, Max, I know that. It's 6:45 in the morning."

"We've got to go see her."

"Oh, my God!" Julien replied and fell back into bed.

Now that he had reestablished firmly in his mind that Bunnie was indeed in the hospital, Max was sure of his course of action, and he did not consider the time. "All right," he said. "I'll call a taxi. If I have to, I'll drive myself."

"Oh, no," Julien said. "Oh, no." He got out of bed and took hold of Max's arm. "Let's go to the kitchen, Max. Have you had breakfast?"

Max searched his mind, but he couldn't be certain. Vaguely he recollected standing at the stove with the burners on full blast and the bacon frying. "I must have," he said. "I cooked it. I remember that."

But most of the breakfast remained on the kitchen table, the excess grease coagulating, milk forming a thin film on the coffee.

"You see," Julien said, "you haven't even eaten. We'll leave for the hospital in a couple of hours. I'm going back to bed."

Once he had finished the cold coffee and another cup that was warmer, Max mixed himself a scotch and sat down in the living room to go over the morning and try to get it straight. The booze helped him to find his bearings, or at least on this morning it did not prevent his thinking logically. Bunnie was sick, and her mind now worked even worse than his did. But he was so much accustomed to depending on her to tell him what he could not remember, he had believed her when she said they were going to the Carlyles'. So it was all right. They had both simply been confused. But then it came to him that Bunnie might have been recalling what he had been recalling, and the guilt he had felt earlier in the morning returned.

That long-ago night, after her outburst of anger, Bunnie had cried. Max, his cheek still streaked with yellow paint, his terrible desire unappeased, his head beginning to ache, had lacked sufficient energy either to arouse himself to self-defense or to apologize. Let her cry, he said to himself, but the sound of her sniffling was as annoying to him as the pings and rattles of his old car. He started to turn on his radio, then remembered it was broken. He thought he might whistle but decided not to risk it. Finally, Bunnie blew her nose and said, "You didn't have to do that, Max. You could have had the decency to wait and take her to a motel tomorrow."

For an instant, the catch in her voice rendered him silent.

"Maybe everybody knows you're hot for her. Probably everybody knows you've been to bed with her before. But God damn it," Bunnie said, "you didn't have to rub my nose in it."

She was right. Max knew that. If she had said, you have no right to sleep with her, you have no right to treat me this way, then he could have replied, Why not? You've screwed John more recently and more often than I've been with Edith. It was just as well. His headache was worse, and he didn't want to argue.

"Okay," he said. "I shouldn't have. I don't know. Maybe it's the life we lead, the friends we have. Maybe we've fallen in with the wrong people."

"Maybe it's us," Bunnie said. She started to cry again, and they rode the rest of the way home without speaking.

For the second time that day, Max thought of purgatory. Thirty-five years ago, when Bunnie had left him and was living in Rome, he had returned to the faith of his childhood. He didn't know why—or rather he did know but didn't like to think about it. He had made such an indecent proposition to Bunnie's niece Susan that Bunnie had gone to Italy to decide whether she could forgive him. For a while, Max had not been certain that he wanted to be forgiven. Belatedly, he had discovered that he had desired children, and it was too late for Bunnie to have them. Max was considering divorce, but with Bunnie away, his life deteriorated. He stopped trying to write. He drank more than usual. He pursued the wives of his friends. Finally he did—or almost did—something that seemed to him so bad, he needed help in finding a way to live with it. He had gone to confession, he had gone to mass, and he had gone to Italy to be reconciled with Bunnie.

He had seen Edith Ross grow old. The time came when he could no longer discern the clean, tightly articulated limbs beneath the broadening hips, the bulging stomach. When Edith died, he mourned her as a friend, and so it had been with other women he had made love to. He had got to the place where he could no longer rehearse in his mind the pleasures he had once enjoyed—until now, when Bunnie's damaged brain brought back those times for both of them. Or did she remember? He was back to the question he had asked earlier. Had she, like Max, relived that night at the Carlyles', or had she forgotten it as soon as Max left and gone back to watching the phantom clock beyond her window? He had to know. It wouldn't be right for her to be hurt all over again. He needed to see her immediately and apologize if he had to and tell her that he loved her.

But how was he going to find out? He recognized his dilemma only after he had aroused Julien once more and they had gone to the hospital. Bunnie sat lightly restrained in her chair, bathed and combed and with teeth in place, ready to receive them. What now? Max wondered. Did he ask her if she had gone to the Carlyles' last night? Clearly he shouldn't bring up what she might have forgotten. He searched her face. It told him nothing, but looking at her made him feel a great tenderness toward her. He kissed her damp, relaxed lips. He pulled a chair next to hers and took her hand. "Sweetie," he said, "how are you this morning? How're you doing, sweetie?"

"I'm better," she replied quickly. Then she said, "Where's your girl friend, Julien?"

"What?" Max asked in surprise. "Who?" What did Julien have to do with him and Edith Ross? Julien hadn't ever met the Carlyles, and anyway, what difference did it make what he did? He wasn't married.

"You remember, Bunnie," Julien said. "Shannon works the afternoon shift."

"Shannon who?" Max asked. "Who're you talking about?" But both Bunnie and Julien ignored him.

"Well, I know that," Bunnie said. "If she were here, I'd know where she was. That's why I asked where she is."

"Who?" Max demanded once more. He had come here to say something important to Bunnie, and this talk of—he had not yet got the name in his mind—was confusing him.

"I don't know where she is," Julien said. "Maybe she's at home."

"You ought to know about those things," Bunnie said, her chin tilted up, her lips pouting ironically. "You won't get anywhere unless you find things out. I bet you didn't even know her first name is Mary."

"Mary who, God damn it?" Max asked.

"Mary Shannon Marsh, Max," Bunnie replied. "You ought to pay attention."

"Well, then," Max said crossly, "where did we know her? Did we meet her in Washington? Did she work for the paper? Is she a writer?"

"No, no, Max," Julien said. "She's a nurse. She's here in the afternoon."

Max, who usually had the nurses straight, couldn't bring his thoughts out of the past. He tried to recall any friend he and Bunnie might have had who was a nurse, but he couldn't think of anybody. "Well," he said, "it's nice of her to come, but I didn't think we knew any nurses."

"No, no, Max," Julien said again. "She's not a friend. She's a nurse who works here at the hospital."

"Well, all right," Max said. He was annoyed at having been kept in confusion, and in fact he was still confused. "Why didn't somebody say so?" he said. "I thought you were talking about Edith Ross."

Hearing his own voice, Max was astonished. Then he was angry with himself for having let Edith's name slip out, and his anger grew to include Bunnie. Whatever he had done that was wrong, he had paid for it. He did not remember having done so, but he was sure that he had apologized to Bunnie for all the times he had slept with Edith and for all the other women he had slept with. He and Bunnie had long ago made their peace with each other. They had lived with the past almost as if it hadn't happened. They had learned to talk about the people with whom they had been unfaithful without mentioning their infidelities, and in Max's case, sometimes without even remembering them. Now Bunnie's sickness had changed all that, and Max resented it. Her stroke had made her mind more fragile than his, and her confusion of present and past was so absolute that it resurrected ancient injuries.

"Edith is dead, Max," Bunnie said softly. "Of all people, you ought to know that."

"I do know it," he replied. He was going to say more, but without warning he felt a terrible grief. His voice broke, and tears came to his eyes. Edith had died twenty years ago, and he and Bunnie had attended her funeral. But now it was as if he had just heard that she was gone; it was as if he now realized for the first time that he would never see her again.

Bunnie patted his hand. "Well, now," she said, "don't take it so hard. You had your fun, Maxie."

# III

The first thing Bunnie felt when she had her stroke was a tightness inside her skull that soon became a terrible headache. Or more than that: a shaft of pain, as bright and ruthless as the sun, that went from her forehead to the top of her spine. Then there was the beginning of darkness. She felt as if she were falling into a black void, plunging like one of Milton's bad angels into chaos. In the instant before she lost consciousness, she was sure she was dying. She knew there was something that she ought to do—pray, say she was sorry for her sins, but her mind refused to focus. The darkness grew darker still, the sense of falling accelerated. Then after a night or a week or a month, she awakened in a hospital room that seemed real enough, the bed palpable when she touched the cold frame of it, but her visions had their reality, too, and both dimensions tricked her.

At times, the bed, even as she grasped it, seemed to disappear. She seemed to levitate, drift about the room with nothing to support her. Then the bed would return, and her father would be standing at the foot of it, a man of thirty-five with a neat black beard and dark eyes like hers. Then a nurse would come, simply appear in the same spot where her father had been standing. Then the nurse would be gone, and there would be Max, sometimes old, sometimes young, sometimes both. Once he came wearing the hat and goggles he had worn when he took flying lessons in the twenties, but when he leaned over her bed, the hat vanished and the goggles turned into spectacles that were clamped at an angle above his ears. Everything shifted and changed, came and went except the giant clock outside her window. It kept its position and ticked off the minutes, night and day.

Time, Bunnie thought. That was the problem. Even with the clock as the one constant of her days, she couldn't get a grasp of time. Her mind darted from past to present, paused and darted back again, moving through her cluttered memory like a restless bird. There were moments when she knew herself for what she was: an old lady in a hospital bed; and there was Max and there was Julien, and there were the flowers her friends had sent her, and outside her window there was the clock. She knew then who was alive and who was dead, but old age was such a silly thing, she could not make herself believe in it. Her faith in herself as a person who had been born when she had been born faded, and she was a girl again or a young woman, and faces that she had not seen in decades came into her vision, voices from the past spoke to her, and the clock that marked minutes and hours, but not years, seemed to suggest that this was 1910 when she had started to school or 1918 when the war had ended or 1931 when everybody was too poor to buy bootleg whiskey and she was the age Julien was now. But that was wrong, too, because in her mind 1931 was now, and she was twenty-seven, and why shouldn't she be the age of Julien or any other age she wanted to be?

When she felt young, she needed to talk to Max. In her mind she saw him as young, but he retained the vagueness that had come upon him in his old age, and it was up to her to tell him where they were going and what they were going to do when they got there and whom they were going to see. She did this, and Max seemed to understand, but then the next day what she remembered was different from what he remembered, or he did not remember anything, and the confusion of time began all over again. Finally, her head began to clear. In the last days before she went home, she knew that Max was old and Julien was young and that the Carlyles and the Rosses and most of their other friends were all dead. She held onto this and was as certain of it as she was of the existence of the clock in the park.

Julien's mother, Susan, fifty years old as Bunnie reckoned and almost as trim as she had been when Max had made his indecent proposal to her, came from Virginia and arranged for a practical nurse to stay with her and Max through the day, and Mrs. Pakenham came from Nineveh to clean the house and cook. Bunnie was able to go home in Susan's car. At the apartment, there was some confusion as both Max and Julien tried to help her from the automobile into her wheelchair. Max pulled her one way, and Julien pulled the other. "Wait a minute, Maxie," Bunnie said. "Wait a minute, Julien." But neither was willing to let go. She wanted to support herself on the car door, but Max wouldn't hold it steady. He held onto her arm instead. The door swung in. It hit Max in the back of the head. Max let go of Bunnie's arm to retrieve his hat. Bunnie fell halfway back into the car, but Julien wouldn't release her other arm.

"Don't worry!" Julien said. "Don't worry! I've got you, Bunnie."

Bunnie was worried. She felt herself suspended, out of control. "Let go, Julien," she said.

"I've got you. I've got you," Julien insisted.

Bunnie thought her legs were going to give way and that she would wind up sitting on the pavement, or, a fate even worse, Julien would pull her arm out of its socket. "Damn it, Julien," she said, "let go!"

He did, and Bunnie bounced back on the seat, her fat behind making a soft splat on the upholstery. She sat and panted a while. Then she said, "All right. Let's try it again." And this time they were successful.

"Well," Max said as soon as they were in the apartment, "we'd better have a little drink."

The nurse and Mrs. Pakenham and Julien's mother gave each other looks of stern disapprobation.

"Wait a minute, Max," Julien's mother said. "Did the doctor say Bunnie could start drinking?"

"It's only vodka," Max said. "That's all she drinks, you know, vodka and water. I'm the one who drinks scotch."

"Yes," Julien's mother said. "I do know. It's alcohol I'm talking about, Max. Did Dr. Harper say she could drink any kind of alcohol?"

"Who?" Max asked.

"Dr. Harper. Did you ask him about Bunnie's drinking?"

"Oh," Max replied, "Tommy never was much of a drinker. I think he was afraid his patients would smell it on his breath."

Sitting in her wheelchair near the glass doors that led to the terrace, Bunnie realized how much she wanted a drink. She had thought about drinking in the hospital, but between the medicine the nurses gave her and the way her mind wandered, she had not been able to concentrate on remembering how booze tasted, the warmth of it in her stomach, the peace she felt when she had had three or four or five drinks. She broke into the conversation. "Drinks all around, Maxie. See what Susan will have. I think Julien would like some of your scotch."

"None for me, Max," Julien said. "I've got to go to the university."

"None for anybody," Julien's mother said, shaking her head. "This is not the way to get Bunnie well, Max. You ought to know that."

Max didn't hear her. He was already in the kitchen, dropping ice into glasses, pouring booze. As soon as Max gave her her drink, Bunnie took a good sip and then another. It was a robust mixture, and the taste of it was better than she had remembered. She drank again, drained half the glass and felt the edge of a splendid lightness in her head. How nice, she thought. How very fine that she was beginning to feel so well so quickly. As the lightness increased, her mind regained its clarity. All on less than one drink, she thought. It appeared that her stroke was going to reduce their liquor bill. She finished her barely diluted vodka and was going to hold out her glass to Max, but Max was crying. Tears were running down his cheeks, and he was reaching for his handkerchief. Bunnie wanted to touch him, but he was sitting on the couch too far away for her to reach.

"Maxie," she said, "it's all right, Maxie. I'm home now." But as she spoke, it occurred to her that she and her stroke and her brush with death might not be what he was crying about. So she said, "We're all doing fine, Maxie," not knowing to whom she was referring. For all she knew he was remembering the past as he had been that day in the hospital and weeping over someone who had been dead for thirty years.

Bunnie had wondered from time to time whether Mrs. Pakenham's husband were related to the British general of the same name who had fallen at the Battle of New Orleans, but she knew Mrs. Pakenham would not know so she never asked. Mrs. Packenham had survived many parties at Nineveh. She was a good cook, and though she was against drinking, she was willing to fix food for as many people as necessary as long as nobody brought booze into the kitchen. At times this had been a problem. People from the South understood, but sometimes northerners, not having had experience with Baptists and members of the Church of Christ, would enter the kitchen, glass in hand, moved by a democratic impulse to socialize with the servants—a term that Bunnie would never use in reference to Mrs. Pakenham. When that happened, Mrs. Pakenham would leave the kitchen, and one night, when a writer from New York followed her out to the back porch, Mrs. Pakenham went home, leaving Bunnie to take care of the dinner.

At Nineveh, there was a wet bar in the library—a nice and perhaps symbolic arrangement, Bunnie had often thought, given the state of modern letters. Once Mrs. Pakenham had finished cleaning there, Max and Bunnie could settle in to drink themselves silly, and Mrs. Pakenham could go about her business in the rest of the house. The apartment in Nashville was another matter. The only bar here was the kitchen counter, and the kitchen was the only place to keep the booze. Bunnie wondered if Mrs. Pakenham would quit, and perhaps Mrs. Pakenham wondered the same thing, but before that issue could be resolved or even discussed, there arose another complication. Bunnie, who could move fairly well on her walker now, became incontinent.

Bunnie was astonished. As she had grown older, her intrepid bladder had been the envy of her female friends, who were constantly looking for or going to or coming from the powder room. When she and Max had traveled by car, she had never had to ask him to look for a rest stop. Now, she might simply get out of her chair and start her slow progress across the room, and it would happen. She would not be aware that she needed to go until she felt the first warm trickle down her leg, and she couldn't stop. Out came whatever was there, which usually was not very much, because her accidents came so frequently. She went through the apartment leaving puddles. It would have been embarrassing under the best of circumstances, but it was particularly so since Mrs. Pakenham had to clean up the puddles, and Mrs. Pakenham blamed the whole unfortunate situation on drink.

The nurse, Mrs. Smith, a tall, rawboned woman with hair dyed red, may or may not have disapproved of drinking in general, but in the matter of Bunnie's drinking, she sided with Mrs. Pakenham. Bunnie suspected that Mrs. Smith had secretly taken the matter up with Tommy Harper, because Tommy paid her a house call unbidden by her or Max, just, as he put it, "to see how she was getting on." That he came at nine in the morning, when Bunnie had just begun on her first drink of the day, was both good and bad. Tommy doubtless thought that Bunnie was starting the cocktail hour early and might get an exaggerated impression of how much Bunnie drank. But at this hour, with the vodka beginning to deal with her daily hangover but not yet blurring her faculties, she was at her mental best.

Max, on the contrary, seemed flustered. He stood to greet Dr. Harper and had half extended his right hand before he discovered that his glass was in it. He looked around uneasily—at the coffee table that was overflowing with newspapers and magazines and at an end table that was equally cluttered. He took a step toward the television set, thinking that perhaps he would set his glass next to his hat. Finally, he shifted his drink to his left hand and extended his right to Tommy Harper. "Bunnie and I are just having a little drink," he said. "What can I get for you, Tommy?"

"Well," Dr. Harper said, "well, well." He looked around as uncertainly as Max had, then lowered his large body onto the couch where Max had been sitting. "Well, now, how are you feeling, Bunnie?"

Knowing that this was what he was going to say, Bunnie had decided in advance to plague him with a joke so old it was sometimes attributed to Socrates.

"Compared to what?" she replied. She was so pleased by the instant of silence that ensued she took a large swig from her glass of vodka.

"I mean," Dr. Harper said drily, "compared to yesterday or last week or when you left the hospital."

"Well, you know," Bunnie said, "I never liked the hospital. The nurses were all right. As a matter of fact, Julien was sweet on one of them. But I didn't at all like being there."

"Look here, Bunnie," Tommy Harper said. "I know you and Max are going to drink. I never knew either of you when you didn't. But try to understand that you've been very sick. You need to give your body a chance to get well. If you drink all the time, you're going to kill yourself."

"No doubt you're right," Bunnie replied. "People have been telling me that all my life. If Max and I go on the wagon, how old do you think we'll get to be before we die?"

"What?" Max said. "Do what?"

"Tommy thinks we drink too much, Max."

"Oh," Max said. "Oh, yes, back then. When they stirred it up in the bathtub, it would kill you. But some of those back-country moonshiners made pretty good stuff. Strong, though. It had a kick to it."

"He thinks we drink too much now," Bunnie said.

"Oh, well," Max said. "A little drink now and then—"

"Bunnie," Tommy Harper said, "I'm serious about this. You stay off alcohol until the cocktail hour, and then you just have one or two at the most. Do you understand?"

"You never said how long you would keep me alive."

"I can't keep you alive at all if you don't do what I tell you," Dr. Harper replied. Then he said a grumpy good-bye and was gone before Max could walk with him to the door.

Bunnie felt betrayed. Her first impulse was to fire Mrs. Smith, call her into the living room and write her a check and send her packing. But this early in the day, her mind was still clear enough for her to see that this wouldn't do. First, there was the matter of Mrs. Pakenham and the puddles. Max had bought a potty chair—he had given it to Bunnie as a coming home present—and Mrs. Smith brought it at frequent intervals and made Bunnie use it. This decreased the number of accidents that Mrs. Pakenham had to deal with. Also, Mrs. Smith bathed Bunnie and dressed her and washed her hair, all personal services that Mrs. Pakenham could not be expected to perform. And Mrs. Smith gave Bunnie her medicine, brought the pills and capsules and saw that Bunnie swallowed them, which was something that Mrs. Pakenham could probably do if she didn't get busy and let the time slip by her. Finally, Bunnie knew that if she fired Mrs. Smith, Julien would call his mother, and Susan would come to Nashville and hire a new nurse who might be worse than Mrs. Smith. In any event, as long as Max was up and moving, neither Mrs. Smith nor Mrs. Pakenham nor the two of them together could keep Max from mixing drinks and bringing them to her.

So Mrs. Smith stayed, but it wasn't, by and large, a happy household. Mrs. Smith and Mrs. Pakenham made remarks to each other about the evils of alcohol that Bunnie and Max were intended to overhear. Mrs. Smith said it was bad for the human system, and Mrs. Pakenham said it was just bad. Both women complained about the way the apartment smelled, and as often as Mrs. Smith brought the potty chair, Mrs. Pakenham got the Lysol spray and released clouds of it throughout the apartment. Mrs. Pakenham gave Max and Bunnie breakfast and lunch and fixed their dinner, but it was up to Julien to get them to the table. This meant he had to be home every night at the time that Mary Shannon Marsh had her dinner in the hospital cafeteria. Bunnie thought this was unfortunate, but apparently Julien had convinced Shannon to see him at another time. He left the apartment at eleven o'clock and was gone for several hours, which made Bunnie nervous, since at night it was Julien who changed her diapers.

She was ashamed of wearing them, of course. They felt and looked strange, not at all like the diapers she remembered seeing on children:

hers were plastic-and-paper contrivances that were like bulky pants. Mrs. Smith wanted Bunnie to wear them all the time, and Susan, down for one of her visits, had agreed. Bunnie was outraged, but finally she had been forced to compromise. Every night when she had finished dinner and got to her room and used the potty chair, there was the moment that she dreaded, though it seemed not to bother Julien. Bunnie could not remove her regular panties. Her limbs were still too weak, and her stomach got in the way. Since she couldn't raise her behind off the bed, Julien had to push at her and pull at the panties until they came off. Then he had to roll her over and then roll her back onto the diaper, and all the time her private parts were on display. It was, Bunnie thought, like a parody of what she and Max and most of their friends had been obsessed with fifty years ago, and she was embarrassed by the whole procedure. Every night she went to sleep swearing that she would not call Julien, no matter how uncomfortable she got, but every night she got so cold and miserable she had to ask him to change her. Then because of the wet diaper, the ordeal was worse, but usually, before he went back to bed, he would bring her a shot of vodka.

She would feel cozy then, warmed by the dry diaper and the booze, and often she would think that Julien treated her as if he were her own son. Depending on how much she had had to drink or how well she had dealt with her handicap that day or how many visitors had come to tire her, she would be comforted or deeply saddened. Sometimes she considered how lucky she was to have someone as kind and faithful as Julien to look after her. He had reason to be grateful to her, since she was supporting him and paying his way through graduate school, but Bunnie was never mean-spirited enough to think that he cared for her only because of what she did for him. She believed he loved her. But he wasn't her son, and she might have had one. Or two. Both of them may have been boys. Would she ever know? Would God tell her if she managed to get to heaven? Would she see them? Or would they be drifting in limbo as the Church once taught? Oh dear, oh dear, she would say to herself as she wept in the darkness.

# IV

While Bunnie was in the hospital, Julien went with Shannon to the cafeteria when she took her break, sat at the table with her while she ate her skimpy supper, admiring her eyes and the way she lifted her fork and drank her coffee. Julien longed to take her out, but she was working seven days a week. She was in debt, she said, and needed to make money. Finally, she agreed to meet him at a bar near the hospital after she got off work. She arrived late, but not, Julien could see, because she had stopped to pin up her hair or put on lipstick. She came as she was, disheveled and weary. Julien was tired, too, from trying to keep up in school and taking care of Max and Bunnie. They drank to each other, fellow victims of fatigue, and smiled across the table at each other and leaned their heads back against the padding of the booth. They met again the next night and the next.

Julien talked to her about Paris, about the things he had seen there, being careful not to mention Justine; he wouldn't have minded Shannon knowing that he had lived with Justine, but he was ashamed of having allowed Justine to support him. She spoke of her patients and her fellow workers. One of the orderlies had been caught trying to steal drugs. The redheaded nurse with the freckled arms had left her husband. It seemed to Julien that, like him, she was speaking warily, being careful not to disclose too much about herself. As the nights passed, her plain face seemed to him less plain. He liked the way she smiled, her lips turning up at the corners in what was almost a smirk. He liked to walk behind her to see the fine articulation of her body, the gliding movement of her hips. On their third night at the bar, he picked up her hand, let it rest in his, bounced it gently, and watched the soft fall of her tapered fingers. After a week of following her home and walking with her to the door of her building, he kissed her, but the pressure of his lips was uninsistent.

"Oh, ho," Shannon said, and gave her ironic little smile. She left

Julien to watch through the door as she made her stunning way toward the elevator.

Finally, she let Julien take her to dinner. She met him in the vestibule of her building dressed all in black—slacks, blouse, jacket. She produced a black derby from behind her back and put it on at a jaunty angle. "All right, Julien," she said, "how about that? Are you up for headwear?"

He was astonished. Her clothes brightened her hair and eyes, enhanced the smooth whiteness of her skin. She looked chic and sexy, and Julien had to resist the temptation to put his arms around her. "You look wonderful," he said, his voice husky and a little breathless.

"Well," she said, "I thought you'd be more help than that. I was wondering if wearing black said something about my psyche."

Having watched her nibble a salad in the hospital cafeteria or make a meal out of a cup of yogurt, Julien was afraid he would have to coax her to eat, but she finished her seafood pasta, drank two glasses of wine, had dessert. After dinner, they walked across the parking lot to the mall that was opposite their restaurant. He considered guiding her toward Victoria's Secret, but he was afraid to. It was crazy. He was older than she. He had been places she hadn't been and was certain that he had done things that she hadn't done. She was twenty-three, but in some ways she seemed very young to Julien. He had half decided that her reticence, the sudden moments when she refused to talk, came from a kind of innocent timidity, but in her occasional wariness, there were traces of experience and mystery. They paused before a window; he put his arm around her waist. They were looking at a lamp shop.

Shannon said, "I used to collect lamps." Her voice was soft, as if she didn't intend for him to hear.

"You did?"

"Yes," she said quickly, "I did a lot of things. Nothing worth talking about."

"No, tell me," Julien said.

"They were lava lamps. Do you remember? They were filled with stuff that kept making different shapes."

"Why did you collect those?"

"To annoy my parents," Shannon said. "But I've already told you it's not worth talking about."

They moved on, paused in front of a women's shoe store, which wasn't as good as lingerie, but it was better than sporting goods or men's apparel. He had never seen Shannon in high heels, but Justine had worn them almost everywhere; he had liked the lift they had given her calf, the trimness of her ankle when she wore them. He started to ask Shannon if she saw any shoes that she liked, but she was staring beyond the window display into the shadowy depths of the store. They went past a pet shop where puppies slept, a toy store, a place that sold greeting cards. Most of the stores were closed. Most of the people were gone. A man lingered in front of a ski shop. A couple, their arms around each other, looked at rings in a jewelry store.

Shannon glanced at her watch. "We'd better go now."

"It's not late," Julien said. "Let's go for a drink."

"No. I need to go home."

He didn't want to take her. He wanted to guide her to a bench and sit down beside her. He wanted to pull her close. He wanted to kiss her. Maybe, he thought, when they got to her apartment, she would invite him in, but he knew she wouldn't. She had been happy through dinner, but now she seemed pensive and more wary than usual. Her mood had changed when she mentioned the lamps. What, Julien wondered, had they reminded her of? He held her hand as they walked back to his car. At her building, he kissed her in the way that he had wanted to kiss her from the beginning, and at first she responded. Her lips seemed fuller, softer when she let them part, but soon she pulled away from him.

"I had fun," she said. "I really did enjoy it, Julien."

"Take another day off. We'll do it again. How about Friday?"

"No. Sometime. But not Friday."

When she entered the vestibule, she took off her hat and shook her head gently. The shimmer of light in her loosened hair touched Julien with joy and longing. He knocked on the glass door. She glanced back and smiled, then stood with her back to him as she waited for the elevator.

Often it was three o'clock before Julien got to bed. This would have been bad enough if he could have slept until eight—he needed more than five hours of sleep—but Max, who unlike Bunnie was mobile, would wake him at seven or even six, depending on how angry he was and what kind of wild idea was possessing his mind. The dispositions of both Bunnie and Max were deteriorating, and everything that happened, or for that matter didn't happen, seemed to make Max mad. He would burst into Julien's room shouting for Julien to get up, his high, thin voice piercing into Julien's consciousness. It did no good to lock the door. Max would bang on it with whatever came to hand—a spatula, a tablespoon, usually something from the kitchen—until Julien went groggily to open it. By then Max would have forgotten what it was that he had wanted in his anger over Julien's having locked the door, and he would goddamn Julien for an ungrateful son of a bitch who didn't care whether his aunt lived or died.

"Go away, Max. Get out," Julien would say, clenching his hands in an effort to control his own anger.

"Don't tell me to go away in my own house!" Max would shout.

Julien would take him by the arm, or sometimes half lift him and move him back out into the hall. "Go see about Bunnie," Julien would say. "Go see if the paper has come. You don't know what's happening in the world. You haven't read the paper."

This often did the trick, because Max would not remember whether he had read the paper or not, but being an ex-reporter, he set great store by the news. When nothing else worked, Julien would say, "Maybe you need a little drink, Max," and Max would become as docile as a pet. All signs of acrimony would disappear from his face, and he would purse his lips and start for the kitchen. Then Julien would feel guilty, and his feelings of guilt along with his anger at having been awakened would make it hard for him to go back to sleep. This meant that he would stumble through another day, half hearing what the professors said, half understanding what he read in his books. His grades were beginning to suffer.

With the doctor harping on the subject, and Mrs. Pakenham and Mrs. Smith eager to help reform Max and Bunnie, booze, when to drink it and how to get it, became sources of contention. Max could no longer be allowed to drive. He got lost if Bunnie wasn't with him to tell him where to turn, and he ran red lights and stop signs and drifted toward the edge of the road until his tires scraped the curb. Sometimes he got two wheels up on the sidewalk. The last time she had been in Nashville, Julien's mother had borrowed Max's car and kept his keys. The next day, she asked to borrow the car again, and there was a great search for the missing keys.

"You must have another set, Max," Julien's mother said. "Everybody has two sets of keys."

"No," Max replied. "One set. That's all it takes, you know, to get it started."

They argued this question until Max got so angry his face turned red, and Julien's mother decided it was dangerous to continue. After she had gone back to Virginia, Max came up with the second set of keys—Julien had no idea where he had been keeping them—and he threatened to use them whenever Julien declined to take him to the liquor store. "All right, by God!" Max would say. He would get his hat and start out the door, and Julien would either have to give in and offer to drive him or for the sake of the public welfare call the police.

Once they got to the liquor store, Julien tried to keep Max from buying too much, and another argument would ensue. Max favored cases of large bottles. "Just get liters, Max," Julien would say. "They're easier to handle. You have better control when you pour."

"No, God damn it!" Max would say. "What the hell do you know about drinking?" Max spoke loudly enough to attract attention. Other customers would stop and look at him and Julien, and Julien would be embarrassed and fall silent.

Why did he even bother? he would wonder, and for a while he wouldn't. "All right," he would tell Max, his voice edged with an irony that Max may or may not have caught. "Let's go to the checkout counter. That's where you get cases. They bring them out from the storeroom."

Beyond the size of the bottles, Max could not remember what he was supposed to buy. Though he always got the same thing, he had to bring a shopping list made out by Bunnie, and it took a long time for him to find it. He and Julien stood at the counter while Max went slowly through his pockets and a line formed behind them. Once Julien tried to prompt him. "Absolut, Max. Two cases of Absolut and two of Dewar's."

Max stopped poking around in his coat and looked up at Julien. "Have you got the list?"

"We get the same thing every time," Julien said.

"Have you decided what you want, sir?" the clerk asked.

"No, God damn it!" Max replied. "This boy keeps interfering."

Finally Max would find the list, but there was still the ordeal of paying. The clerk called the order to the storeroom, and the four boxes would be waiting beside the door long before Max got out his pen and checkbook. Laboriously he scribbled his name. He showed his driver's license. Finally the booze would be stored in the trunk of Julien's car, and for a long time that was the end of it. But one afternoon Max discovered that there was a convenience store next to the liquor store. Julien had opened the car door for him, and Max was about to get in when he glanced up and saw for the first time what on previous trips he had been looking at without seeing.

"Whoa!" Max said. "Hold on there a minute, Julien. I need to go in that store."

Caught by surprise, it took Julien a moment to figure out what Max was up to. "Why?" Julien asked, but Max was already entering the convenience store. "Wait," Julien said. "Wait, Max."

Max didn't wait. He stepped out rapidly on his short legs, got a shopping cart and was at the ice chest before Julien caught up with him. "Wait, Max," Julien said again. "We've got ice at home. We don't need to buy that."

"I'm not at home," Max said. He tugged with both hands and got a small bag of ice into his cart. "Find the glasses."

Oh, my God, Julien thought. "They don't have glasses, Max. You have to get those at a department store."

Max was not deceived. He found the plastic glasses, got a bottle of club soda, and pranced up to the counter, his smile adding a jaunty touch to his small gray mustache. "Well, now," Max said as Julien, carrying the purchases, followed him back to the car, "we can have a little drink on our way back to Nineveh."

"We're not going to Nineveh," Julien replied. "We're going to the apartment."

"Well, that's all right," Max said. "We need a little drink wherever we're going."

From that day, Max, who forgot everything else, remembered the convenience store. While the whiskey was being put in the trunk, he bought his ice and the package of glasses and the soda, all of which would be thrown away when he got home, and retrieved a bottle from one of the cases and made a mess of Julien's automobile. He put the ice on the floor, ripped it open with his pocketknife, put some in his glass, and scattered some on the floor mat. Julien learned to wait until the drink was mixed before he started his engine. He offered to help, but Max declined his offer. "No, no," Max would say, "I know how I want it done. You just hold the glass until I get the bottle open."

The large bottles were too much for him to maneuver with one hand: sometimes he missed the glass entirely. Always liquor splashed— on Max's trousers, on the upholstery, into the ice that melted on the floorboard. Alcoholic vapors would fill the automobile, the odor so strong that Julien's nose tingled.

"You'd better have one, my boy," Max would say.

"Sure I had," Julien would reply, "that's all we need to get us both a trip to the slammer."

Even that would not be the end. When he got to the apartment, Julien would have to endure the opprobrium of Mrs. Smith and Mrs. Pakenham, who would remind him in tones both tragic and stern that the doctor disapproved of Max's drinking. What can I do? Julien wanted to say, but usually his energy was at too low an ebb for him to argue.

"My God," Shannon said one night a few hours after Julien had made a liquor run with Max, "what's happened in here, Julien? Do you operate a distillery?"

She had opened the car door, stepped back and closed it quickly, and looked at Julien with her half-smirking smile. "We can't ride in there," she said. "If we breathe hard, we'll have to be detoxified."

"I aired it out," Julien replied testily. "What did you want me to do? Spray it with Lysol?"

"Oh, my. Oh, my," Shannon said, "I seem to have touched a nerve. Well, let's see." She wrinkled her nose as if in preparation for the smell, opened the door, put her hands in the car and waved them vigorously in the fragrant air. "All right," she said finally, "but try to hold your breath until we get there."

In their booth at the bar with their wine in front of them, they looked at each other for a moment saying nothing. He reached across and took her hand. He would have liked to kiss her, but the table was between them.

"Julien," Shannon said, "what do you think? Do my mother and father love each other?"

"What?" Julien said. "Good God, how do I know?"

"Well, think about it," Shannon said. "Of course you don't know until you've given it some consideration."

She looked toward the other side of the bar. The piano player had finished his last set. A single customer gazed indifferently at the television. "Let me give you the background. My mother's forty-seven. My father's fifty. Now pay attention. That's three years' difference. Not five like there is between us."

"I'm only four years older than you are," Julien said. "Maybe four and a half. I'm too tired to figure. Damn it, Shannon, why do you ask me things like this?"

"Now don't get impatient, Julien. That's the trouble with your generation. You want to know everything at once. Is this the way you act at the university? Do you expect to learn everything about a course the first time the class meets?"

Dear God, Julien thought, how had he come to fall in love with this strange girl? She was giving him her little smirk now, but that didn't mean anything. She might be joking. She might be serious— even about such a strange question as the one she had just asked. Sometimes she talked about finding meaning in her life and getting control of her destiny as earnestly as if she were still in high school. Julien sighed. "All right," he said. "Tell me about your parents."

"My father's a lawyer. In Jacksonville. I mean, you'd expect that, wouldn't you, since that's where I'm from?"

Not necessarily, Julien thought, but he didn't say anything.

"And my mother is—" She tilted her head slightly. "Well. My mother. So, what do you think?"

"I think they adore each other," Julien said. "I think they've got the greatest love affair since Romeo and Juliet. Except . . ."

"Except what?"

"Except for us. Ours is the greatest love affair ever. When I'm fifty and you're forty-six, we'll put our children out for adoption and start all over again. How about that? We'll have a second honeymoon in Tahiti. We'll sit under a palm tree and eat coconuts. Can you paint? I think we ought to be careful that our work doesn't look too much like Gauguin's."

"Damn it, Julien," Shannon said, "that's what's the matter with you. You just don't take things seriously."

"I couldn't be more serious. Let's get married. I'll move in with you. How big is your apartment, anyway?"

She stared at him and frowned. For an instant she seemed to be genuinely angry. "That's gross, Julien. That's nothing to joke about."

"I wasn't joking."

"Yes, you were. At least you were looking for a way to change the subject."

"Okay," Julien said in resignation. "Tell me some more about your parents."

"Well," Shannon said, "it's a mixed marriage. That's one of the reasons I brought the subject up."

Mixed? He looked at her white skin, her thin nose, her eyes that most of the time were green. He couldn't fancy how what she said was true, but this was a delicate matter, and he wanted to get his own feelings on record. "What difference does that make, if they love each other?"

She shook her head. "Julien, you really are hard to converse with. Of course it doesn't matter if they love each other, but that's what we're talking about—whether they love each other. Concentrate. Try to keep that in mind. Now, what do you think?"

"Well," he said, "does the difference . . . the fact that it's a mixed marriage cause any trouble between them?"

"I don't know. It never seemed to. The one it caused trouble for was me."

"How?" Julien asked.

"On Sunday mornings, for one thing. He played golf, but I had to go to mass with my mother. Which wouldn't have been so bad by itself, but he let her send me to Catholic schools, too. That was a bitch, Julien."

"Wait a minute," Julien said. "When you said mixed marriage, did you just mean that your parents don't have the same religion?"

She gazed at him with her eyes wide, her lips parted. "Well, my God, Julien, what else could I have meant? Look at me. I mean, it would be great if I looked less like me and more like Robin Givens. Or what if I were half Oriental? That's a terrific combination. But you ought to be able to tell I wasn't that lucky. For one thing, my eyes are blue."

"Shannon," Julien said, leaning toward her, his arms resting on the edge of the table, "you know damned well your eyes aren't blue. You look at yourself in the mirror, and girls can't be color-blind. Why the hell do you do me this way? You're the most exasperating girl I've ever known."

"You see," she said, "you didn't mean it when you asked me to marry you."

"Yes, I did. But right now I'm glad you said no."

"Well," she said, "my apartment's too small, anyway. I tell you that because the way things are going now, you're never going to see it."

"Look," he said, "why can't we be serious? How can we get into an argument over whether your mother and father love each other when I've never even seen them? It doesn't make sense, Shannon."

She lifted her wineglass, but then set it back down and pushed it a few inches away. "Hm," she said, looking at Julien, her lips pressed together. "I guess that's a good question."

She was silent for a moment. "Did you ever hear of Teresa of Avila?"

"What?" He was unprepared for this sudden turn in her conversation. "Who?"

"Well, she was a saint—the Church says she was, anyway—and she lived in Spain, as you might guess, a long time ago."

My God, Julien thought. He got enough of this kind of talk from Max and Bunnie. "Has this got something to do with your parents' mixed marriage?"

"Listen," Shannon said. "It's a story, a legend. One winter day she was crossing a creek, and the mule she was riding threw her into the water. Well, saint or not, she didn't like this, so she said, 'God, why do you treat me this way?'"

So far the story was worse than Julien had expected. He didn't want to hear any more of it, but he didn't know how to stop her.

"So God said—I don't think she saw him, you understand; there was just a voice from the sky or something—God said, 'I treat all my friends this way, Teresa.'"

Shannon paused; Julien waited.

"Teresa said, 'Then no wonder you have so few of them.'"

Shannon gazed down at the table, at the ring her wineglass had left on the vinyl. Then she looked up at him, her face pleasant but serious, the sort of expression she might assume if she were posing for her portrait.

"Well?" Julien said.

"Well, what?"

"Is that it? That's the whole story?"

"Call it a parable," Shannon said.

She turned her head slightly. It seemed to Julien that her expression softened, but this may have been a trick of the light: now one side of her face was in shadow. A parable, he thought. Maybe so, but he was too tired to guess at its meaning.

"You see," Shannon said, "I'm worse off than God. I think you're the only friend I've got, Julien."

Then she said, "We have to go." And she was up, out of the booth, moving as always a few steps ahead of him.

# V

Sitting in front of the glass doors, watching an occasional chipmunk scamper around the edge of the patio, Bunnie thought about literature. When she was in the hospital, she thought it might help her get well if she put her mind to work, and she did this by trying to remember all the books she had read. Mostly, she had read novels and poems, but the poems were hard to get a handle on. She would think of a couplet or a quatrain or a line, but they would never be from the same poem, and when she put them together, they made no sense. *With rue my heart is laden* she would think, *For golden friends I had.* But then her thoughts would skitter off, and she would think, *They also serve who only stand and wait.* Or, *I shall wear the bottoms of my trousers rolled.* Or, *We must love one another or die,* which seemed to her a silly line, because at the time she thought she was probably going to die anyway, whether she loved anybody else or not.

She quit trying to remember poetry, but her memory of novels was not much better. She knew very well that *War and Peace* was about Napoleon's invasion of Russia, but she was certain too that there was a white whale involved somehow, and for the life of her—whatever that meant to a person in her condition—she could not imagine how such an animal could have been got to Moscow in 1812. Or was it 1813? And there was Becky Sharp, a little schemer who, Bunnie was sure, had lived in England, but in Bunnie's recollection, she kept turning up in rural France. Hans Castorp, she thought, was a boozer—she was on familiar ground here—who had been sent to a sanitarium to dry out, and in that same book there had been a woman, as there almost always was, whom Castorp called his Dulcinea, but Bunnie couldn't remember anything about her or imagine what she looked like.

Now that she was at home and much improved, Bunnie understood that she had been confused, but she wondered what would happen if you took the characters out of one novel and put them in another. The moment she began to consider this, she came up with many interesting possibilities. Suppose Nick Adams had not done all that hunting and fishing and fighting in the war, but had gone to Harvard and met Quentin Compson. She tried to conceive of them talking all night about the South, but Shreve was there, listening and talking, too, and three characters broke the symmetry of the narrative. It was really quite a difficult game to play. Once she tried to have Daisy Miller marry Willie Stark, which didn't work at all, and she saw without having to think much about it that there was no way Emma Bovary could be recast as Jay Gatsby's girl friend. Finally it occurred to her that she might be better off writing her own novel—or at least planning it, thinking about it until her mind got clearer and she was ready to put it all down.

The easiest thing to do, Bunnie decided, would be to write about yourself, which was what most novelists did anyway in one fashion or another. She and Max would be the main characters; their friends would have supporting roles. She might even put in Julien, though she was miffed at him because he wanted her and Max to drink less. The plot would be her life and Max's life and their life together. She saw the design of the book as an inverted Y. Her life in Virginia and his life in Mississippi were separate roads that joined when they met in Tennessee. It seemed simple enough, but then she didn't quite know where to begin. Maybe she could do what Dickens did in *David Copperfield* and begin with her birth. But where would that leave Max while she was telling about her childhood? She saw that writing about herself was not going to be as easy as it had seemed when she first thought about it. She would have to find the form in her material, she decided; she had read somewhere that this was the thing to do. She would ask Max.

"Maxie," she said, "you wrote books. How did you decide where to begin?"

Bunnie timed the question poorly. It was afternoon: Max had drunk well before lunch, and he was drowsing in his chair.

"What?" he said testily, not quite awake.

"When you wrote novels, I mean. How did you know where to start the story?"

"What story?" Max asked.

"Whatever story you were writing."

"God damn it!" Max said, "I'm not writing any story. I'm too damned old."

Bunnie thought about this for a moment and concluded that it was probably true. Max was four years older than she was, and she was having trouble trying to write a novel herself. But that was no excuse for him to be cross. "Well," Bunnie said, "I'm not."

"Not what?"

"I'm not too old."

"Too old for what?"

"To write a novel."

Max raised his voice. "Damn it, I've already told you, I can't do that anymore."

"Don't disturb me, Maxie," Bunnie replied with dignity. "I'm working on a book."

Remember, she thought. That's what she had to do. She would recall as many things as she could about herself and Max, and she would sort them out, put the happy things on one side, the sad things on another, and see what she had. She tried to recollect her wedding, and for an instant she saw herself in her white veil. Ha, ha, she thought, the costume for virgins. If people had only known. But the memory slipped away from her almost as soon as it came. Once more her mind was bouncing around beyond her control. She assumed she would have to wait until the next day to begin her book, but as soon as she stopped trying to remember, the thoughts that sometimes haunted her at night took over: every detail of her first abortion, every event that pertained to it was clear in her mind.

It was in the thirties, when Max was still working for the newspaper and knew everybody, including the politicians and the whores and all the cab drivers who would bring him home when he was drunk. Max had been working on a novel then, the second book that won the prize, and he knew that he would not be able to keep his job at the paper and write his book with a baby in the house. It wasn't a matter of money. Along with the house at Nineveh, Bunnie had inherited enough to keep them going. But babies were disruptive. They cried and had to be taken care of. Most of the writers Bunnie and Max knew didn't have children. John and Edith Ross had slipped up, but Edith's mother had taken the baby off their hands. Bunnie knew that her mother would not do that for her. She had agreed with Max that she needed an abortion. Had she simply done it for Max? she wondered now. No, she was involved, too. She had thought Max was going to be a great writer, and art was more important than children. Max would write great novels. She would be the wife of a famous man. And she was teaching at the university: she had her own career to think about.

She was amazed at how clearly the details came back to her. Hers had been no back-alley job, done in a fetid room with dirty equipment. Late one night, they went to the office of a real physician, a man of some prominence in Nashville. Did this go on every night? Bunnie wondered. Riding up in the elevator, entering the doctor's waiting room, she had a sense of unreality. For one thing, she and Max had had a few drinks before they left home, which only seemed natural, given their apprehension over what was going to happen and the time they had to kill before their appointment. They took a last little pull out of Max's flask walking down the hall to the doctor's office.

In the waiting room, there were the usual chairs and couches and magazines, there was the receptionist's desk; but without people, it looked more like a set for a movie than the functional place it was and would be tomorrow when it filled up with patients. Bunnie felt as if she were an actor in a play, or a character in one of Max's novels.

The doctor arrived, a tall man already decked out in white; he spoke to Bunnie and Max, his manner formal, his tone distant. Max handed him some money. The doctor led Bunnie into one of the examining rooms, put on his rubber gloves, and relieved her of her baby. It was quicker than she had imagined it would be. It had hurt. She bled for a while. When they were back in their car, she and Max had another drink, but this was too much for her. On the way home, she got sick. Max had to stop the car to let her lean her head out the window. The next day, she felt nauseous and a little depressed, but these were the usual symptoms of her hangovers.

For a few weeks, she wondered if she had done the right thing. Then Max's book got good reviews and sold well and won the prize, and what was a baby, the memory of which was fading as the days passed, compared to the career Max seemed to be launching? Those were the best times Bunnie could remember; she had no inkling that Max's fame would fade as quickly as it did and that one day he would hold against her the fact that she had borne him no children. They had kept the house in Nineveh, her house, handed down to her through her family who had built it, but Max had quit his job with the newspaper and they had moved to New York. The Rosses had been there for more than a year, and they introduced Bunnie and Max to critics and novelists and poets and editors. There were always people to drink with, and the weekends were disasters, but Max managed to work on a new novel while they lived on his prize money and the royalties he got on his last book.

Even in her mind-damaged and somewhat inebriated state, Bunnie wondered now how she and Max could have been so innocent. They had believed that one prize, one book that sold well, would lead to another, except the sales would get better and life would get easier, but Max's next book was a flop, and they were out of money, and she was pregnant again. Max was distraught. He continued to believe that his new book was good. He felt that he had been betrayed by some of the critics he had met through the Rosses. He told Bunnie that New York was bad for both of them. They needed to go back to Nashville, Max said. They did, and there in the same office, at the hands of the same doctor, Bunnie had her second abortion. Then Max got his job with the senator and moved to Washington. He would keep his eyes open, he told Bunnie. He would make notes for a political novel. The time wouldn't be wasted. She was rehired by the university, but the only classes they had for her to teach were sections of freshman English.

Well, Bunnie thought, as the vodka began to make a muddle of her brain and she neared the end of her working period with little written on the yellow pad she had filched from Julien, it's not supposed to go like this. The happy part is supposed to come at the end, but theirs had come early, and then the bad luck had set in, and the times of anger and recrimination. She had gone to Italy to give herself and Max a chance to decide whether they would forgive each other. After several months, Max came to Rome—to take her back to Nineveh, he said, which was some of the truth, but not all of it. In her absence, he had returned to the Church, and in his new enthusiasm he had come to visit the center of his religion.

Though some of the hurt she had felt when he had spoken of divorce remained, Bunnie had been glad to be reunited with him. By the time she and Max got home, she could joke mirthlessly about what had happened. Lunching with one of her friends, she said, while I was gone, Max took up with another woman. Oh? the friend said, surprised and a little embarrassed. Yes, Bunnie replied, the Virgin Mary. Two years passed before Bunnie entered the Church, too, and she and Max were married again in a ceremony at the cathedral. They invited all their friends and had a reception afterward.

And now what? Bunnie asked herself the next day or the day after that—she couldn't keep up with the passage of days— how did all this fit into her novel? Every morning she wrote what she could remember on her pad, but the next morning when she consulted her notes, there was less there than she expected. Most of what she thought seemed to stay in her mind, and the narrative of her life became more and more complicated. She kept returning in her thoughts to what seemed to her to be the major problem with her story. She wanted a happy ending, and she didn't see how she was going to get it, given the fact that she and Max languished now in their drunken old age. All the good things were in the past. Now all there was to do was to wait to see not what would happen, but when and how. Maybe that was what life amounted to, anyway.

Thinking this way depressed her, but now that she had started her memory working, it wouldn't stop. She kept remembering the past and getting more and more gloomy, and she was feeling very sad a few days later when Father Freeman came to bring her and Max communion. The priest was tall and slightly stooped; his thinning brown hair was streaked with gray. Mrs. Smith or Mrs. Pakenham, whoever answered the door, greeted him cooly, and then both of the women went into the kitchen and stayed there until his visit was over. Among other things, they held him and his church at least partially responsible for Max's and Bunnie's drinking.

"Well," Father Freeman said, "how are you today?" He noticed that Bunnie was wearing a new robe and told her she looked pretty.

"Ha," said Bunnie, knowing better.

The priest asked Max what he was reading, and Max didn't know. He had to look at the cover of the book he was still holding in his hand and check the title. "But listen," Max said, "It's a good book. It's about creation."

"Oh?"

"Yes," Max said. "Father, you know, don't you, that it's not like they say in Genesis?"

The priest looked at Max for a moment, started to say something and apparently thought better of it. After a pause, he said, "Well, let me give you your communion, and then we can visit."

"No," Bunnie said.

"What?" Father Freeman was startled.

"I've got to talk to you, Father." She looked at Max who met her gaze with placid eyes, his youthful old face relaxed to the point of blankness.

"Maxie," Bunnie said, "I need to talk to Father Freeman."

"Well, all right," Max replied.

"Privately," Bunnie said. "I need to talk to him privately."

"All right," Max said again.

"If I'm going to talk to him privately, you'll have to leave the room. Would you mind doing that?"

"Oh," Max said. He picked up his book and looked around. For a moment it appeared that he would reach for his hat, which was in its accustomed place on the television. At last he went shuffling out of the room.

"Well, Bunnie," Father Freeman said.

"Father, you know I'm a convert."

"Yes."

"Well, I've been working on a novel."

"How nice," the priest said. "I knew Max was a writer, but I didn't know you wrote fiction."

"I don't," Bunnie replied. "I mean, I haven't before."

She paused. She hadn't begun in the right way. Once more her mind was betraying her. "What I mean is, I started to write a book about Max and me. I've been thinking about our lives, what we did a long time ago, and the best years we ever had were before we came into the Church. Do you see what I'm getting at?"

"I know it's difficult for you now," the priest said. "It's hard for anybody to be old and sick. But this is when God can give you the most comfort, Bunnie."

She shook her head. "No, that's not what I'm talking about."

The priest waited.

"Listen," Bunnie said, "it's all been a lie. For a long time, Max and I weren't faithful to each other—" She stopped. This was true, but it wasn't what she wanted to say. It didn't lead to wherever it was she wanted to go. Her mind came and went, lost and regained and once more lost its focus.

"All dead," she said. "All the people we committed adultery with. Like in Eliot's poem."

"Excuse me?" Father Freeman said.

"What I mean is, all that's over. We did what we did, and I confessed it before I was confirmed, and most of the time I can't remember how it was to be young like that, to have all that passion."

Father Freeman put his hand on hers. "Don't worry. It's all right. You've done all the Church expects you to do."

She felt very tired. Maybe if she had another vodka, her strength would return, but the priest was here to give her communion. She wasn't supposed to be drinking.

"In the thirties," she said, "over fifty years ago, I had an abortion."

"But you confessed to that, too."

"Yes. And I regret having had it now. People need children when they get old. I have a niece, a great-nephew—" She was wandering off course again. "No. When I look back, it was the time after the abortion that was the best time of my life. I think it was that way for Max, too. So I don't really regret it, you see. I know what I did was wrong, and I know I would be better off if I had children now, but I can't be sorry for a period in my life that was so good. I can't be sorry to have had that blessed time, Father."

"That's all right," the priest said. "If you were happy, remember being happy. God knows, there's little enough happiness in the world. There's no sin in remembering."

She wanted to believe him, but like her thoughts that kept drifting off the mark, what he was saying did not exactly fit her case. When she was young, she had believed that old people must think a lot about the hereafter and devote their waning energy to making the best accommodation they could with God. But for her, it proved to be different. She thought of death every waking hour, sometimes every minute. She felt her life slipping away, time going too fast for her to sort out her thoughts, but she didn't worry about the final judgment. She dwelt on the past—on as much of her life as she could recall—and tried to make sense of it. This was her most urgent desire: to see some order, some logical pattern, in the years she and Max had spent together. This, she saw now, was why she was trying to write her novel.

"Do you understand, Bunnie?" Father Freeman said.

She nodded, but she didn't know. Her weariness had almost completely overtaken her.

Max came back into the room and was surprised to see Father Freeman.

"Forgive me, Father," he said. "I didn't know you were here."

# VI

That night, she kissed Julien at the door, told him to go home and get some sleep, and went up to her apartment thinking that she would have to stop giving him so much grief or he would quit seeing her. He would have enough of her teasing and he would stop calling and she would be back where she was when she first came to Nashville: alone and afraid not to be alone and in agony because of her loneliness. But after what had happened at the hospital today, she knew that she would have to hold herself absolutely together, keep her defenses strong against any word or gesture that might arouse the old pain and the old habits that had got her into the sanitarium five years ago. The doctors had discharged her as cured, assuming that she would behave herself. But there were times when she felt as fragile as an egg.

What if she simply told Julien everything? This thought was too heavy for her to deal with immediately. She put it out of her mind, achieved a kind of vacancy in her brain that made her pause inside the door and look around as if she had never before been in her own apartment. It was small, as she had told Julien, and sparsely furnished. There was a tiny entrance area, a living room with a space for dining, a bedroom, a narrow kitchen. She had a scattering of furniture: a couch, a chair, a table, a television set. Except for a single lamp, the walls and the surfaces of the furniture were bare: no pictures, no ashtrays or vases, no magazines or books or newspapers. Shannon occasionally bought a magazine, read it in a night, and threw it away as soon as she was finished with it. She borrowed books from the library—sloppy historical novels mostly—took them home one at a time and kept them on a shelf in her bedroom closet when she wasn't reading them. Her kitchen was as clean as if no one ate there, and often no one did. She slept late, had juice and coffee around noon, occasionally a croissant, washed and dried her dishes and put them away, cleaned her already clean apartment, ran the few errands she had to run. Then she went to work, and when her break came, she had dinner in the hospital cafeteria.

Her closets were filled with clothes: five-year-old dresses and shoes that she had never worn and probably would never wear, though she should wear them, she supposed, even if many of them were out of style, in order to keep herself normal. Toward the end of her stay in the sanitarium, shopping had been a part of her therapy. Her mother, who had moved to Atlanta as soon as Shannon was allowed to have visitors, took her on the appointed days to Nieman Marcus and Saks, and Rich's and Lord and Taylor and the specialty shops at Phipps and at Lenox. At first, she simply let her mother choose. With all the drugs and alcohol that had been the sources of her energy now out of her system and with tranquilizers working in their place, Shannon had moved through the world as she moved at night through dreams. She had never cared much for downers. In the days when she and Mason had been stoned always and drunk often, she had preferred speed and acid and sometimes coke. She had wanted to feel that the world moved and that she moved within it even when she sat with her back against the wall, too wasted to lift herself off the floor.

Now it seemed that nothing moved at all, or rather that things, people, the cars and escalators, her mother and the clerks and the other shoppers moved so slowly that nothing was focused or connected: everything paused and turned and drifted as if all creation had been transformed into a large and peaceful sea. Her mother tried: Shannon had to give her that. She smiled and talked—my God, how she could talk—and worked her way through racks of dresses, carousels of blouses and sweaters, as if the years of bitter enmity between them had never been.

"Darling," she would say, "isn't this precious? It's a perfect color for you. It goes with your eyes."

Stupid, Shannon would think. Stupid. Stupid. The words would rise sluggishly through her brain, and she would feel anger, but there was no edge to it. It was a general ache that she often confused with her sense of loss.

It occurred to Shannon later that if she had joined in the shopping, they would have bought less. It would have been easy to do: to say no, no, no, no, and then pretend to like something barely often enough to keep the process going. But that would have meant giving in: maintaining her sullen silence was the only way she knew to continue punishing her mother. So they made their way through the stores, the beautiful, stylish, forty-two-year-old woman, and the plain girl who refused to wear makeup and who spoke only to say "I don't know," or "I don't care."

At first, she had hoped that her father would run out of money or at least get tired of spending it to keep her in the sanitarium, but at their Saturday morning family counseling sessions he showed no impatience. They sat in a rough circle in a bright room where the furniture was all chrome and glass and leather and the blinds were tilted just enough to deflect the summer sun. There were Shannon, her parents, her doctor, a social worker, sometimes other members of the staff. They drank coffee. Her mother smoked. Their orchestrated conversation repeated itself with different nuances: they spoke of the present and made a cast now and then into the future, but mostly they talked of the past. The Saturday mornings were not much different from her private sessions with the psychiatrist, and she knew what in both cases was wanted from her: for her to talk of Mason's death, so they could tell her that what had happened had not been her fault. But for a while, her guilt seemed the only comfort she had, the only certainty in her life, and she clung to it.

After the shaky days of her detoxification, which she remembered only in fragments, Shannon refused to speak. When she was introduced to her roommate, a small dark girl who kept her gaze on the floor, she turned away and lay down on her bed and closed her eyes. She let the questions that her psychiatrist asked hang unanswered in the air. The psychiatrist, a slight, pale man about the age of her mother, with brown hair and monograms on the cuffs of his shirts, was patient. He seemed to endure the silence as well as she did. Sometimes he talked, not specifically about her case, but about feelings of guilt and bereavement, about how the psyche could heal if given the opportunity. Finally he said, "You need to get well, Shannon. But we can't help you unless you talk."

She considered this for three days. What she wanted was not to get well, which meant letting them change her into something she didn't want to be, but to get out and to go somewhere as far away as possible where she had no relatives, no acquaintances, where nobody would even want to know who she was. She thought of it as playing a game, but the doctor was better at the game than she was. All right, she told him, I'm ready to talk now. I want to get well. Ask me anything. He pretended to believe whatever she said, and it took her a little while to discover that believing or not believing was not how the game worked. He knew the facts of her case already: how she and Mason had got themselves expelled from Saint Monica's so they could go to public school where they could smoke pot between classes and keep booze in their lockers and trip through the school day when they wanted to. He probably knew where they had gone at night and the names of some of the people they had seen, because after the accident, in the interval between Mason's death and the night Shannon tried to kill herself, the police had attempted to find out where they had been getting their drugs and who was selling beer and whisky to teenaged girls.

She saw that if she lied to the psychiatrist, the lie was to him more significant than the truth. He wanted to know what she felt, what went on inside her, and after a while she wanted to help him because she wanted to know, too. "All right," she said, "I'm really ready this time." But then her memory started to play tricks, as if she were on acid again. It came and went in segments, vivid scenes that were incomplete and that did not connect. Had her mother once locked her in her room? Did she truly remember that? Her father was the one who raged and threatened, but now and then her mother did something wild.

"Yes," Shannon told the doctor, "she did. It was after she found the condoms. She's Catholic, you know. They're scared to death of sex."

"How old were you then?"

"Thirteen. Maybe fourteen."

"Were you sexually active?"

"That's what she wanted to know, but she put the question differently."

"Well?"

"No, but it seemed time to get started. Mason and I talked about it. We were awfully ignorant. You can only get so much out of watching movies and reading books."

"What was it that you and Mason were trying to decide?"

Shannon wasn't sure that she knew. She thought for a moment. "How to get started, I guess. We wanted to lose our virginity at the same time, and . . . well, we didn't know much about boys. I worried because Mason was better looking than me. Taller and brunette. I thought, what if we went out one night and her date wanted her, but mine didn't want me? That sounds crazy, doesn't it?"

"No," the psychiatrist said, "but do you know why you wanted to do this when you were fourteen instead of waiting until you were sixteen or seventeen?"

After a pause, Shannon said, "It all goes back to your parents, doesn't it?"

The pale psychiatrist smiled. "That's one theory."

"A theory," Shannon said. "Jesus, I don't know. Was there a time when everything between us, my mother and father and I, I mean, when everything went to hell and we didn't even know it? There's a lot I can't remember. Mason and I started to school together, and we were best friends from the first morning. From then until she was killed, we were together so much some people thought we were gay."

"Is that one of the reasons you thought you ought to start sleeping with boys?"

"I don't know. What I'm trying to tell you is that Mason was the person I talked to and listened to and trusted. So I didn't talk to my parents, and I didn't listen when they talked to me. Then there was all the business with dope and booze, and it seemed that all my parents and I could do was get mad and yell at each other."

"How do you feel about your parents now?"

Shannon looked at the psychiatrist and felt her lips form the beginning of the first smile she had attempted since Mason's death. "How do I have to feel," she said, "to get the hell out of here?"

On the night of the accident, they had ridden around for a while, Mason driving her mother's Honda, Shannon filling and lighting the pipe that they passed between them. They were in a part of town they didn't know very well and were ready to turn around when they came upon a long, low building with a sign that advertised live music and Busch beer. "Well, now," Mason said. She pulled into the parking lot and rolled down her window. What they heard coming through the concrete-block walls was not heavy metal or even rock, but country, and not very good at that. Guitars uttered the same few chords over and over, and a high male voice sang about fickle women and broken hearts. They were ready to drive away when Shannon spotted the motorcycles and pointed them out to Mason.

"What do you think?" Mason said. "They're probably big and have tattoos and smell bad."

"Wow," Shannon said. "Let's have a hit or two before we find out."

They smoked another pipeful and then another. When they got out of the car, Shannon had to hold onto the door for a moment before she could make her legs work. She and Mason went crunching across the shell parking lot, weaving, bumping against each other. They opened the door to a blast of tepid air and cigarette smoke and amplified sound. The cyclists were sitting at a long table, unmistakable in their sleeveless denim jackets and earrings and wide belts. While Shannon and Mason hesitated, looking around for a table, two women came out of the ladies' room and joined the cyclists—one of them quite plump, the other tending that way, and both dressed not much different from Mason and Shannon: jeans, tank tops. Mason and Shannon were not wearing boots.

"Too bad," Mason said.

"Maybe not," Shannon replied. "There are only two of them. With four men. Let's give it a try."

They sat down and went into a routine that they knew well by now, having practiced it often, usually with success. They pretended to talk. When they paused to drink, they looked across the tops of the beer cans, letting their eyes hold for an instant after the men glanced up. The way the cyclists were sitting, it was hard to tell which of the men the two women belonged to. "Maybe that's the arrangement they have," Mason said. "Maybe two women are all they want."

"Everybody wants more of everything," Shannon said. "Just keep working."

She and Mason ordered another beer, drank, and Shannon began to feel both worse and better. Her vision was out of kilter. The table where the cyclists sat seemed to be surrounded by at least a dozen people. Shannon knew what to do about that, but as soon as she closed one eye, she felt dizzy. She was still giving what she hoped was her come-on look, but when she squinted and managed a moment of hard concentration, she discovered that she was flirting with one of the women. Jesus, she thought, I've got to pull myself together. Sometimes when she was like this, another beer would help. It was like getting a second wind when you were running. She turned her head to see if the waiter were nearby, but she couldn't tell. People moved among the tables in pairs and foursomes—bodies and images of bodies indistinguishable to Shannon. She raised her hand. She watched it with interest as it went up, watched it wave, and sure enough, there were two more Buds on the table, and the grumpy garçon waiting for his money.

Mason paid and said, "I'm drunk . . . Or stoned . . . Or something."

"Me, too," Shannon said. "Can you see all right?"

"Well," Mason said. She shook her head slowly. "I mean, no. Not very well."

It appeared to Shannon that the world was slowing down. Seconds seemed to elapse between beats of the music. When Mason spoke, the words came slowly through the air, one straggling behind the other. But then, Shannon thought, there were times when Mason's speech got pretty lazy. It occurred to Shannon that with the night getting on and things with her and Mason being the way they were, they had better put a bold move on the cyclists.

"Listen, Mason," she said, "since we can't see, maybe we'd better get closer."

"All right," Mason replied, her voice serious, which seemed right to Shannon because getting from where they were to the table across the room where all those other people were sitting was going to be a serious undertaking.

They started to get up, but on the first try, neither of them made it. They put their hands on the edge of the table for support, but the table was unsteady. It tilted toward them, and Shannon was barely able to stop her beer from sliding off. She looked at the red and silver can knowing what it was but uncertain what she was supposed to do with it. Then it came to her that she was going to need her beer. She had better take it with her, but first she had to get to her feet, and so far she hadn't made any progress. She pushed against the bottom of her chair and got some action. She came up slowly, but when she had to stop pushing and rely on her legs she went back down again. Well, now, Shannon thought, this is worse than I realized. She saw that Mason was still sitting, too, so she assumed they were both in the same predicament.

Shannon considered the problem for a while. Then she said, "Mason, we need to do some planning here. I'll hold the table while you get up. Then you can hold it while I get up."

"What?"

"Look," Shannon said, "I'm going to push up on the table while you hold onto it and get out of your chair. Then you can hold it for me."

"I don't know," Mason replied. "Are you sure that's feasible?"

"Well, of course I am," Shannon said. "I don't suggest things without thinking about them. First, let's put the beer in the middle of the table."

For a moment, it was touch-and-go. Shannon slid her chair closer to the table, braced her elbows on her knees, and pushed. Mason rose, hesitated, gave ground, then gave a shove and was standing.

"Now, hold it for me," Shannon said, but it was soon apparent even to Shannon that this part of her plan wasn't going to succeed. It was one thing to hold the table up when you were sitting and braced: standing and pulling up on it was another matter. Shannon tried to get to her feet, the tabletop dipped, the beer cans came sliding down, and this time Shannon couldn't catch them. They fell and went rolling away, leaving foamy trails behind them.

"Hell," Shannon said. "This won't cut it. Get behind me and push on me."

Shannon raised herself off her chair. Mason put her hands under Shannon's buttocks and tried to lift, but the angle was wrong: the leverage was not so much up as it was forward. Shannon had to sit down again to avoid falling across the table.

"I tell you what," Mason said. "I'll sit back down, and then we can start all over again."

"No, wait," Shannon said, "you'd just have to get up again. Are you pretty steady?"

"Ah . . . well . . . actually, I don't think so."

Shannon looked at Mason, and Mason seemed to be weaving, but Shannon couldn't be sure she wasn't moving her own head. Mason was holding onto the back of the chair she had vacated. Shannon decided that Mason wasn't going to be much help, but seeing Mason gave Shannon an idea. "All right," Shannon said, "here's what I'm going to do. I'll slide around in my chair. Then I'll hold onto the back of it and pull up."

Let's go carefully, Shannon told herself. She decided she had better watch her feet as she turned. She looked down, but for a moment she couldn't find them. Were those Adidas hers? They must be, she decided, but unless she closed an eye, one of them looked larger than the other. Now, she thought. She began to turn, the seat of her jeans moving easily against the smooth wood. Fine, she thought, fine.

But suddenly, it was not fine at all. She got too close to the edge, the legs of the chair tilted and began to slide, and she was sitting on the floor, not sure how all this had happened. She didn't feel any different down here than she had felt sitting at the table, but she thought she had heard a splat when her buttocks hit the floor. That's terrible, she thought. She couldn't believe that she was getting fat: she didn't eat that much. Then she was being pulled to her feet by hands and arms too strong to belong to Mason. She turned around and focused and looked into the face of the plump woman who was with the cyclists.

Shannon considered what might be proper to say under the circumstances. Thank you. That must be it, but she couldn't quite get her tongue in position to say it. She got a whiff of pot. Ah, ha, she thought, but then it occurred to her that what she smelled might be coming from her own hair and clothes or from Mason's. Anyway, a couple of hits might improve the situation.

"Honey," the plump woman said, "both you girls are wasted to hell. You better get out of here."

"Well, actually," Mason said, "we wanted to meet your boy friends."

"You don't want to meet those bastards even when you're straight," the woman said. "Now, come on. Fresh air will make you feel better."

The woman got between them, took each of them by the arm and led them past the tables, through the door, and into the parking lot. "Take some deep breaths," the plump woman said. "Can you walk? Walk around out here until you straighten up a little bit."

"We have an automobile," Mason said with dignity.

"Yeah. I know you do. But you'd damn well better walk a while before you get into it."

"Jesus," Shannon said when the woman had left them. "She sounds like my mother."

"Well, more like mine," Mason said, "but who's counting?"

Shannon felt halfway sick, but she didn't tell Mason. If she needed to, she could put her head out the window on the way home. Better still, she could throw up in her own bathroom where her parents could hear her. It seemed to her that Mason was better off than she was—or worse depending on how you looked at it. Anyway, Mason seemed more in control of herself, but she still appeared to have to concentrate to make her feet go where she wanted them to. By the time they got to the car, Shannon felt perspiration running down her cheek. Her faint nausea was constant at the back of her throat.

"Maybe we ought to get some coffee," Mason said. "We could have some doughnuts."

Oh, God, Shannon thought, she wasn't ready for that, but she didn't say anything. They got in the car. Mason started the engine. The air conditioning came on, feeling cool on Shannon's skin, drying the dampness. Mason raced the engine, but the car didn't move. Then she got the transmission into drive, and they churned the shells as they left the parking lot. Shannon thought she might go to sleep, but the edge of sickness that was still in her mouth made her afraid to. She nodded, jerked her head up, and nodded again. Her mind was blank. She was conscious only of the music that blasted from the speakers and the fuzzy glow of the lights of cars that approached them. It was, Shannon thought, a nice ride. She was aware that they were drifting, moving from one side of the street to the other. They scraped the curb, and Shannon thought she heard a horn blow, but she couldn't be sure because of the music. Then there were lights directly in front of them. For an instant, Shannon thought this was nice, too: her dilated pupils refracted the beams into flashing colors. In the last second, some part of her brain remembered that she ought to be afraid, but it was too late for her to say or to do anything that might have saved them.

The pale psychiatrist put the point of his pencil on his pad and balanced it there, his finger on the tip of the eraser. "When did you find out that Mason was dead?"

"It wasn't just Mason," Shannon said. "There was a woman and a six-year-old girl. They were in the other car."

"When did you hear about Mason?"

"I don't know. I mean I remember the moment, but I don't know when it was. I was banged up myself. I was only unconscious for about a day, but when I came to, I couldn't get things straight. When they cut down on the pain-killers, I think I hallucinated."

Shannon looked out the window at the sunlight, the walks, the grass. "Why do I have to go through this? Remembering all this hurts, don't you understand that? It's like if you burned your finger and then stuck it in the flame again trying to make it get well. What kind of way is that to practice medicine?"

"Try to trust us, Shannon."

"Yeah," she replied, "that's what they all say, isn't it? Your parents, the nuns, priests, you. Even if it doesn't make any sense to me.

Even if it's the last God-damned thing in the world I want to do."

"Let's try another image," the doctor said. "It's not like putting your finger back in the fire. It's more like draining an infection. It causes pain temporarily, but it gets rid of what's been causing the pain."

"Okay," Shannon said, "my mother told me. As I told you, I don't know whether it was morning or afternoon or whether I had been in the hospital two days or a week. But I remember that she was wearing a blue dress and a gold Saint Francis medal. She leaned forward, and I could smell tobacco on her breath. She called me darling and told me how sorry she was and said that Mason had not survived the accident. Those were the words she used: not that Mason had been killed, but that she 'had not survived the accident.'"

"Do you remember how you responded?"

"No, but badly, I suppose. The nurse was standing by with a syringe of Demerol. She zapped me with it, and the world turned rosy and I slept for a long time."

"When did you hear about the woman and the little girl?"

"A while later. When you've been hit on the head, strange things happen to you. The doctors told me that I shouldn't drink or use drugs for at least a year, so as soon as I got home, I got my extra pipe and my extra bags—I had hidden them in my mother's room, which I thought was pretty smart—and I lit up, and it was like nothing I had ever felt before. I mean even my first toke on a joint didn't blow me away like this did. Two more hits, and I had just enough sense left to put the pipe and the dope under my mattress and lie down on top of them. It's a wonder I didn't burn the house down."

"After that, you found out about the woman and the child?"

"I'm getting there. I thought you wanted to know everything."

He smiled and nodded.

"For a while, I don't think my parents knew that I was doping again. I looked terrible anyway, pale, circles under my eyes, and they had been told that maybe for a year I would have trouble remembering and concentrating. I wasn't back in school yet. I wasn't allowed to drive. I kept asking them about the accident, and all they would say was that they knew I was very sad and that they were very sorry. Finally, I rode the bus to the library and got the old newspapers, and that's when I found out about the little girl and the woman."

"Was that when you tried to kill yourself?"

"I think so. Mason was gone, and I kept thinking I might have saved her. I mean, if I had pulled myself together in time, I could have told her to get on her side of the road. Maybe I could have jerked the wheel and got us out of the way. The whole thing was wrong, you see. It wasn't right that Mason and the woman and the little girl should die and I should live. It wasn't right that I didn't save all of them. If they had to die, it wasn't right that I didn't die, too."

"Are you all right now? Can you tell the rest of it?" He was offering her a tissue.

"Am I crying?" She touched her cheek and found that she was. How could that have happened without her knowing it? Belatedly, she felt tightness in her throat, a sting in her eyes. She blew her nose, and a sob escaped. She took a deep breath and swallowed and waited until she was sure that she could go on.

"I told you that I never liked downers. But my mother took sleeping pills. I got the bottle out of her bathroom and broke open the liquor cabinet and got a bottle of vodka. I figured that if I were going to do what I meant to do, I might as well make it pleasant, or at least easy."

"Did you think of writing a note?"

"Who to?" Shannon said. "There was nobody left on earth that I had anything to say to."

"All right."

"I decided against playing music. I opened my windows so I could hear anything that might be going on outside. I took one of the pills and had a slug of vodka. That didn't seem so bad. I had another hit of vodka and then another pill and more vodka. I know now it was pretty dumb to go at it that way. I should have taken all the pills at once and then as much vodka as I could handle. But I thought there might be an experience in what I was going to do, and I wanted to get the most out of it."

"Maybe you really didn't want to die, Shannon."

"Ah, ha," she said. "That's what you're paid to find out, isn't it?"

"How many pills did you take?"

"Not enough. I passed out before I got enough of them down. It was funny. I had a good time trying to kill myself."

"Do you still want to kill yourself?"

"I don't know," Shannon replied. "I need somebody to help me figure it out. I wish to God I could talk to Mason." Her voice broke, and she was sobbing, her face in her hands, tears wetting her fingers.

Now she sat in her bare apartment in Nashville where she kept no booze and no dope and none of the crazy lamps she had collected when she was in high school. She guessed that her old room in her parents' house in Jacksonville was in its own way as stripped of reminders of the past as her apartment. It was as if she and her parents and the doctors had all agreed without ever saying so that she *had* killed herself that night. That the old Shannon had died, and they had brought the corpse to the sanitarium and used the shell, the body that had once been inhabited by a wild and destructive girl, to make a new person. But not quite. The old Shannon lurked still in the corners of her brain and occasionally asserted herself.

This afternoon at the hospital, a woman who was dying of cancer got out of her bed and came down the hall trailing monitor wires and catheters. She stopped at the station and looking at Shannon with a face already cadaverous, said, "You have to help me. You can't let me die. Don't you see? My husband has left me, and I have two children."

Shannon had seen death before, but never this way. Under her gaze, sick people had gone struggling out of the world or simply stopped breathing as quietly as a falling leaf. But the dying people she had known had been too weak to protest what was happening to them. Oh, she thought, this was what it was really like to die when you knew there was life left—a future, if only you could survive to see it.

The pain of Mason's death, the guilt she felt about the deaths of the woman and the little girl came back to her. Sorrow and remorse hammered at her heart. She wanted somebody to help her, somebody to listen to her say how sad she was and to tell her that she would soon feel better. But for reasons that she did not understand, she could not tell Julien about the dying woman anymore than she could have told her parents, from whom she was as estranged now as she had been in the old days when they had argued about booze and drugs and her general misbehavior. All she had been able to do was to annoy Julien with a silly inquisition and tell him that he was her friend by means of a story that had confused him completely.

Well, she thought, score one for the old Shannon. She was more fully alive than the new Shannon had thought. Sooner or later, the new Shannon would have to tell Julien about her old self—that is, if he didn't give up and stop going out with her.

# VII

Bunnie was having dreams that frightened her and sometimes caused her to scream in the middle of the night. She said she wanted to sleep with Max, and Mrs. Smith put her in Max's bed, and that caused trouble. Max slept on a single bed, which was ample for his short, spare frame, but having Bunnie in the bed with him was another story. It seemed to Max that Bunnie was fatter at night than she was in the daytime. Mrs. Smith had placed her on one side of the bed, and Max had to admit that she was still lying where Mrs. Smith had put her, but there was only a narrow strip of mattress left for Max to occupy. "Well, now, Bunnie," Max said, "I don't think this is going to work. Maybe I'd better go sleep in your room."

"No, Max," Bunnie replied. "I came in here because I didn't want to be by myself. If you go to my room, you'll defeat the whole purpose."

Thinking about it, Max had to admit that what Bunnie said was true, and there was the further consideration of whether he wanted to be in her bed under any circumstances. Usually her diapers worked, and the mattress was covered with a rubber sheet, but still the bed never smelled quite fresh to Max, and Max was far from sure that he wanted to lie down on it.

"Well," he said, "all right, but you're taking up the whole bed. You're going to have to make a place for me."

"I'll try," Bunnie said, "but you'll have to help me."

Max attempted to figure out what was the best course for them to take, and Bunnie must have been doing the same thing, because for a while both were silent. Max concluded that Bunnie would have to turn one way or the other. She was lying on her back. Even though her stomach was big, if she were on her side she would occupy less space. Or so Max thought, and Bunnie agreed with him. They assayed the possibilities. If Max could lift her or if she could move herself, she could turn where she was, but since he couldn't and she couldn't, they would have to roll her. Max got his hands under her buttocks, which were bigger than ever with the diaper covering them. He shoved and Bunnie pushed with her legs; they got her halfway over, and for an instant her fleshy body was balanced on the edge of turning, but the strength in Max's arms gave out, and Bunnie flopped back into her starting place.

"God damn it, Bunnie," Max said, "you need to help."

Bunnie had been trying to help, and the effort had exhausted her. "Oh, oh, oh," she said in a breathless voice, "oh, oh, oh." Her full lips were rounded, and she was panting.

Now what? Max wondered. He needed something like a pole that he could put under Bunnie and get some leverage, but he didn't see anything in the room that would serve the purpose. If he had a pulley, now, and a piece of rope, but he had never kept things like that in the bedroom. Looking at the bed, Max saw that when they had tried to turn Bunnie they had made the situation worse: falling back, she had slipped into half the narrow space that Mrs. Smith had left for him.

"What I need," Max said, "is something to roll you with. A two-by-four maybe."

"Max," Bunnie said, "you can't prod me around as if I were a hog. Get your hands under me again and push harder."

"Maybe the broomstick," Max said. "I'll look in the kitchen."

"No, damn it," Bunnie said, "let's try again like we did last time."

This time Max put one of his hands under Bunnie's shoulder. He set his legs so he could lean his weight against her if they could raise her body off the bed. "Now," he said. "Push now, Bunnie."

Bunnie pushed and Max pushed. Once more Bunnie's body reached a point of equilibrium. She began to tremble, and it seemed to Max that they were going to fail to turn her again. "Push," he said. "Push." His arms were aching so much that he thought he would have to give up. He flexed his knees and shoved with his legs. Bunnie rolled. She flopped over face down on the edge of the bed. She gave a soft grunt of surprise. The springs squeaked, and Bunnie kept rolling. There was no hesitation, no time for Max to try to catch her. Over she went, landing with a soft bump beyond Max's field of vision. Max did not immediately know what had happened. First Bunnie was on the bed, then she was gone. He heard her voice, but he couldn't see her, and even though she seemed to be talking loudly, he could not understand what she was saying. At last he made out his own name.

"Max!"

"Well, yes," Max replied, still not certain what he ought to do.

"Damn it," Bunnie said, "you pushed me off the bed. Come around here and help me."

It was true. She was on the floor. Max leaned across the bed and looked at her for a moment. Then he turned on the ceiling light and walked to the other side of the bed where she was lying. There was no mistake about it. Bunnie was on her back peering up at Max with her eyes narrowed into what Max thought was an unaccountably angry expression.

"Help me!" Bunnie said, her voice sharp.

"To do what?"

"To get up, you idiot."

Max had a sense of déjà vu that slowly shaped itself into a memory. "I can't do that, Bunnie. I couldn't do it last time."

Bunnie began to say things she did not ordinarily say, most of which were names she was calling Max. Max ignored her and tried to get his thoughts in order. His memory continued to grow. The last time she had been on the floor, Julien had telephoned for somebody to come help, but Max couldn't recall who. He went to Julien's room to ask him, but Julien wasn't there. He returned to his own bedroom and asked Bunnie.

"What?" Bunnie said.

"You remember. When you fell in the living room. Julien called somebody to help, but I can't think who it was."

"Max," Bunnie said, "are you talking about when I had my stroke? Don't you know I was unconscious?"

"Well, the principle's still the same," Max replied. "You were on the floor like you are now, and I couldn't lift you."

"Damn you, Max, find Julien."

"Where?"

"Try the hospital. He's probably there waiting for that nurse to get off."

"What hospital?" Max asked.

"What hospital! The one where I was when I had my stroke."

"Oh, yes," Max replied. He couldn't place the name of the hospital any better than he could remember whom Julien had called for help, but he didn't want to tell Bunnie this. She was, it seemed to Max, getting unreasonably disgruntled. He decided that he would look up hospitals in the yellow pages to see if the name would come to him, but suddenly his old mind, which so frequently betrayed him, came to his rescue.

"It was the fire department, Bunnie," Max said. "Julien called the fire department."

"The fire department? What are they going to do, bring a ladder?"

"No," Max replied patiently, "they bring one of those little beds that rolls along. I don't know what you call them."

When the paramedics arrived, there was a moment of confusion. They lifted Bunnie onto their gurney and then asked Max where he wanted them to take her.

"Just right there," Max said. "It's my bed, you know, but she wants to sleep with me."

The paramedics looked at each other. Then one of them, who was almost as short as Max but stocky and strong-looking, said, "You don't want to take her to a hospital?"

"No," Max replied. "What happened was, she fell out of bed. She can't get up, and I can't lift her."

"You don't want her transported?" the paramedic said.

"No, God damn it," Bunnie said. "Just put me in that bed and turn off the light. It's past my bedtime."

The paramedics didn't do any better job of placing Bunnie on one side of the bed than Mrs. Smith had. Max lay down on the small space that was left for him, but there wasn't room in the bed for both of them. The only way Max could keep himself from falling out was to push against Bunnie, but Bunnie had become very cross, and she spoke harshly to Max and told him to quit shoving her.

"I don't have any room," Max said. "It's my bed, and you're taking up all of it."

"Max," Bunnie said, "you always were selfish."

Though Max knew that her muscles were almost useless, somehow she contrived now to push back against him, and this increased Max's sense of outrage. Fair was fair. He was willing to share his bed. He was willing for Bunnie to have half of it. But it wasn't right for Bunnie to take the whole damned thing. "Get over," he said.

"Get over yourself!"

Max tried to make more room for himself, but Bunnie's body, soft as it was, was unyielding. They argued again, shouted at each other. It seemed to Max that Bunnie was growing. It was as if her body were being inflated. He shoved and shoved again. She was trying to shove back, but mostly she held him where he was with the inert mass of herself.

"Move, God damn it!" Max shouted.

"I wouldn't if I could," Bunnie replied.

"Move!"

For a moment, there seemed to be silence. Then, could it be? Faintly it came to Max that Bunnie was singing. He listened closely. Sure enough, there was a tune; there were words. Bunnie was singing a church song, a hymn out of her Methodist past. "Brighten the corner where you are," Bunnie sang in tones that resembled those of a badly tuned oboe. "Brighten the corner where you are. Someone far from harbor you may guide across the bar . . ."

Max was furious. His heart pounded. He felt his pulse surge in his neck and head. Even though he was lying down, he was dizzy from the force of his own blood. His anger became laced with fear. Was he having a heart attack? A stroke? God damn her! Was she going to kill him?

"You're not in a corner," he shouted. "You're taking up the whole bed, and you're going to move over!"

He braced his hands on the frame of the bed, pulled his legs up and around, placed his feet against Bunnie's thighs and pushed. Her legs slid across the bed and got tangled in the sheet. Then she was off the bed, lying once more on the floor with the covers wrapped around her.

"You bastard!" Bunnie shouted. "You son of a bitch! You're trying to kill me!"

Subdued by what he had done and embarrassed at the thought of what he had to do, Max made his way to the phone and called the paramedics. The same two men arrived with what Max assumed was the same gurney. "What now?" the stocky man who seemed to do all the talking asked.

"Well," Max replied, his eyes not meeting those of the paramedic, "it's pretty much the same situation that we had last time."

"You mean she's on the floor again?"

"Not exactly," Max said.

"Where?"

Max could find no way to put a good face on the matter. "What I mean is, she is on the floor, but she's not on the same side of the bed. She went over the other side this time."

"Jesus," the paramedic said.

"He did it," Bunnie yelled as the two men pushed the gurney into the room. "He's trying to kill me."

The men looked at Bunnie and then at the aged and shrunken Max and clearly did not believe her.

"Lady," the short one said, "I think we better take you to the hospital."

"Oh, no," Bunnie said. "Oh, no."

The paramedic looked once more at Max. "Mr. Howard, we want to be helpful, but this is beginning to look funny on our log. I mean, we can't keep coming back to the same place without transporting the patient."

"Well—"

"Get me up," Bunnie said loudly. "Don't stand there talking. Get me back in the bed."

"That bed?" the paramedic asked.

"Oh, no," Max said. He knew that couldn't be allowed to happen again. "Oh, no. She'd better go to her own room."

"You mean this ain't her room?"

"This is my room," Max replied. "You see, she's been having these dreams—"

"Get me back in bed!" Bunnie said, her voice louder than ever. "Move your asses!"

Suddenly, the second paramedic spoke. He said, "You mean we'd better move yours, don't you, lady?"

Taller than his partner, with fewer muscles and longer hair, he appeared to be astonished that he had been the author of this witticism. His eyes widened, his jaw dropped. He looked at Max and then at Bunnie, who had been shocked into temporary silence. Then he caught the other paramedic's eye and began to guffaw. It was as if laughter that he had hoarded for a lifetime was now being spent. Rich and sonorous ho, ho, ho's rose from his diaphragm. He held his stomach. He wiped his eyes. He tried to repeat the line, but mirth disabled him.

"Hey, Charlie," he managed to gasp, "I said . . . I said . . ." Then he was laughing again as loudly as ever.

"Yeah," Charlie said when he could make himself understood. "Now we better move this lady."

The paramedics took Bunnie to her own room. Max brought her a drink. He had one himself. He hadn't meant to push her out of bed. He felt terrible.

"I'm sorry," he said. "We can leave a light on. I'll stay here with you until you go to sleep."

Bunnie was not pacified. "I don't dream when I'm awake, Max. It's after I've gone to sleep that I get frightened. You're confused, as usual."

"I'll stay here all night. I'll doze in the chair."

"Do what you want to," Bunnie said coldly.

They didn't speak for a while, but Bunnie was restless. She moved her legs and turned her head from side to side. Max knew that she probably wanted another drink but was still too angry with him to ask for it. He thought of offering to get it for her, but he didn't know quite what to say, and he couldn't quite bring himself to utter the words that came to him. He had never been good at this sort of thing. It seemed to him that once he had said he was sorry, the dispute ought to be over. With Bunnie, with most women he had known, it was different. They wanted something beyond the apology, something that Max was unable to give. But he had to try.

"Bunnie, would you like another drink?"

For a moment, she didn't answer. "All right," she said finally, her tone neutral. She didn't look at Max.

He fixed a drink for himself, too. Bunnie thanked him. Then they sipped in silence until both drinks were gone. Max felt relaxed and tired. The edge of his guilt was dulled. He decided that as soon as Bunnie went to sleep, he would return to his own bedroom. But Bunnie was still restless. She smoothed her hair. She put her hands under her head and stared at the ceiling.

Finally, Bunnie said, "I was thinking about beds, Max. The beds here and the beds at Nineveh. I was trying to remember all the beds we ever slept in."

What? Max started to say, then stopped himself. The events of the night seemed to have clarified his mind or at least made him more wary. There was no need to ask Bunnie to repeat herself. Ever since her stroke, she had been trying to create lists out of her memory: poems, novels, people. Max decided he would help, give her some hints as a kind of peace offering.

He said, "Have you thought of the guest room at Susan's?"

"Hah," Bunnie replied, "why would you think of that? That's not the bed you would have taken her to, Max. She was visiting us at Nineveh when you propositioned her."

"God damn it!" Max said. "That was a long time ago."

Bunnie was still looking at the ceiling. "Yes, it was all a long time ago. But it happened, didn't it?"

Jesus, Max thought. He was too old for this. Here it was again, the same thing he had been pondering a few minutes before. With women, nothing was ever finished. With them, it was as if the whole world, the whole scheme of creation, was as confused as he was. When Bunnie was in the hospital, his memory had tricked him into thinking the past was the present. For a few awful minutes he had thought his botched seduction of Edith Ross had taken place the night before, and he was so unnerved that he cried when he got to the hospital. He was not confused now. He knew that his invitation—was that the right word?— to Susan had been made thirty years ago. Why wouldn't Bunnie leave it alone? Why couldn't they be done with it?

Some of the anger he had felt when he and Bunnie were fighting over space in his bed returned to him. "I wasn't the only one," Max said. "You had your men. We were both doing it."

"Oh, no," Bunnie replied. "The whole point was that I couldn't do what you wanted Susan to do. You'd missed your chance with me. You didn't want children when I was young enough to have them."

"I told you I was sorry," Max said. "I never stopped loving you. I went to Italy to bring you home again."

"Yes, but what you did was the reason I was in Italy in the first place."

What? Max wondered. What exactly had he done? What had he said to Susan that afternoon at Nineveh? He tried to remember, and a few details came back to him. They had been in the library, he was sure of that. She had been on a couch, reading, her legs pulled up under her. Had he planned it? Had he thought beforehand that she might consent to have a child for him? It seemed to Max that he must have planned what he was going to say in advance. He would tell her that, being too old to have babies herself, Bunnie wouldn't mind, but there would be no use to tell her until they knew that Susan was pregnant.

Could he have done this? He wasn't considering the morality of it.

He was pondering his own stupidity. At the time, he was past fifty: half a century of living, and part of that time spent trying to be a writer, trying to create characters that resembled real people. Had he still been too dumb to think of how what he was saying might sound to Susan? What possibly could have made her want to do something so bizarre? What motives would have compelled her to have a baby and give it up just to satisfy Max's desire to be a father? No, Max told himself, he had not been that stupid.

He had wanted a child, but he had wanted Susan, too. She had been visiting them for a week. Every morning, Bunnie went to Nashville to teach summer school. Max was supposed to be working on a book, but as the week passed, his concentration lapsed. Sitting at his typewriter, he listened for Susan's footstep. He was conscious of her being somewhere in the house. His sense of her presence overwhelmed him. She treated him as if he were really her uncle, a blood relative like Bunnie. She came to breakfast in her nightgown and paraded before him in shorts and halter. He longed to touch her. Her breasts, the smooth firm flesh of her legs, were constantly in his imagination. Max recalled now that it was only after he had made his pass and been rebuffed that he gave her his line about wanting children.

That afternoon in the library, he had put his hand on her thigh, and for a moment she gazed at him in astonishment. He remembered the questioning look in her eyes, the wrinkling of her forehead. What had happened then? Had he withdrawn his hand? Had she jumped up and left the room? Had she stayed to scold him? He didn't know. He thought he could see her standing in the middle of the library, the book still in her hand, her finger marking her place in it. He could make himself see her lips move, but whatever she might have said was irretrievably lost in his failing memory.

"You're wrong, Max."

At the sound of Bunnie's voice, Max jumped. He had forgotten he was in the same room with her.

"It wasn't just sex," Bunnie said. "You wanted her, all right. You wanted most women. But you wanted a child more. It was partly all that Old South business. You remember how it was when we visited the Rosses? John writing a novel about the Civil War. Maps pinned on the walls. All that talk about battles. And of course, talk of families. All the men wanted sons so their lines would continue. But, Max, what if Susan had said yes? And what if the baby had been a girl? Did you ever think about that?"

Tears stung Max's eyes. They wet his cheeks. Sadness gripped his heart, but he was not sure what he was crying about. Was it guilt that made him weep? Or was it the memory of those days with John and Edith Ross, their house in the country full of poets and novelists and critics, all of them talking of the books they were working on? This had been long ago. Bunnie was confused about the time. These wonderful days had come twenty years before he had tried to seduce Susan. They had all been equal back then. There had been no one to warn them of the future, to predict that some of them, like John and Edith Ross, would succeed and others, like Max, would fail. But he had failed, and the knowledge of his failure had almost destroyed him. However mixed his motives had been when he put his hand on Susan's thigh, he *had* wanted a son. Bunnie was right about that. But not merely because of family pride. He had also needed the promise of another chance. He had needed someone to redeem his own failure. Now he didn't know. Nothing was as clear to him as it used to be.

Bunnie spoke again, and once more he started.

"It wouldn't have changed anything, Max. Oh, it would be nice to have children, of course. But, Max, we are what we are. We did what we did. It's us, Max. We're the culprits."

# VIII

God damn the bed, Bunnie thought, and God damn the wheelchair, and God damn being old in general. She had a friend, a poet, who liked to say that old age was the most ridiculous thing that could happen to you, but how did he know, being no more than seventy-one or -two and suffering from nothing more than cold feet and heartburn? Bunnie longed to be up and about. Once or twice a week, a friend would come and take her for a ride through the park or even for lunch at the University Club. But getting her out of the apartment and into the car and out of the car and into the club sometimes made these outings more trouble than they were worth. And there was always the chance of embarrassment. Going into the cathedral one day, she had lost her diaper. She had come in a back door and was crossing in front of the altar when it fell around her ankles, and she was obliged to step out of it. After that, she had just about quit using her walker.

Max, of course, was still mobile, for which she supposed she ought to be thankful. He made the whiskey run with Julien. He could walk around the apartment complex, usually without getting lost, and because he could walk, he could go with Mrs. Pakenham to the grocery store or get her to take him to the bank, where he had learned to use the automatic teller, or to the mall, where he enjoyed strolling among the shoppers and looking in the windows, and where now and then he bought a book. Unlike Bunnie, Max could go to funerals, and did, but they made him edgy. He always went to the cemetery, always stayed until the gravediggers had filled the grave, even though hearing the clods of dirt thump against the vault upset him. Bunnie wondered why he put himself through this. It seemed unlikely to her that Max could think of attending burials as an act of penance. Was he attempting to prepare himself for what he knew was his own fate? Was he trying to figure the unlikely odds of escaping when his time came? When he got back from the cemetery, he paced the floor and looked out the windows as if he had just had a close call and was still not certain of his own safety.

Since visitors usually came in the afternoon, Bunnie spent her mornings alone or sitting with a silent Max, her yellow pad on her lap, thinking about her novel. Most of the time she was deep in thought, but when she was thinking, she stared in the direction of the patio, and Mrs. Pakenham and Mrs. Smith thought she was watching the chipmunks. For Bunnie's sake, they wanted to encourage the chipmunks to play on the patio and knew that the best way to do that was to feed them, but they didn't know what chipmunks ate. They discussed this topic full time for two days, or so it seemed to Bunnie. Every time she heard conversation from the kitchen, it concerned such things as the sizes of chipmunks' mouths and what kind of teeth they had and whether they ate worms and snails or just seeds and acorns. Mrs. Pakenham wondered if they liked raisins. Or strawberries, Mrs. Smith suggested, but immediately concluded that feeding them strawberries would be too expensive.

"Peanuts," Bunnie said finally, trying to get some peace in which to do her work. "They like peanuts."

"Well, of course," Mrs. Smith agreed. But this did not bring the silence Bunnie had hoped for.

Bunnie listened with increasing annoyance as the two ladies searched the kitchen. Cabinet doors opened and shut. Jars and cans scraped on counters. "I thought we had some," Mrs. Smith said.

"Well, we usually keep them," Mrs. Pakenham replied, her tone a little defensive because it was her job to buy the groceries.

They continued to look and to declare their mutual frustration until it was clear that the house was bereft of peanuts. There was a blessed silence. Bunnie studied the notes on her pad. Where was she now? What had she been trying to remember when she stopped yesterday? Before she could get herself oriented, a voice filled with the joy of discovery came from the kitchen.

"Peanut butter," Mrs. Smith said. "We can give them peanut butter."

"Well, I suppose," Mrs. Pakenham said warily. She seemed still chagrined to have been caught without peanuts. "How will we do it? Put it on a dish?"

"Why not on bread?"

"Why, yes," Mrs. Pakenham said, "a peanut-butter sandwich."

Interrupted again just as she felt that her mind might start to work, Bunnie was furious. She threw her pencil at the glass doors, shoved the pad off her lap, and gripped the arms of her wheelchair.

"Finger sandwiches," Bunnie shouted. "Give them finger sandwiches with currant jelly. And don't forget the napkins."

"What's that?" Mrs. Smith asked from the kitchen door. "Do you need something, Mrs. Howard? Oh, I see. You've dropped your pad and pencil."

God damn having strokes, Bunnie thought. God damn Mrs. Smith for being a busybody. God damn Mrs. Pakenham, whose husband's great, great, great-grandfather, Bunnie fervently hoped, had been the very one who had lost his entrails on the field at Chalmette. Mrs. Smith gave her the pad and pencil and shifted Bunnie in her chair, which was another annoyance because she put Bunnie's weight on her bruised hip. God damn falling out of bed, she thought—or had she been pushed out? She hadn't quite kept track of exactly how she received her injuries. Well, she thought, one or the other, but that shouldn't have happened. After all their years of marriage, after all they had gone through together and all they had forgiven each other for, here at the end of their lives she and Max ought to make peace with each other. But of course as far as novel writing went, fighting in bed was the very ticket. Somebody—as usual, her mind declined to furnish a name—had said that happy families were all alike, meaning only unhappy families were interesting and worth reading about. If that was the case, Bunnie thought, her life with Max was the stuff of great literature.

Poor Max, Bunnie thought. When he propositioned Susan, he had probably been going through his male menopause. Maybe she should have been more patient with him, but at the time she had had no disposition to indulge him. The next morning she sent Susan home, and two weeks later she was in Rome in a little third-floor apartment in Trasteveri that seemed to Bunnie cold even in the summer. John Ross, who was at the American Academy that year, found it for her. John met her plane, and the moment she caught sight of him coming toward her down the wide, gloomy corridor of the airport, she knew what was going to happen. It crossed her mind that, like some character in mythology who had offended a minor god, she was doomed to spend the rest of her life sleeping with dapper little men who took sex seriously.

John, who like Max sported a well-trimmed mustache, wore a blue paisley ascot, an ivory-colored shirt, and a magnificently tailored houndstooth jacket. He was carrying a cane, something Max could never have brought off without embarrassment. A Freudian symbol? Bunnie wondered. Did he think of his life in imagistic terms as if his very existence were a grand narrative still being constructed? He approached her with arms outstretched; he spoke quick Italian to the cab driver; and then they were on their way to Rome, past flowers that bloomed along the roadside.

"Well," John said, "let me look at you. More beautiful than ever, if I may say so."

Ah, so soon, Bunnie thought. Weren't women supposed to be given time to recover from broken hearts? Surely, considering what Max had done, she ought to have one.

"You'll love your apartment," John said. "It reminds me of the flat where Keats died."

Died? Bunnie thought. Died? She turned her mind from her supposedly broken heart to the grimmer notion of consumption.

"Keats?" she said. "Died?"

"Well, he was in a better neighborhood," John said. "Over by the Spanish Steps, though God knows what it was like when he lived there."

He paused. Then he said, "I'm so glad you're here. Edith and I have separated, you know. I assume you heard that before you left Nashville."

She hadn't heard. Did this make them two of a kind? she wondered. She had not so far decided whether she had officially separated from Max, though clearly for the time being at least they were not living together.

"No, I hadn't heard," Bunnie said. "What happened?"

"Oh, you know, the same old thing."

"Your women?"

"Now, Bunnie," he said in his deep and, she had to admit, enormously attractive voice, "you know things are always more complicated than that. Yes, there was an Italian girl involved, but that's just a symptom of something more fundamental."

"Or so men like to believe."

"Don't think about Edith and me, Bunnie. She's gone to London to do some work in the British Museum. Look." He swept his hand toward a piazza, a fountain. "You're in the Eternal City."

He put his arm around her and moved closer. She kept peering straight ahead. Soon the cab stopped. John got out and helped the driver unload the luggage.

It seemed reasonable to Bunnie that her apartment should have reminded John Ross of a moribund Keats. They mounted steep, dark steps—the men carrying her suitcases, thank God—to one room and a bath with the most primitive facilities. There was a daybed, a desk, a table, a few straight chairs; at one end of the room, discernible beyond a half-drawn curtain, were a small stove and a sink.

"Everything's here," John said happily. He opened cabinets that contained a small collection of shabby dishes, a few utensils. There were sheets and towels. In a corner, behind another curtain, there was a rod where she could hang her dresses.

"You've a wonderful view," he said. "You can see the river."

It was true. Peering through the dusty glass, across the decaying tiles of rooftops, she could make out a stream, a bridge, a line of plane trees. Though to her it was exotic, the sight depressed her. She knew that the river was dirty, and she doubted that it would be safe for her to walk alone beneath the trees even in daylight. John sensed her mood and blamed it on weariness.

"You're tired from the flight. Get some rest. I'll come back tonight and take you to dinner."

She *was* weary, but she couldn't sleep. She dozed fitfully, but asleep or awake, her mind kept creating variations of old themes. John Ross, perhaps because she had seen him so recently, intruded on scenes in which he had played no part. Bunnie recalled the day she had returned to Nineveh and found Max drunk in the library and Susan sitting white-faced in the living room, her fists clenched, her bags packed. On that afternoon only the three of them had been in the house—where had Mrs. Pakenham been when Max put his hand on Susan's thigh?—but in her dream, John Ross waited for her just inside the door. He said, Don't worry about Max. Don't worry about Susan. Then she heard her own voice, saw her own lips move, as if she were at once spectator and actor. Of course, replied the acting Bunnie, of course. She thought she heard other spectators murmur their approval, as if the house at Nineveh were a stage with an audience unseen beyond the footlights. The idea that she was being observed pleased her. She took John's arm and moved with him up the long curve of stairway to—where? The dream ended. She jerked awake. She was in Rome.

Ah, she thought, if she and Max and Susan *had* been performing before a crowd that afternoon, far from appearing tragic, they might have elicited some laughs. Susan, who must have been waiting quietly all afternoon, her feelings repressed, her fury building, was too angry to say what had happened. Every time she attempted to speak, she began to cry. Max had drunk enough to dull, if not obliterate, his sense of guilt, and he claimed not to know what the fuss was about.

"Well," he said, "I didn't mean to get her all upset. I never knew any other woman to respond this way."

"What did you do to her?" Bunnie asked, surprised at the calmness of her own voice.

"Not much," Max replied. "I guess I touched her thigh."

"God damn it, Max. How could you have done such a thing? That's incestuous!"

"Yes, in a way," Max said judiciously. "That's what I had in mind. I thought that if I could get her to have my baby, it would be kin to you, too. I was thinking of both of us."

My God, Bunnie thought. Had he actually said this? Was this what she was supposed to put on her yellow pad and incorporate into her novel? Unfortunately, she was sure that this was exactly what he had said, even though she knew that often her memory was inaccurate. One day recently when she had been remembering her exile in Rome, she had imagined a scene that clearly could not have happened. She had been in her apartment in Rome, lying on the daybed, and John Ross was making love to her. To be sure, this had occurred many times, but without intervention. What her remembering or dreaming mind made up was a knock at the door and then the voice of Max, stronger than in real life, saying, "Open the door! Open the door! I know what you're doing."

"Oh, oh," Bunnie heard herself say, "oh, oh," her tone both startled and eager.

John stopped moving. There was a moment of silence. Then Max spoke again. "Open up. You can't fool me. I wasn't born yesterday."

Oh, no, Bunnie thought, surely not. Max had never been a good novelist, but he wouldn't use such dialogue as that. Lying motionless and frustrated beneath John, Bunnie was a little ashamed for him.

Even so, the Max of the dream would not give up. "I know you're there," Max said. "I'm not going to leave. You're going to have to come out sooner or later."

Again for an instant there was no sound. Then to her utter astonishment, John Ross, who recently had won a Pulitzer Prize for fiction, spoke in clear falsetto tones and said, "No use for you to wait. Ain't nobody here but us chickens."

"Chickens, my—"

Whatever expletive Max had used was lost in John Ross's crowing. He raised his head, opened his mouth, filled his small lungs with air, and emitted a great cock-a-doodle-do, a piercing sound that filled the room. He leapt out of bed and crowed again. He put his hands on his chest and flapped his bent arms as if they were wings, and sure enough, he rose. He was flying.

Impossible. Impossible. No such thing had ever happened. But she saw him in her memory. His nude body drifted awkwardly in space like a figure in a Chagall painting. The image was clearer to her than the room in which she sat, more real in her mind than the glass doors, the bricks in the patio, the chipmunks that declined to eat their peanut butter. She heard another shrill crow. She saw John turn as he reached the wall. He banked and straightened up again, flying as a chicken would fly, clumsily, without grace: he was a bantam beating the air, his appendage undiminished, a proclamation of his pride and his virility.

Had she cackled in response? Had she tried to fly? Had her then leaner and firmer body joined his in transport through the air? There was hardly space enough in the small room for both of them to levitate. Their wings would have brushed. They might have crashed with thumps and groans that would have given their game away to Max. Hearing them, he would have known they weren't chickens.

Dear God, Bunnie thought, upset by the memory of this crazy sequence. I'm eighty-six years old and I've had a stroke and I've gone crazy. She needed a drink. She called for one. Reluctantly, Mrs. Smith brought it, and Bunnie took half of it at once. She was frightened. Her hand shook. She hadn't had such hallucinations since she left the hospital. Was she all right now? she wondered. She made herself look at the lawn beyond her patio; she was afraid that she might see a clock that didn't belong there. She finished her vodka and decided that she had not had another seizure. She was all right—or what passed for all right in her case. She must have dozed off. Once more, she must have been dreaming.

Bunnie lit a cigarette and tried again to get her thoughts in order.

Then she remembered. Of course Max had come to Rome. He had said so last night. He had come to get her. Gradually, it all came back. She had not met his plane. The few letters they had exchanged after she left Nashville had been noncommittal. Did he still love her? Did she still love him? She didn't know, and she didn't want to find out in a place as public as the airport. Early in the afternoon, she heard his steps on the stairs, his bags scraping the wall and bumping the railing. Did he assume that he was going to move in with her? The idea made her press her lips together in annoyance. He knocked. She opened the door. There was Max, plainly himself: the flesh, at least, was unaltered.

This was not what she had expected, but she didn't know, either then or now, what she did expect. He was wilted from his journey, his collar not quite fresh, his tie poorly knotted. A mist of perspiration covered his pink forehead. His mustache, his small blue eyes, were so utterly familiar to her that for a moment she had the strange sense that they had not been apart; it was as if for the last several months she had encountered this face every morning as usual. She was disappointed. Without realizing it, she had prepared herself for a moment of high drama: of operatic anger or a sudden rediscovery of passion, neither of which gripped her heart. She hugged him—it seemed the proper thing to do—and stood aside for him to come in.

Apparently, she would not need to tell him that he could not stay there. He looked at the poor furnishings, the curtains that served imperfectly for walls. He let his eyes linger on the daybed, looked away and turned back to the daybed again. It was obviously too small to accommodate two people for any purpose other than making love. She wondered if Max were considering what might have happened here, what men Bunnie might have entertained while he lingered at Nineveh. Again she was angry. He had been the cause of her leaving. After he was sober enough to discuss the proposal he had made to Susan, he had told Bunnie that he might want to divorce her. He needed time to choose between staying married to her and finding a willing younger woman who might give him a son. After that, did he still have a claim on her? Even though they were still married, did he have any right to question what she might have done?

But all this was in her mind. If Max were thinking such thoughts as she was imagining for him, he did not divulge them. He left his bags in the middle of the floor and walked the few steps to the window.

"You have a nice view," he said. "That must be the Tiber."

Bunnie had a sense that she was reprising her own arrival in Rome, but with less-skilled actors. "Leave your luggage here," she said. "There's a *pensione* around the corner. Let's go see if we can get a room for you. I don't have a telephone."

That night they had dinner together, treating each other with great courtesy, and the next day she went with him to see the sights of Rome. At Max's suggestion, they began with Saint Peter's, which was not one of Bunnie's favorite places. She admired the building, but it was always cluttered with what she thought of as pilgrims—devout tourists who had come from far and near to genuflect and cross themselves, duck into confessionals and kneel before altars. She considered these public exhibitions to be in bad taste; she was embarrassed when she saw someone kissing the foot of a statue. Nothing could have surprised her more than seeing Max do the same things. He lingered on his knees in one of the side chapels until Bunnie could wait for him no longer. The room was neither small nor crowded, but sitting there made her nervous. She felt as if the ceiling were lowering, the walls moving together. She went out of the chapel and on through the doors into the Roman sunlight.

When Max joined her, she peered into his face. Clearly something about him *had* changed. His face must show something that she had missed when she had looked at him yesterday. But no. Insofar as she could tell, he was absolutely the same: rosy cheeks, white hair. He had missed a spot under his chin when he shaved this morning. Finally, she could contain herself no longer.

"Max," she said, "what's the matter with you? What the hell is all this rigmarole you've been engaged in?"

"Well, now," he replied, sounding like the same old Max indeed, "let's go over here and have a drink. We can talk better."

It took them a while to get around the corner to a café, where Max, who would have liked something more stimulating, had to settle for wine.

"What about it?" Bunnie said.

But Max was in no hurry to confess. They were at a table on the sidewalk. Max leaned back in his chair and looked around like any other tourist—at the other customers and the waiters and the cars and people passing. An Italian girl in spike heels and a short skirt walked by. In Bunnie's judgment, she was too plump, but Max apparently didn't think so. Seeing him stare at the girl brought Bunnie to the edge of fury.

"God damn you," she said, "stop looking for whores and talk to me."

The words were more harsh, her tone more bitter, than she had meant them to be, but she had no notion of apologizing. She was still angry. When Max didn't answer immediately, she spoke again. "Tell me. What the hell's going on?"

Max's mind had evidently been wandering. "What?"

"Why are you doing all this kneeling and crossing?"

"Oh. It's all a part of being Catholic, you know."

"No, I don't know," Bunnie said. "That's what I'm asking you."

"Well," Max replied, "it makes sense once you understand it. There's a reason for everything we do."

"We?"

Max emptied his glass and touched the pink tip of his tongue to the edge of his mustache. "I was lonesome," he said. "You were gone, and the house was empty, and I was lonesome. It seemed the right thing to do under the circumstances."

"You became a Catholic?" She heard the note of astonishment in her own voice. "You joined the Catholic church because you were lonesome?"

"I rejoined. Took it up again. It got me out of the house."

"Got you out of the house!" Bunnie said. "Max, that's the worst reason for getting religion that I ever heard of."

Max had poured himself another glass of wine; now he finished this one off, too. "Well, you were gone, and I didn't know whether you were coming back. If you think of it that way, it makes sense."

Makes sense, Bunnie thought. Makes sense. That was what Max had said, but it hadn't. Not then and not now, which was some kind of commentary on the condition of her own mind when a year later she had become a Catholic. But one thing at a time. She needed to deal with Max first. He had gone into the Church first, and she needed to know why. She needed motivation for her novel. She had about quit asking Max for help, but there was no one else to appeal to. He was sitting across from her now, on the end of the couch, reading the *Wall Street Journal*. Recently, he had been mixing his drinks in a coffee mug. Bunnie didn't know why. Perhaps because the handle on the mug made drinking easier. He took a sip from his mug now and sighed.

Bunnie caught the sweet odor of scotch penetrating the stale air of the apartment.

"Max," Bunnie said, "when I was in Rome, why did you return to the Church?"

"It was the family," Max said. "The Howards, you know. Even under Henry the Eighth, we never left. We've always been Catholics."

"But, Max," Bunnie said, "you had given it up. You weren't a Catholic when I married you."

"Well, yes," Max replied, "but it's all different over here. In America, I mean. We don't have a king over here. We have a president."

Bunnie peered down from her wheelchair into his innocent blue eyes. Then she threw her pencil to one side of the room and her pad to the other so it would be twice as much trouble for Mrs. Smith to pick them up and give them back to her.

# IX

I'm dying, Julien thought. He was succumbing to fatigue, to a weariness that was certain to be fatal. His case was so advanced that only the time and place remained in doubt. Maybe in bed, he thought. That would be all right. Dying in bed would be traditional and proper. Perhaps one night he would fall into a sleep so profound that he could not awaken from it. He would slide from sleep into death, feeling no pain, causing no more than the usual amount of trouble people cause when they leave the land of the living. But then, he thought, Max wouldn't allow him to do that. No matter how soundly he was sleeping, Max would find a way to wake him up. Still, on the morning of his death, coffee would not save him. He would go staggering out of the apartment, drive in a daze to the university, park, and move down the sidewalk and probably collapse in the middle of Twenty-First Avenue.

This was an awful thought. There he would be, lying on the street, both his frame and his face grown so gaunt from lack of rest that his eyes would seem darker and his nose longer than usual. Traffic would be stopped for him, he supposed, horns blowing now and then, though in Nashville drivers seldom used their horns. And what would they do with him? Well, some level-headed citizen would call an ambulance, but in the meantime, what do ordinary people do with a strange body? If his fellow students passed, would they pretend not to know him? Would somebody try to give him CPR? It was a terrible scene to contemplate: he, being dead, would be oblivious to all proprieties. He saw himself, his legs bent at the knees and extended like broken spokes, his face smudged by his fall. There might even be blood, and a crowd would be jostling each other to get a look at him. He was so deeply embarrassed by the notion of his lifeless body on display in the middle of the street that he came to his senses. My God, he thought, what's the matter with me? He was in the library, surrounded by his fellow students, all of whom were reading books or staring at computer screens. He wasn't going to die. Surely not. But the idea kept going around in his brain, haunting him.

"Listen, Shannon," Julien said that night. They were in the bar. The piano player was working through his last set. Shannon was taking delicate sips of wine. My life is continually repeating itself, Julien thought. Only the conversation, the terms of annoyance, were ever different. "Listen, I'm dying."

"What?" Shannon asked. "Right now? This minute?"

"Yes, God damn it," Julien replied. "Or tomorrow. Or the next day or next week. I'm telling you in advance so you'll know when I don't show up. They'll probably send my body to the medical school."

"Dear me," Shannon said. "Let me feel your pulse." She held his wrist, looked at her watch, then turned to him with her eyes opened wide in mock seriousness. "How long has this been going on?"

"How long has what been going on?"

"Julien, your pulse is a dead giveaway. I should have been taking it earlier."

"What?"

"Do you know what your trouble is?" Shannon said. "You're in love." She smiled at him. "I can help you, Julien. You won't need a doctor."

"For God's sake," Julien said, "I know I'm in love. I've told you I love you a thousand times. But love's supposed to make you feel good, not like you're dying."

"That's not true," Shannon said.

"What's not true?"

"All of it. You haven't told me you love me a thousand times. It's more like ten. And love can make you feel lots of different ways. You ought to know that, Julien."

He did know it. He had loved Justine, but not the way he loved Shannon. His love for Justine had been calm, sensible, mature. His love for Shannon was a form of insanity. Even when she was hassling him, asking him outrageous questions, he took delight in watching her lips move, hearing the sound of her voice. And always, every minute that he was with her, he wanted her.

"I tell you I love you ten times a night," Julien said. "My real trouble is that you won't let me come home with you."

"You never asked."

"Never asked! of course I did."

"Well, it was the way you did it, Julien. You said, 'Can I come up and see your apartment?' or 'How about letting me come up for a drink?' But you never said, 'How about letting me spend the night with you?'"

"All right," Julien said, "try this. I want to spend the night with you. I want to make love to you. Let's go to your apartment."

"When?"

"Tonight. Right now."

"Maybe," Shannon said, "but first I have to tell you something."

Julien was holding her hand, clinging to it as if now that she had agreed to let him make love to her, she might try to escape. "You've already told me what I want to hear. Let's get out of here."

"No," she said, "listen. It's like they say in books, Julien. I've got what they call a past. I need to tell you about it."

"It doesn't matter," Julien said.

"Yes, it does. Nothing's ever finished, Julien. Life goes on, time goes on. Things happen that you can't change. But the wrong things you did stay with you."

"I've got a past, too," he said. "Sometime I'll tell you about it, if you want me to. But not tonight. All I want to think about tonight is you and how much I love you."

"I'm not a virgin," she said, and except for the tone of her voice and that her eyes would not meet his, he would have thought she was joking.

Julien smiled. "Neither am I, thank God. Those books you're reading are off the wrong shelf, Shannon. Queen Victoria's been dead for almost a hundred years. We're about to enter the twenty-first century."

"It's more than that."

"I don't care what it is. I don't care what you've done. Sometime we can tell each other everything about ourselves. Right now all that matters is that I love you. I want you. Let's go to your apartment."

For a moment, her dark mood seemed to linger. She was silent, her gaze on the table. Then she looked up and said, "You still haven't done it, Julien. You still haven't told me that you love me a thousand times. Maybe I ought to resent that."

He kept his arm around her as they moved out of the bar. On the sidewalk, he kissed her, then walked with her to her car and kissed her again.

"Hurry," Julien said.

"What if I don't go home? What if I drive back to the hospital?"

"I'll follow you. You know what people say goes on in hospitals."

On the way to her apartment, she teased him, driving slowly, stopping and waiting at every deserted intersection. He tried to kiss her in front of her building and again in the lobby, but she pushed him away. Her good humor had returned. "Damn it, Julien," she said, "we're almost there. And don't try anything in the elevator. You've been seeing too many movies."

She did let him kiss her in the small vestibule of her apartment. He pulled up her skirt, ran his hand up her leg. He wanted to undress her step by step as they moved toward the bedroom. She told him to stop. She caught his wrist, and he was surprised at how much strength there was in her slender fingers.

"For God's sake," she said, "behave yourself, Julien. You act like you're still in high school."

She led him to the couch and let him kiss her again. Then she pulled away. "Wait here," she said. "I'm going to take a shower."

"A shower?" He couldn't believe he had heard her correctly. It was almost as if she had said she was going to take a walk or vacuum the carpet or do the laundry.

"Think of it as an ablution. I've been at the hospital all day."

"Damn," he said, "how long will it take?"

"A few minutes."

"You're going to wash your hair, too, aren't you?" Julien said gloomily.

"Just wait," Shannon said. "You'll be surprised how fast I can do it."

She stepped away before he could kiss her again, moved through a door and shut it. Did he hear the click of a lock? Was she afraid he would follow her? He checked his watch. It was ten minutes until two. He couldn't believe they had stayed so long in the bar. For a blank instant, he watched the second hand creep around the dial. Then he sat down and looked at the apartment that she had once told him was too small to accommodate both of them. There was very little to see. Besides the couch on which he sat, there were two tables, a lamp, a chair, a television. Everything was clean, the surfaces free of dust, the paint unsmudged around the doorknobs and switchplates.

The room was as quiet as it was clean. Julien leaned back on the couch and strained to hear any sound that might come from Shannon's bedroom. At first, he heard nothing and knew there would be nothing to hear. What did he expect? The click of metal when she unhooked her brassiere? The rustle of nylon? Still he listened, and finally he thought he heard the hiss of water. The sound was very faint, perhaps a product of his imagination. He tried to imagine her with the water falling over her head, her hair hanging dark and wet over her shoulders. He wanted to go find her. He longed to slip into the bathroom, to look at the blurred contours of her body through the opaque shower door. When she came out and saw him, she would probably try to cover herself with her hands like the naked women in Renaissance paintings. He forced himself to stay where he was. He needed to calm down. When they made love, he did not want to disappoint her.

He concentrated on trying to hear the shower and convinced himself that he heard it, a noise constant and faint, a whisper. He shifted his position, leaned further back on the couch until his head rested more comfortably. He thought of watching television, but he didn't want to move. Whatever he might see was probably not worth the effort. He was calmer now. His heart that had raced a moment ago was beginning to slow down. He looked at his watch. Ten minutes had passed since he had looked at it before. Was she out of the shower? He listened for the sound of a hair dryer and heard nothing. He listened for the hiss of water that he thought he had heard a moment earlier. At first, he could not hear anything. Then he believed he caught the hissing sound again, but he wasn't sure. He slipped further down on the couch and listened once more, but heard only the sough of his easily drawn breath in the silence.

Once or twice, he moved in a strange, white landscape. Or did not move, but drifted, hung suspended in an alien world, plain and dimly lighted. Then he was back in darkness for minutes or hours, before he opened his eyes and kept them open and did not know where he was or remember what he had done the night before for a few comfortable seconds. Strange, he thought, strange. This was not his room. There was no sound of Max banging on his door. Then not slowly, but not quite suddenly either, he awakened fully to the horror of what he had done. Oh, Jesus, he thought. Oh, my God, my God. What time was it? He was afraid to know. He had to make himself look at his watch, but at first he couldn't find it. His left hand was under a blanket that he had never seen before. He sat up quickly, got his arm free. It was 3:25.

Shannon! He didn't dare call out to her. He had to find her, apologize to her. He leapt from the couch and collapsed on the floor. His right leg was asleep, numb, devoid of feeling. He rose and hopped around the room, his clumsy foot going thump, thump, thump against the floor. His leg began to tingle, but when he tried his weight on it, he fell again, sprawled on the floor as he had imagined he would sprawl on the street when he died of weariness. Finally he was able to limp around the room. His coat was draped over the chair. His shoes sat neatly on the floor. Oh, Christ, he thought. He hadn't done this. He looked once more at his watch: 3:30. Shannon went to work at 3:00. "Oh, my God," he said, and the note of agony in his voice made him feel worse. He was ruined. He was disgraced forever.

He thought he heard a footstep. Could she have taken the day off? The idea that she might still be in the apartment filled him at once with hope and desperation. He would apologize. But what could he say? How could he even face her? He tried to imagine the scene: himself with a silly expression on his face, his hair uncombed, his clothes wrinkled. He couldn't look at her. He would never be able to look into her eyes again. He would stare at the floor and say, *Forgive me for going to sleep. Really. I do love you. I really do. I just couldn't stay awake while I was waiting to make love to you.* No. It was too awful. It hadn't happened. He hadn't gone to sleep. He couldn't have. But he had.

Once more he thought he heard a footstep. He gathered his courage. "Shannon?"

There was no answer. He waited. "Shannon." Afraid, his heart pounding, he moved toward the bedroom door. "Shannon," he said again. After a moment he slowly turned the knob, pushed the door open, and looked in. No one was there. He saw a bed, a table, a radio, a telephone, a lamp. There was a chair, and a dresser with absolutely nothing on it, the top as clean and pristine as if it were still in the furniture store. There was no evidence that Shannon or anyone else had ever slept here. The bathroom fixtures were dry. The towels were fresh. The apartment was too neat to be real, and for a moment

Julien entertained the hope that he was living in a dream. I'll wake up, he told himself, and then knew immediately that he was awake, standing in Shannon's bedroom. His embarrassment was undiminished, but now he wanted to see her. He had to tell her how sorry he was. If he had to, he would get on his knees.

He walked around the bedroom. He put his hand on the bed, but there was nothing to feel there except the mattress beneath the spread. He opened one of the dresser drawers and found her underwear. The sight of her neatly folded slips, her panties, jolted him with feelings of guilt and desire. He wanted her, he ached to have her, and he was ashamed of himself for what he was doing. He closed the drawer. He had to talk to her, but not from here. He needed at least to get out of her bedroom. After what had happened, it was indecent for him to be here. He found another phone in the kitchen, which was as neat as the bedroom and had the same unlived-in look. He called her station at the hospital. While the phone rang, he tried to plan what he would say.

But she wasn't there. "I'm sorry," the voice at the other end of the line said. "She's taking some time off."

"Oh, no," Julien said, "she couldn't do that."

"I beg your pardon."

"Do you know where she is?"

"Try her at home. Do you want her number?"

"No, thank you," Julien said and hung up.

He sat down at Shannon's kitchen table and put his head in his hands. She hates me, he thought. She's hiding from me because she hates me. She never wants to see me again.

# X

Bunnie was planning a party for her and Max's sixtieth wedding anniversary. Although it was only April and the anniversary was not until August, she had booked the party room at the apartment complex, which had a wet bar and a kitchen and glass doors that opened onto a large patio, and she planned to pack the room and the patio with her and Max's friends—the few that were still living—and their friends' children and grandchildren and great-grandchildren too if they were old enough to behave themselves. She intended to invite some of the people from her old parish at Nineveh and some she had met at the cathedral, including a couple of priests and perhaps the bishop. She hadn't fully made up her mind about the bishop. She was going to send invitations to members of clubs she had belonged to before her stroke and to some writers who lived out of town and probably wouldn't come, but who Bunnie thought should be invited anyway. The list kept growing. She would think of people to invite at odd times of the day or night; she had to write the names down immediately or she would forget them, and that caused some friction—or to be precise, more friction— between her and Mrs. Smith and Mrs. Pakenham.

Invitations had been printed, and Mrs. Smith and Mrs. Pakenham, both of whom wrote decent, or at least legible, hands, were willing to address them, but they couldn't keep up with Bunnie's list. She tried to write the names on the yellow pad that she used when she worked on her novel, but often she had to use whatever was handy. She put names on old envelopes and on the covers of magazines and on scraps torn from the margins of newspapers and inside empty books of postage stamps. Once she wrote a name on the label of a vodka bottle, and a few names were on the toilet paper that she kept beside her potty chair. It was, Mrs. Smith and Mrs. Pakenham repeatedly pointed out, a losing battle. They were sure they were not finding all the names, and those they found were sometimes incomplete and sometimes unreadable. Mrs. Smith made her own list of all the names she could find and took up a morning of Bunnie's novel-writing time trying to get the matter settled.

Once they got the names that Mrs. Smith couldn't read out of the way, Bunnie's memory was tested. There were five Marthas on Bunnie's list, and she could only remember three of them. Had she listed two of them twice as Mrs. Smith seemed to think? That was possible, but Martha was a common name, and Bunnie didn't want to leave out anybody. Also, she needed to be careful about generations. There were three Carsons to be invited, all of whom were women—mother and daughter and granddaughter. Names that you seldom heard anymore, such as Cyrus and Dorcas, were repeated because people were named after each other. These Bunnie was able to sort out, but she got so frustrated trying to get the five Marthas straight that she asked Max for help.

"Maxie," she said, "try to think. How many people named Martha can you remember?"

Max was in his usual place on the couch perusing the *New York Review of Books*. "I don't know," he replied. "It depends on which one you're talking about."

Bunnie had found that one of the bad things about being in her condition was her inability to shut up when she knew she ought to. The part of her mind that had survived her stroke intact and that had not yet suffered its daily assault by alcohol warned her that if she kept trying to get assistance from Max, he would probably become more confused than he was now, and she would lose her patience. This would not help solve the mystery of the five Marthas. But whether from drink or sickness, the part of her mind that controlled her tongue seldom acceded to reason.

"Listen to me, Max," Bunnie said. "I'm talking about all of them. How many women can you think of who are named Martha?"

Max put his paper aside and took a sip from his coffee mug. "Well, there's one in the Bible, you know. She was the sister of Lazarus. And one of Hem's wives was named Martha."

"Who?"

"Ernest Hemingway," Max replied amiably. "I'm sure her name was Martha."

"Damn it, Max, we're not talking about Hemingway's wives!"

"It'll come to me in a minute," Max said. He paused, but before Bunnie could express her outrage, his eyes that had been narrowed in concentration sparkled with the joy of recollection. "Gellhorn! That's it. Martha Gellhorn. I met her once in New York. John Ross introduced me to her."

Why does this make me so angry? Bunnie wondered. What was it about their intimacy, their having lived together for almost sixty years that allowed him to annoy her so? She tried to get control of herself, but when she spoke, her words were louder and more distinctly enunciated than usual. "Max, we are not going to invite Hemingway's wives to our party. Hemingway is dead. Most of his wives are dead. We didn't really know them, anyway. Now who are the women we do know who are named Martha?"

"All right," Max said. He peered through the glass doors toward the April sunshine, the newly green grass. "There was Martha Livingston. And you remember the Italian girl Simmons Carlyle had an affair with. Her name was Martha something. It began with an *S*. Martha Speroni."

"They're both dead, Max."

"Yes," he replied, without surprise. He was on a roll. He was apparently behind in his morning drinking, and his mind was clicking away. "Martha Livingston died of pneumonia before they had sulfa drugs. I don't know what killed Martha Speroni. I think she died in California."

Bunnie tried to remember the women and managed to see two faces in her mind: one a brunette, one a blonde, both with the snugly waved hairstyles of the thirties. She didn't know if she were recalling the right faces; and if she were, she wasn't sure which was which. Logically, the brunette ought to be Speroni, but her vague mind insisted that Speroni had been a blonde. Thinking of the dead women made Bunnie sad. She hadn't known either of them well. She hadn't remembered either of them in years. They had meant nothing to her, but hearing Max talk about them and recalling all the other people they had known who were gone now took her out of the mood for planning her party. Caught up in her own thoughts, she was startled when Max spoke and failed to understand him.

"What?"

"It's an unhealthy state."

"What?" She had no idea what he was talking about.

"California," Max said. "Where Martha Speroni died. They have all those cases of AIDS, you know. There's something wrong out there."

Oh, dear, Bunnie thought. "Max," she said, "I believe Martha Speroni died from peritonitis, a ruptured appendix."

"Yes," Max replied. His voice was triumphant as if he had just made the winning point but didn't want to brag about it. "Yes. In California."

Maybe I'm doing this all wrong, Bunnie thought later. She had had lunch and had dozed in her chair. Now she was awake and reasonably alert, and it occurred to her that maybe August wasn't the right month and maybe this would not be their sixtieth anniversary after all. Maybe her first marriage to Max had not been valid, and she ought to start counting from the day they were married by a priest after their conversion. Perhaps, she thought, both anniversaries ought to be counted. She had read about a fundamentalist preacher who was ninety-nine, but who claimed to be one hundred and seventy-eight because he celebrated not only the day that he was born, but the day he was born again. If she and Max counted both of their wedding days, they would have been married for almost a hundred years, which would astonish their friends and relatives.

Well, Bunnie thought, her weddings had been two hopeful occasions, though the first one still largely escaped her memory. All she could recall of it beyond the white dress that she had worn was a kind of vague and amorphous joy, a sense, perhaps augmented by the alcohol in the punch, that disappointment and unhappiness had been evicted from her life forever. The second time, twenty-five years after the first, she had worn a pink silk dress and known better. Still, she had been excited. She walked down the aisle at the cathedral feeling eager and foolish as if she really were a bride. There was music: the organ, a clarinet, a pair of violins. There were flowers on the altar— again not white, thank God—and the priest handsomely vested with an altar boy to serve the nuptial mass. Bunnie had communion. Max had communion. Their Catholic friends—not so many of these, given the size of the company—had communion. The stirring music took up again. Out went Bunnie and Max. Out came John and Edith Ross, Bunnie's and Max's attendants, who themselves had recently been converted to Catholicism. Max, it seemed, had set out to convert the whole world and was having some success, though most of his and Bunnie's friends still took a dim view of religion. There was much kissing and handshaking in the narthex of the cathedral. Then all present, fortunately still sober and at themselves on this summer afternoon, got in their automobiles and set out for Nineveh.

Bunnie had planned the party. Since the wedding had been Max's idea, she had let him choose the date and hire the musicians and deal with the priest. She had stocked the bar, booked the caterer, chosen the menu. At Nineveh, she and Max and John and Edith stood in line and received the guests, most of whom they had already hugged and kissed at the cathedral. The guests started drinking, as did Max and Bunnie and John and Edith as soon as they were free to do so. There they were in the lingering twilight, people who were mostly in their fifties and sixties—old enough to know better, old enough to know how awful a hangover could be when you achieved advanced middle age and how long one could last—drinking as if they were in their twenties again and able to carouse all night on the riverbank.

My God, Bunnie thought, what days those were when they were young and their weekends were one continuous party. They had had what they called "camps," houses built on stilts near the water, shabby, three- or four-room affairs where they had danced and sung and paired off to go out and make love on a blanket. Had they really done that? Oh, yes, they had. Once a couple had gone without a blanket and called it splendor in the grass, but they had gotten chiggers and itched for several days in awkward places. Why had someone not drowned? Bunnie wondered, looking at the fellow revelers of her youth, now twice the age they were then, but revelling still. Several times every weekend, there would be a splash and a shout, and someone would have to be pulled out of the water. To the best of Bunnie's recollection, Adelaide Tomkins, a tall, very thin blonde who played the piano and could not swim, fell in every Saturday. She got drunk easily, and when she went out to walk around and clear her head, she tumbled down the bank. Bunnie remembered how placid she seemed as she came up for the first or even the second time, her dress billowing around her. Like Ophelia, Bunnie thought, but not so pretty.

The river was treacherous, filled with undercurrents and whirlpools that dragged at swimmers and made canoes tip over. The canoes were a nuisance, because when they swamped, they would go floating off downstream while those who could swim rescued those who couldn't.

Then somebody would have to get the other canoe and chase the canoe that had turned over. Usually they couldn't find the paddles. Because they were young and drunk, all this had seemed funny, and every rescue called for more drinks in celebration. But one night Simmons Carlyle simply disappeared. Or rather, late in the evening when people were settling down on beds and hammocks and anywhere else they could find to sleep, his wife Vera noticed that he was missing. Those who could still walk went outside with her to tramp through the weeds and shine flashlights at trees and look in the cars in case Simmons had bedded down in one. There was much shouting. Everybody was calling Simmons, men and women yelling his name, their voices so loud and constant that they couldn't have heard him if he had answered. "Simmons!" they screamed in tones deep and high, shrill and controlled: in rare cases the word was surprisingly well articulated.

Downriver, Bunnie remembered, dogs took up the call. There was barking and howling answered by shouts of "Simmons, Simmons!" which made the dogs bark louder. John Ross, no more sober than the rest of them, but smarter, whether drunk or sober, called the sheriff and got scant satisfaction. The sheriff had been asleep, and when he answered the phone, he could hear the shouting of the searchers. He accused John of being drunk, which John had the impudence to deny.

"Well, if you ain't drunk," the sheriff said, "why's all them people yelling?"

John had responded by quoting a line from Virgil, or it could have been Dante, something about a friend; Bunnie didn't know whether he had said *amicus* or *amico,* and apparently neither did the sheriff. There was considerable asperity on both ends of the conversation. The sheriff offered not to find Simmons but to arrest those who were searching for him. John Ross called the sheriff a piss-complected son of a bitch and hung up the telephone.

"Complexioned," Bunnie had said.

"What?"

"Complexioned," Bunnie repeated. "There's no such word as *complected.* Maybe you ought to stop using all those other languages and learn English."

"God damn it, Bunnie," John Ross said, "*complected* scans better. Art always comes first."

Outside, the shouting and the barking continued. Adelaide Tomkins, who had taken her tumble into the river earlier in the day, was admonished to stay behind, but made bold by drink, she set out down the long flight of wooden stairs toward the water. She made a zigzag course, bumping against the flimsy rails, waving her flashlight and pointing it at the sky as if she expected to find Simmons up in the air, levitating. At the landing, Adelaide lost her flashlight. Bunnie saw it sail through the air and disappear, and she was sure that Adelaide had gone with it. Bunnie started to yell for help, but people were still calling Simmons. "Simmons, Simmons!" they shouted, though some of their voices were getting hoarse. "Woof, woof!" replied the dogs, their tones clear and strong as if they could go on barking forever.

Bunnie started down the steps knowing she would be too late: by the time she reached the landing, Adelaide would have billowed up for the third time and floated off into the darkness. Oh dear, Bunnie thought. To lose two friends in one night would be dreadful. She got to the bottom of the stairs. Without much hope she called Adelaide's name, and Adelaide, who had fallen into one of the canoes, answered.

"Oh, Adelaide," Bunnie said and started to cry.

Seeing that Bunnie was crying, Adelaide began to weep too. Bunnie stepped into the canoe, almost turning it over. She wanted to put her arms around Adelaide's skinny shoulders, but she was afraid to move. She held Adelaide's hand, and they cried for a moment longer, while around them people still called for Simmons.

"I don't know why I fall so much," Adelaide said. "It's a good thing this canoe was here. It's just chance I hit it, you see. The other one is missing."

"What's missing?" Bunnie asked.

"The other canoe."

Bunnie thought for a moment. Then she said, "Why, that son of a bitch!"

"I'm sorry, Bunnie," Adelaide said. "I just seem to miss my step. I don't fall when I haven't been drinking."

"No," Bunnie said, "not you. I thought Vera would have looked here first. I assumed she had before she got us all searching for Simmons. I don't know which one of them I'm the madder at."

Bunnie stepped carefully on the landing and steadied the canoe while Adelaide made a shaky progress behind her. Bunnie led Adelaide by the hand back to the camp and told her to go to bed. Then she went into the raucous evening and found Vera. "One of the canoes is missing," Bunnie said, and Vera began to say things that ladies were not supposed to say even in the relaxed society that she and Bunnie moved in.

"Well, why didn't you look at the canoes in the first place?" Bunnie asked.

"Why didn't you?" Vera said.

He's not my husband, Bunnie started to say, but there was no use pursuing this line of thought. Vera's head was as empty as a gourd, which seemed to Bunnie fair enough since she had a body that all men lusted for. Bunnie and Vera went to tell the others that the canoe was missing. There was more cursing, some of it containing words, or at least constructions, worse than those Vera had used. Finally, all the human voices were quiet, though the dogs could still be heard in the distance.

The merrymakers, who had not been very merry when they were searching for Simmons, gathered on the porch of one of the camps to talk things over. "Leave the son of a bitch where he is," somebody said. "Let him stay there all night, and maybe a snake will bite him."

"That's all right," another voice said. It was dark on the porch, and Bunnie couldn't always be sure who was speaking. "But we ought to get the canoe. There's a good chance he didn't tie it up properly when he got there."

John Ross said, "Take Vera over there and leave her and bring the other canoe back."

The sentiment of the group was divided. Some of the men, who were the ones who would have to do the paddling, wanted to get the canoe. Others said that if the canoe hadn't drifted away by now it would stay where it was until morning. Vera, whose anger was undiminished but no longer directed at her husband, demanded that somebody go get Simmons. "God damn it," she said, "he's a great artist. You can't just leave him there."

"He's a damned fool," a voice from the shadows said, "and so are you for not looking to see if the canoe was gone before you told us Simmons was missing."

"You're jealous!" Vera shouted. "He's a genius, and you're all jealous of him."

This seemed unlikely, Bunnie thought. Were writers, not to mention ordinary people like her who at that time had never thought of writing a novel, jealous of painters? She had meant to take that up with Vera, but two of the men, neither of whom either wrote or painted, said they would go get the canoe and bring Simmons, too, but being newcomers to the group, they needed directions.

"It's right across from here," John Ross said. "There's a bluff where a spring comes out. Just below that, there's a little clearing and a path that leads to the top of the bluff. He goes up on the bluff to watch the sunset."

"The sunset?" one of the men said.

"Yes," John Ross replied. "He takes a bottle of whiskey with him. You might have to slide him down the bank."

"But the sun sets over here, too," the man said.

"He says the color is better over there. Remember, he's a genius."

And here they were now, Bunnie thought on the afternoon of her second wedding, the remnant of the same group, those whom time had spared during the ensuing thirty years, gathered at Nineveh and drinking as much and as fast as ever. But more today. This was what she didn't understand. The wedding seemed to have done something to them. Except for Simmons Carlyle and a few others who drank all the time, most of them had gradually slowed down. Usually now, they stopped before they collapsed on the floor or wandered away as Simmons had done that night or otherwise made fools of themselves. For a long time, Adelaide, skinny as ever, had taken only white wine, but now, for reasons Bunnie could not guess, she was drinking martinis. Harry Goldman, grown rich in real estate and usually prudent, swayed gently and surveyed the world through glazed eyes. Elizabeth Manly had removed her shoes and put them on the mantel in the library, one on each arm of the Celtic cross Max had bought in Ireland. Young Elizabeth had loosened several buttons of her blouse so that the tops of her great Rubenesque breasts showed forth like those of an eighteenth-century courtesan. As Bunnie watched, both Elizabeths took hardy pulls from their drinks. Harry Goldman and Adelaide put their glasses to their lips. The same thing seemed to be happening among most of those present, and there was a crowd around the bar demanding service.

Everyone seemed to be well along toward total intoxication, and even those who were not yet drunk were misbehaving. Jennings Harper, who to the best of Bunnie's knowledge had never flaunted his sexual preference, stood in the middle of the living room with his arms around—what? where had he come from? who had brought him?—an Indian with an immaculate white turban and a wispy little beard. Others, men and women, were embracing, too. Harry Goldman was hugging Adelaide, whose looks, Bunnie had to admit, had improved with age. A few feet away, Stella Goldman was too busy kissing young Roger Cantrell to notice what her husband was doing. Vera Carlyle, as dumb and almost as sexy as ever, was also engaged with a boy half her age. Except for Harry Goldman and Adelaide, all the couples appeared to be mismatched: young men with older women; younger women with older men; people heretofore thought to be chaste in the arms of known lechers.

It seemed to Bunnie that something dreadful had happened. It was as if someone had put a powerful aphrodisiac in the liquor or as if, as in a fairy story, some evil spirit had cast a spell over all the guests. Whatever they were doing, drinking or petting or, like Jennings Harper and his Indian friend, climbing the stairs toward the bedrooms, they exhibited what appeared to be purposeful determination. Their movements lacked grace; their mouths were set in grimaces or ugly, joyless smiles. Young Elizabeth Manly was in a chair. Frank Wilson knelt beside her. He—or had it been she?—had loosened her brassiere. He held one of her breasts and lifted it slightly as if he were testing the weight of a cantaloupe. Adelaide sat motionless on the floor, her back against the wall, her eyes closed. Harry Goldman sat beside her, too drunk, apparently, to lift a finger. What is this? Bunnie asked herself. What's happening here? Where was the joy they had known when they were younger?

She had to find Max. She couldn't allow him to get involved in whatever was happening. Before she could start to look for him, she felt John Ross's hand on her shoulder. He was calling her name and smiling at her—a terrible wide smile that showed too much of his teeth and made him look, she thought, like a gargoyle. He held her where she was and brought his face closer to hers.

She said, "I've got to find Max."

"Oh," John Ross replied in his deep and sensual voice, "don't worry about Max. He's probably with Edith."

He'd better not be, Bunnie thought, but in the midst of this strange party, she couldn't be sure of anything. John Ross had his arm around her waist.

"Stop it!" Bunnie said. "What's the matter with everybody?"

"It's the wedding," John Ross said. He wet his lips, then stretched them once more into the same awful smile.

How could that be? Bunnie wondered. What could have happened in that vast, ugly church to make her mostly mature and civilized guests behave so badly? What had happened beyond what all of them had seen happen dozens of times before? She and Max had stood at the altar. The priest had led them through their vows. Surely the ceremony couldn't have engendered this mingling of bodies.

"I've got to find Max," Bunnie said again.

"Not yet," John said. He held her more tightly, but she struggled free.

She made a slow progress through the crowd of people. They seemed to be moving always, shifting, even as they held each other, from one place to another. The floors and carpets were spotted with spilled drinks. Bunnie stepped on a glass and almost fell. Above the murmur, she heard something solid fall and bounce. "Excuse me," she said. "Excuse me."

The faces that surrounded her seemed at once strange and familiar. They were the faces of her friends, but they were drawn and wrinkled with expressions of intense concentration. The conversation she caught in passing was fragmented—single words, short phrases: *yes; no; oh God; yes, like that.* Bunnie pushed her way out of the library, crossed the hall, and went into the living room. She walked through the dining room and back into the hall. She could not find Max, and she had not seen Edith. Were they together as John had said? The thought that they might be, that either of them would betray her on this ceremonial day, made her weak with sorrow. Were they upstairs? She made up her mind to go and see, but when she got to the stairs, her feet would not carry her up them. She stood with her hand on the newel-post, shivering as if she were having a chill. Someone must have turned up the air conditioning. She halfway felt as if she were going to be nauseated. She got to the front door and onto the warm porch, and there, discernible in the last light of the afternoon, were Max and Edith.

They were sitting in chairs across from each other, not close enough to touch. They looked at Bunnie without change of posture or expression. They were innocent. Thank God, Bunnie thought. She was ashamed that she had suspected them. She found her own chair, and for a moment none of them spoke. Finally, Bunnie said,

"Are you all right, Maxie?"

Max seemed to miss the serious tone of her voice. "I don't know," he said and smiled. "Edith thinks I'm a heretic."

"Thinks you're what?" Bunnie asked.

"She thinks I read too much Teilhard de Chardin."

"Yes," Edith said. "He ought to stick to novels."

Inside, the sound of the party rose and fell. Once when the porch was almost quiet, Bunnie thought she could hear tree frogs or perhaps crickets, but immediately the noise from the house grew loud again. She knew that she ought to go inside, that it was rude for her and Max, host and hostess and honorees too, to abandon their own celebration. But she was content where she was, and she didn't move. She waited and listened to Edith and Max talk until some of the departing guests found her. Things seemed to be returning to normal. The guests expressed thanks. Bunnie and Max said how glad they were to have had them. A procession of drunk people found their cars and drove carefully or with abandon out the driveway. Soon, Bunnie knew, she would have to go in and survey the damage. Would she come upon a body hidden in the shadows? Would the caterer overcharge for the glasses that had been broken? Would the pictures still be on the walls? Had somebody spilled a drink on the piano keys? Finally, she wondered where John Ross was, and at that very moment Edith excused herself and went to find him.

"Well," Bunnie said, "we're married for sure now, Maxie."

"Yes," Max said and laughed softly. "We're on our honeymoon."

# XI

It seemed to Max that people were dying at an alarming rate: old friends and some not so old—and in one case, the grandson of a man younger than Max—giving up the ghost. Every month and sometimes more often, some person Max knew went down with a heart attack or got cancer or had a stroke. Max was depressed by all this dying and even more depressed by the funerals that most of the time were not really funerals but parodies of a proper service, empty ceremonies that started from no premise and promised nothing at the end. Percy Holcomb was given a proper Presbyterian service, and Leo Bernstein was buried with chants in Hebrew and a ritual tearing of clothing, but for the most part, what passed for funerals these days was a series of eulogies with some gloomy music interspersed. For Adelaide Tomkins and Herschel Witherspoon—and this according to their own directions—there had not been funerals at all, but cocktail parties, food and booze and people to eat and drink them in celebration of the deceaseds' now-terminated existences.

Max thought that if the country should go into a depression it would start with the casket business, because nobody was using caskets anymore. Like Adelaide and Herschel, almost everybody was being cremated, and although sometimes the ashes were buried or more likely put in a niche in a mausoleum, they could be put anywhere: dumped in a lake or scattered in a garden or thrown from an airplane so they could mix with the other impurities that tainted the air. Even worse, some people were leaving their bodies to the medical school. Max knew about this—or had known about it sixty years ago when he was a reporter and kept up with how everything in Nashville worked. In those days, cadavers came from a different class of people: prisoners whose relatives had disowned them and drifters fetched out of alleys and rummies who had made a deal with the school when they were still alive. It would have been unheard of in the old days for somebody like Jimmy Lucas—who was a member of Belle Meade Country Club and Saint George's Episcopal Church and lived on Chickering Road and drove a Jaguar—to have given his body to be dissected, but Jimmy did exactly that, and insofar as Max could determine he had escaped all criticism. How awful, Max thought. What a total invasion of one's privacy to be laid out naked on a table and have a group of students take you apart and examine your pieces.

Being himself close to extinction, Max was disturbed by what he considered a widespread disrespect for the dead. Now, when he woke in the morning and decided that he was still alive, he worried about his own funeral. Before Vatican II, knowing he was a Catholic would have been enough to put his mind at rest, but the Church allowed cremation now, and what would a requiem mass be without a body? Would they bring in an urn and let the priest sprinkle it with holy water? Could he trust Bunnie to see that the proper arrangements were made? Given the state of Bunnie's mind, the real question was, could he trust Susan and Julien? One day he told Bunnie to be sure and bury him properly when he died, but she misunderstood and told him he wasn't dead yet, and that led to an argument. As usual, she was staring at the yellow pad she kept on her lap, and her lack of attention made Max angry.

"God damn it," he said, "listen to me. I want to be sure you take me to the cemetery."

"Why?" Bunnie asked, her eyes still on the yellow pad.

"To bury me," Max replied, trying to contain his exasperation. "I want to be put in the ground. I want a Christian funeral."

"But you're not dead yet," Bunnie said once more. "If we buried you now, we'd have to give you a breathing tube and dig you up every now and then to feed you."

Max's voice rose. "I mean when I am dead. I'm talking about my funeral."

"Why not bury you at sea? You could be resurrected from the briny deep." Bunnie paused and gave him a tight, malicious smile. "You always did like swimming."

Max said some things he shouldn't have said, then suddenly fell silent, stunned by the thought that he might not have made his plans properly. Years ago, before he had come back to the Church, he had bought space for him and Bunnie in the cemetery at Nineveh. Was this all right? Could he be buried in unconsecrated ground? He was pretty sure that he could, but might somebody use this as an excuse to have him cremated? Maybe to be safe, he ought to buy another lot, get space in the Catholic cemetery in Nashville, so when he died there would be a choice of places for him to go. Nobody could say that his lot was too far away or of the wrong persuasion. What now? he wondered. Should he call the office at Calvary? No, he wanted to do this in person. He wanted to see where he and Bunnie would lie. He needed to take care of this now, but transportation was a problem. Julien was at the university. Mrs. Smith had the day off, and Mrs. Pakenham could not leave Bunnie. He would have to drive himself, but he had better get a map and be sure he knew where he was going.

Ah, Max thought, he had to be careful. Silence, exile, and cunning. He wasn't sure he had the words exactly right, and in any case, exile did not suit his situation, but the rhythm of the phrase enhanced his sense of adventure. Where would he find a map of the city? He went to his room, looked through the papers on his desk, searched his bookcase, rummaged in his closet. He knew he had one—or had had one. Things got lost. It might be at Nineveh. Or maybe in his car: that was logical. If he didn't find it there, he could buy a map at the bookstore.

Max was already attired for business. When he dressed in the morning, he put on coat and tie, made himself ready for whatever the day would bring, which was usually nothing more exciting than visitors. He could get out of the house all right. He frequently went for walks, though usually Mrs. Smith or Mrs. Pakenham went with him. Max moved into the living room as boldly as his shuffling footsteps would allow, retrieved his hat from the top of the television set, announced his intention to sample the morning air, and stepped out the sliding glass doors, going in the direction opposite the parking lot. He got around the corner of the building feeling clever and vigorously alive, found his car, opened the glove compartment, and there it was: a map of Greater Nashville. Max spread it on the hood of his automobile, found his own location, found the cemetery. Should he try to make a short cut along the Interstate? No, he would go by what he briefly remembered as a way he had gone before: into town and then south when he reached the river. He got out his pen and traced a route. It would have been better if he had had a colored marker, but he could see the black line if he looked carefully. That would have to do.

He started his engine, bounced over the speed bumps, left the apartment grounds, and went past the fire station where the paramedics waited, ready to come pick Bunnie up should she fall again. Max turned right on Hillsboro Pike. This was easier than he had thought it would be, though the honking of horns close behind him made him nervous. On Max went, stopping when lights turned red, waiting until they turned green, behaving himself, staying far below the speed limit, being a good citizen, a careful driver. Well now, Max thought. He was exhilarated, enjoying himself in spite of the horns that continued to blow and the occasional screech of tires on asphalt. He looked around. A street sign said Twenty-First Avenue, which was right, Max knew, because Hillsboro Pike became Twenty-First Avenue as you moved toward the city.

But where on Twenty-First Avenue was he? At the next red light, he looked at his map, but for a while he couldn't find the line he had drawn. Then he did find the line, but it only told him where he was supposed to be going. He needed the name of a cross street to know where he was. He looked around for a sign, but his attention was diverted by a great bleating of horns that rose behind him. He peered up at the traffic signal, which turned as he looked at it from yellow to red. The rude chorus of horns rose in volume. Then there was a great blast of sound, a noise so loud that Max temporarily released the steering wheel. In his mirror, he saw the front of an enormous truck, the bars of the grill like a giant set of teeth that were about to devour him. The horn of the truck blasted once more. Then there was a blow, a thrust against the rear of Max's car so severe that he lost both his hat and his glasses. And he was moving. Max's foot was still on his brake, his wheels were locked, but in spite of that, his car went shuddering, squealing forward.

"Whoa!" Max said. "God damn it, whoa!"

But the car continued to move. It picked up speed. The locked wheels bounced and began to skid. "Whoa, damn it!" Max said again. The front end of his automobile was swinging toward the oncoming lane. Max pulled at the wheel, but the car continued to move to the left and squeak and tremble. The truck's horn sounded a note so long and loud that Max jerked in his seat. His foot came off the brake, and he got control of his automobile. It would steer where he wanted it to steer, but it was going faster.

"You son of a bitch!" Max shouted.

Still looking at the road, he shook his fist toward his rear window, but he knew the truck driver neither saw nor heard him. In his mirror, there were only the ugly teeth of the truck's grill, but Max couldn't stop to contemplate them. Ahead of him there were other traffic signals, other cars moving in what seemed to be all directions. Directly in front of him, he saw a white van with deeply tinted windows. It was stopped, its brake lights on, and Max was closing on it. The space between Max's car and the van was diminishing at an alarming rate. Max tried his brakes again, but his shuddering car barely slowed. He blew his own horn, but the sound of it was lost among all the other horns that were blowing. My God, Max thought. He was about to have a wreck. He was going to die, his funeral plans unmade, his cemetery lot unpurchased. His car would crash into the back of the van; the truck would continue to push him forward; his own poor Chevrolet, and not a very new one at that, would be crushed between the two larger vehicles. It occurred to Max that he ought to pray, say an Our Father or a Hail Mary or an Act of Contrition, but there was no prayer in his heart to match his anger.

"You son of a bitch!" he said, taking his eyes off the road for a moment to scream over his shoulder. He hoped the truck driver would be killed, too. Maybe the collision would start a fire, a sudden burst of yellow flame and black smoke that would fry that bastard who was pushing him. But wait. Maybe not. The traffic light had changed. The van was moving. Max was still closing on it, but not as fast. A block or two ahead of him on the right, Max saw the parking lot of a restaurant. He decided to go for it. He needed to get into the right-hand lane, and though there was a solid line of traffic there, he couldn't hesitate. He flipped his blinkers, he blew his horn. Slowly he turned his wheel to the right. His car drifted over. Was that a scrape? Had he bumped another car? He could worry about that later. He wanted to shake his fist at the truck driver again, but that would wait, too.

Many, many horns were blowing again, most of them coming from his right, but Max persevered. The truck was still pushing him, but he was slipping away from it. In his mirror, he saw a fender now as well as part of the grill. He thought he felt another slight bump. An angry voice came to him, but it was too indistinct for him to make out the words. There was more squealing of brakes, and then Max was free of the truck. He was slowing down, but here was the parking lot. He pushed his brakes, jerked his steering wheel. His car made a quick but wide arc. A metal light pole appeared, and Max didn't quite miss it. This time the bump was hard enough to give him a jolt, but he held tight, watched what he was doing, and brought his car to rest between two lines as neatly as if it had been parked by a professional.

"The son of a bitch," Max said, still holding the steering wheel, not trying yet to move. He could feel the pulse in his temples. He was panting, and his mouth was dry. "The son of a bitch!" Max said again. "He tried to kill me." Max found this thought arresting. He turned it over in his mind. The truck driver had tried to kill him. Or at least he had taken a chance on killing him, had been willing to kill him— out of anger or a warped sense of humor or a desire to make up for lost time. The truck driver had tried to kill him, but Max was still alive. The knowledge that he had survived both comforted and excited him. He had escaped a great danger. He had had a brush with death, and he had lived through it. The air he breathed seemed sweet to his lungs. The sun shone with unaccustomed brightness. The pale red bricks of the wall in front of him seemed to glow.

Well, Max thought, this calls for a drink. Luck was still with him. The restaurant where Max was parked was open. He found his spectacles on the floor and clamped them above his ears. He retrieved his hat from the back seat and adjusted the brim. Then, still a little weak in the limbs but in the best of spirits, Max went into the restaurant and took a seat at the bar.

But then there was more trouble. Max had hardly made a dent in his second scotch when he was surrounded by a policeman and two angry citizens. The citizens, a man no taller than Max but half Max's age and a blond woman even younger, began to yell at Max, their combined voices making a considerable racket in the otherwise quiet restaurant. Then the policeman started to yell too, and though the noise rose to a more unpleasant level, the dispute gave Max time to take a good pull at his drink, and that made him feel better. The policeman got the citizens quiet, but when he asked Max if the black Chevrolet parked outside belonged to him, the citizens began to yell again before Max could answer.

"Wait a minute," the policeman said, and when the citizens seemed inclined not to do so, he took their arms and led them to a booth and made them sit in it.

All to the good, Max thought. During this small hiatus, he had time to finish the drink he had and order another.

"Now, sir," the policeman said to Max, "if that is your car, those people say you scraped their fenders."

"Well," Max replied pleasantly, "it's hard to be sure one way or the other under the circumstances."

"Come again?"

"The lamp post, now," Max said. "The lamp post gave me a pretty good jerk. I know I hit the lamp post."

"Sir," the policeman said, "may I see your driver's license?"

Max had a license, he knew, but he had trouble finding it. He took out his billfold and thumbed through the compartments, but the license didn't seem to be there. "Wait, now," Max said. He removed his credit cards and put them on the bar. Could the license be with his money? He lined up his bills beside his credit cards: two one-hundreds, two fifties, some twenties and tens and ones. Max believed in going well heeled; he wanted to be ready for any emergency. Still no license, and for some reason the money appeared to make the policeman uncomfortable.

"Put the cash away," the policeman said, his voice flat but with an edge.

Max heard him but didn't touch the money. He knew he had a license and was frustrated that he couldn't locate it. He took the last of his drink, peered at the bottles on the back bar, and tried to remember. He emptied his pants pockets, dropped change, a penknife, two handkerchiefs, two sets of keys onto the bar. He started on his coat and found his notepad and two pens and at last a wallet that held more credit cards and several automatic-teller receipts and his driver's license.

With the matter of the license settled, Max went with the policeman and the two citizens—both calmer now—to the parking lot to examine Max's car. Sure enough, on his right front fender there was a streak of red paint. On the right rear fender there was white paint. On the left side of the car there was evidence that Max had hit the light pole, but none of this much mattered to Max because the car was old and he didn't drive it very often. The policeman asked questions and completed forms. Max told the policeman how he had been pushed by a truck. It was clear that the policeman didn't believe him, but Max didn't argue. He wanted to get back on the road to the cemetery. Max was given a paper to sign: a ticket? a summons? would he have to go to court? Max was still eager to leave. There would be time to worry about the ticket later. Max gave the citizens the name of his insurance company, but the male citizen was not content to let bygones be bygones.

"He's drunk," the male citizen said. "You saw him drinking."

"Yes," the policeman said, "but that doesn't prove he was drinking before the accident."

There was another short argument between the policeman and the citizen. Then the policeman told the citizen that the investigation was over and advised the citizen to leave. A good idea, Max thought. That was what they all ought to do. He glanced at his watch: 11:30. The parking lot was beginning to fill up. Max would have liked another drink, but he thought he ought not to have one, given the conversation between the policeman and the citizen. He put his mind back on the reason he was driving in the first place and realized that his run-in with the truck and the scene with the policeman and the citizens had knocked the directions to the cemetery out of his memory. He needed to look at the his map again. It occurred to him that the policeman could help him.

"Officer," Max said, "I'm trying to get to the cemetery."

The policeman, who was tall, peered down at Max. His eyes were narrowed, his lips tight. "Yeah," he said. "I can see you are. You keep on running into people, and you'll get there."

"No," Max said, "all that was because of the truck. Maybe you can help me."

Max got his map, spread it once more on the hood of his car, and tried to show the officer where he had started and where he wanted to go, but the policeman paid no attention.

"Listen, Mr. Howard," the policeman said, "I'm going to help you. I'm going to call a cab and put you in it, and you can go to the cemetery or home or wherever else you want to go. I'll have to have your car towed. When you're sober, you can pick it up at the tow-in lot."

Max thought that he ought to object to this. He had a driver's license. He was properly insured. He paid taxes. But the idea of riding in a cab stirred old memories. In his days as a reporter, cabs had been his only means of transportation.

"All right," Max said.

Max may have gone to sleep. He didn't know. Sometimes his mind went vacant. When he came to himself, he would be unable to recall where he was or what he had been doing for the last five or ten or thirty minutes. Now, he discovered that the cab had stopped at a fork of narrow roads. The cabdriver, a portly black woman in a chauffeur's cap, was looking at him. "Mister," she said, "are you okay? You'll have to tell me where you want to go now."

Where are we? Max wondered, trying to make his mind work. A cemetery, of course: he could tell that from the sweep of grass and the headstones and the statuary. He was pretty sure that this was Calvary, but why was he here? For an instant, he suffered the same uncertainty about whether he was still alive that he felt when he awakened in the morning. It seemed unlikely that he would breathe his last in a taxicab, but that was exactly what had happened to Cal Lowell. He had been on his way to Manhattan from Kennedy, and out he went. The face of the driver was wrinkled with concern. That he could see her and hear her made him think that he had not yet passed away.

"Mister, you want me to call for help?"

"No," Max replied. "I forgot for a minute. Somebody I know is buried here."

The driver seemed to be reassured by this. "Lots of people," she said, swinging her arm toward the cemetery. "Lots of dead people. I lost my own baby sister three months ago."

Max wanted to express his sympathy, but before he could get the words straight in his mind, the driver asked where his friend was buried.

Max didn't remember. For an instant, he thought he recalled that he had not come here to visit. He had the vague notion that he had come here to do business, but he couldn't recollect what. The driver, apparently satisfied that Max was himself again, waited for directions. Max glanced over the rolling ground of the cemetery and a name came to him: John Ross. He recalled that John had been buried at the top of a knoll. Early in his career, John had written a book on the American Civil War, and forever after, he considered himself a military expert. He had joked that when he died he wanted to occupy the high ground. How could this old memory come back so clearly, Max wondered, when the rest of his mind did not seem to be functioning at all? He could see himself and John at a table at the University Club. *Drink to me, Max,* John had said, lifting his glass. *I've picked out a place to be buried. I tried to get the best terrain in case I have to fight off the devil.*

That was it. Max had come to buy a cemetery lot. To do this, he needed to go to the cemetery office, and he almost told the driver to take him there. But the sound of John Ross's voice lingered in his mind. He wanted to visit John's grave. He needed to go there in the hope that John's soul might see him there and know that he cherished John's memory, that he had long ago forgiven John for what John, full of booze and facing death, had said to him. His mind was returning rapidly now from wherever it had been. He recognized the lie of the land, saw here and there statues that he remembered: a figure of the Virgin, an angel with wings fledged and spread like those of some gigantic bird. He gave the driver directions, and soon he was standing above John Ross's grave, reading the inscription on John's headstone.

John William Rutledge Ross
April 20, 1902–January 12, 1973
Sancta Maria Ora Pro Nobis

For us, Max thought, pray for us. Well, Max thought, that was what you put on tombstones, that was what you said in the Rosary, even though there was only one person dying or praying. Looking at John's single grave with the empty plot beside it, Max fell back into his funerary mood, and on John's behalf he felt a sense of loneliness. Edith should be here. But until his health gave out, John had been unable to stop chasing women, and Edith had divorced him. His forced reformation had come too late. But John had had a proper burial. His body had been put in a casket. There had been a mass and incense and holy water. Handsful of dirt and flowers had been dropped into the grave. Then Max remembered. There had been something else. Yes, Max's manuscript. The pages of his book.

The last time John visited Nineveh, short of breath and thinner than ever, his face drawn, even his wonderful voice grown weak, Max asked him to read a novel that Max had just finished, the last one, Max knew, that he would ever write. After his bright beginning as a writer, Max had lived with his long period of failure by trying to write himself out of it. At first he dreamed of writing the great novel that he had always felt he could write. As time passed and his manuscripts remained unpublished, he was willing to compromise. It would be all right, he told himself, if only he could bring out one more book.

111

John read Max's manuscript, and for a while he wouldn't talk about it. "I don't know yet, Max," he said. "I'm not sure what to say."

What this meant, Max realized, was that John knew exactly what to say but was looking for a way out of saying it or, failing that, for kind words to convey the bitter truth. Max knew later that he should have let the matter drop, but he was unable totally to suppress his hopes.

One afternoon in the library at Nineveh, that setting in which, as Max had thought many times before, most of the important scenes in his life seemed to have been played out, Max and John, whose doctor had told him not to drink at all, opened the bar too early in the afternoon and visited it too often. John was doubtless thinking of his own end; the liquor he had drunk had sharpened his sense of his own mortality. But whiskey had affected Max, too. He was not dying, but he longed to be told that his life hadn't been wasted. "Tell me the truth now," Max said. "What do you think of my manuscript?"

There had been, Max remembered, a moment of silence. Or more than a moment, long minutes undisturbed by even the ticking of a clock. "Your novel," John Ross said at last. "Your novel."

"Yes."

"It's like everything else you've ever written," John Ross said. "You never were a writer, Max. Nothing you ever did was worth reading."

Max was sick with anger and disappointment. He felt the afternoon's booze burning in his stomach. Tears that would disgrace him as a man if he shed them gathered in his eyes. Because of them, he dared not speak. He looked away from John, studied the bookshelves where books by his friends, many books by many friends, reproached him. Others had succeeded where he had failed. And why? Max wondered. Why had God given him such an overwhelming desire to write well and not given him the talent with which to do it? He turned his gaze toward the bar, looked at the bottles and glasses until they began to blur. He wanted to leave the room, but he wasn't sure that his legs would carry him. With both hands, he pounded the arms of his chair. Then he rose and made his way into the hall and went to his study.

John Ross died in January, and this made it convenient for Max to hide the box he was carrying under his coat. There was snow on the ground and a wind that swept in vicious gusts across the knoll on which John was buried. Few people had come from the church to the cemetery, and those who had come were anxious to get back to their cars. As soon as the last words of the service were spoken, the crowd dispersed, but Max lingered. Bunnie urged him to leave. She told him she was freezing.

"Go on," Max said. "I'll be there in a minute."

Bunnie left. There were a couple of gravediggers anxious to get started with their shovels, but they didn't matter to Max. In the box under his coat, he was carrying the manuscript of his last novel. He took it out and tried to bury it with John. He wanted to drop the pages of his book into the grave as if they were the petals of roses: the manuscript would be an offering of peace, a memorial to his and John's friendship, and Max hoped, a symbol of his having come to terms with his own failure. But when he tried to drop them in, the wind snatched the pages out of his hand. Sheets of typing paper fluttered away, scattered among the graves, caught briefly against tombstones and were swept away once more. They lifted high against the gray sky, snapped among the branches of bare trees. They twirled and dipped and skittered along the brittle grass. Some of them twisted back through the canopy that had sheltered the mourners.

Max leaned over the grave, reached down into it in an effort to leave at least a part of his book on top of John's casket, but the wind dipped beneath the surface of the earth and caught these pages too and lifted them. A particularly strong gust dug some of the paper out of the box and sent it scattering. With only a chapter left, Max looked into the startled faces of the gravediggers. They were improperly dressed for the weather. They were shivering. Their cheeks were red from the cold. Their noses were running.

"Help me," Max said.

They didn't answer but continued to stare at him, their eyes wide.

"Help me."

One of the gravediggers licked his chapped lips. "What? Help you do what?"

Max held the box out to him. "Put this in the grave. Hold it and put some dirt over it so the wind won't catch it."

"All right," the gravedigger said, but he was not up to the task.

Max held the box out to him. He took it briefly in his trembling hands, then the wind snatched it away. The last of Max's novel lifted and twirled, ascended toward the bleak sky then fell again. The pages darted and tumbled like great white leaves and dropped on the frozen ground of the cemetery.

# XII

"Where the hell have I been?" Shannon said. "Have I missed something here? Is that the new way to say, Welcome back, Shannon?"

"Oh, my God," Julien said. "I've been worried to death. Listen, do you know they told me not to call the hospital anymore? They said I was interfering with their work. They threatened to have me arrested."

"Well, Julien, you know the nurses need to tend to the sick people—"

"I'm coming over now," Julien said. "I'll be at your apartment in ten minutes."

"No."

"Yes. I'm on my way."

"Damn you, Julien, I won't let you in. Listen to me. If we weren't talking on the phone, I'd tell you to read my lips. I'm going back to work this afternoon."

"Shannon, it's only eleven o'clock. Look, I'm sorry I went to sleep. I apologize. I'll make it up to you. What do you want me to do? Tell me what you want me to do so you'll forgive me."

"Go to bed early. Study hard. Make good grades. Take care of Max and Bunnie."

"For Christ's sake, Shannon, that's what I've been doing for the last week. I'm coming over."

"Julien," Shannon said, "if you come over here, I won't answer the door. I'll disconnect the buzzer. I mean it, Julien."

Jesus, Julien thought, what did she want him to do? He was talking on a phone at the business school into which, during the last week, he had dropped a hundred quarters. He had kept calling the hospital, even after they had threatened to have him thrown in the clink; he had called her apartment so often that when he went to bed at night, the rhythm of the ringing phone echoed in his mind. It had been the worst week of his life. He had spent most of his waking moments telling himself what a fool he had been to have allowed himself to go to sleep. He should have paced the floor; he should have pinched himself; he should have stuck his head out the window and breathed the night air. He had composed a speech of apology and thought he had it memorized. But after so many fruitless phone calls, her voice at the other end of the line surprised him and he forgot what he had planned to say.

"Shannon," he said, "I *am* sorry. I had a speech made up to tell you how sorry I was, but I've forgotten it."

"All right."

"Do you forgive me?"

"All right."

All right? What the hell did that mean? Julien wondered. "Well, do you?"

"What?"

"Forgive me, damn it," Julien said. "What else were we talking about?"

She was silent. She was still there. At least the line was still live, but no sound came to him through the phone.

"Well, of course I forgive you, Julien," she said finally. "It was partly my fault that you went to sleep. But maybe it was fate, you know. Maybe we weren't supposed to be seeing each other."

Oh, no, Julien thought. Here we go again. Is this what he had been longing to have back in his life during the last week when he had missed her so desperately? He hadn't even seen her since she returned, and already she was hassling him.

"If fate had had anything to do with it," Julien said, "we wouldn't have gotten together in the first place. Why won't you let me come to see you?"

"How are you fixed for sleep?"

"Don't worry," Julien said. "I've learned my lesson. Your couch is damned uncomfortable." He started to tell her that while he was lying on it, his leg had gone to sleep, but since he had been asleep all over, there were too many jokes she could make about that.

"Yeah. Well, it's not my couch I'm thinking about."

"That's not what I'm thinking about, either," Julien said. "I'm thinking about you. I want to see you."

There was another pause. "Meet me at the bar after I get off from work."

"I'll meet you at the hospital."

"You can't come to the hospital. If the guards see you there, they'll shoot you."

"Look," he said. "One more time. I didn't mean to go to sleep. You know that, Shannon."

They were in their usual booth, and nothing had changed. The week of her absence had seemed interminable to Julien, long enough to take the world into a new geological age, but here they were, ordering from the same waitress, listening to the same piano player, drinking what might as well have been the same wine.

"Oh, ho, ho," Shannon said. "How am I supposed to know that? You may have been setting me up, Julien."

"What?"

"Well, think about the way you acted that night, how eager you were before I left the living room. Suppose I let you go home with me again. I'd figure that I'd better get with it before you went to sleep."

"Shannon—"

"It's true, Julien. At least, you can see the logic of it."

"Be serious, Shannon."

"I am, but you're not paying attention."

"I'm paying attention," he said, "and I want to know why you ran away that night. It wasn't just because I went to sleep."

Her lips assumed their familiar posture of not quite smiling. "Well," she said in her teasing voice, "I was embarrassed."

"What?"

"Remember, Julien, I hadn't planned to let you come home with me. It sort of happened after I made you tell me that you loved me."

"I wanted to tell you. I'd already told you."

"Whatever," Shannon said. "Anyway, it occurred to me when I got out of the shower that I didn't have anything to wear."

"Didn't have anything to wear!" Julien said. "Shannon, the idea is that you . . . I mean, under those circumstances, people don't usually wear anything."

"Julien, I'm beginning to think you made that up about living in France. There's more to it than, well, what you were just talking about."

"Oh, my God," Julien said. "What is it you think you need? I'll buy it for you."

"Not need. Needed. As long as it's just me, what I have is all right. I mean my underwear and robe and stuff. But for romance, I ought to have sexy things like they sell at Victoria's Secret."

"Shannon," Julien said, "how could you be embarrassed about not having sexy underwear when I'd gone to sleep? That's not the reason you left. Level with me."

"I'm trying to," she said. "The clothes did matter, Julien. If I had had something special to wear, it would have helped to make what we almost did special. You know, get our affair off to a good start."

"Let me get this straight. You went off and sulked for a week because you didn't have the proper underwear for me to take off of you before we did what we never got to do because I went to sleep."

"Well, I wasn't really sulking, but that's the gist of it."

"Okay," Julien replied, nodding his head, "that's fine. That makes exactly as much sense as almost everything else you've ever said to me. Why should I try to understand what you're saying now?"

"Julien, you really shouldn't be cross. After all, you were supposed to wait for me. Remember?"

"I'm not cross," he said with mock patience. "I'm not cross at all. I'm just crazy. I love you." He leaned toward her. "And get this. In spite of the fact that I don't know what you're talking about most of the time, I want you to marry me. How about early in June, as soon as I graduate?"

"Julien—"

"No, it's worse than that. When I do understand what you're saying, I don't like it."

"Julien—"

"Think of how happy we'll be. Twenty years from now, you'll still be saying things that don't make any sense to me, but it won't matter because I'll still love you."

"Julien, you mustn't get upset like this. I'm afraid getting enough sleep might not be good for you."

"Did you hear what I said?"

He waited while she took a sip of wine.

"Well?" Julien asked.

"Well, what?"

"Did you hear what I said?"

"As a matter of fact," Shannon said, "I did."

"Well, what about it?"

"About what?"

"Damn it," Julien said, his voice louder than he had meant for it to be, "you said you heard me. Will you marry me or not?"

"Julien," Shannon replied, "you shouldn't be asking that question now. You're annoyed with me, and that may make you think you want to marry me. You know what Freud said about love and hate being the same thing. When you get over being mad, you might not want to marry me at all."

I'm getting out of here, Julien thought. I'm going to get up and walk out and never see her again or think of her again or admit that I ever heard of her. For the rest of his life, if anybody asked him whether he knew Shannon Marsh, he would say no. No, I don't know her. I never want to know her. She's probably almost blond and not very pretty and crazy as a loon. I'm gone, he told himself, I'm leaving now. But nothing happened. His muscles didn't tighten; his legs didn't move. It was as if his nerves didn't work anymore, or more likely, the sensible part of his brain had been overruled by whatever it was that had made him foolish enough to fall in love with her in the first place.

He took a deep breath. He drank wine. He wished he smoked, because in old movies at moments like this people lit cigarettes. Poor, dear Justine, he thought. He hadn't realized how easy and comfortable his life with her had been. She had talked sensibly, loved him when he wanted to be loved; even at the end when she had sensed that he would soon be leaving, she at least had made sense. I should have stayed there, Julien told himself. He could have married Justine and got a green card. He might have become a businessman or a diplomat or—stranger things had happened—an actor or a television star. Maybe he would have become so famous that when he died people would look for his grave in Père Lachaise and forget about writing graffiti on Jim Morrison's tombstone. But he had come home and fallen in love with Shannon, who sat in the other side of the booth smirking at him.

He breathed deeply again. Then he said, "I am not mad," but his voice, as grim as a funeral bell, betrayed him.

"Oh, dear," Shannon said. She took his hand in both of hers. "I'm sorry, but it's all a part of why I left, Julien."

He couldn't resist her. He loved her and wanted her. He had not stopped wanting her since he had awakened and found her gone.

Now, when she touched him, all the passion of his anger turned to desire. "Let's get out of here," he said. "Let's go to your apartment." "No. Listen, Julien, I'm trying to tell you something. Things happen to people that they don't expect to happen. I mean, like Saint Paul. He was living a perfectly normal life persecuting Christians, and then he got zapped on the road to Damascus. Think about this, Julien. What if he hadn't been going to Damascus? Do you suppose if he had been going somewhere else, the zapping might not have taken place?"

Oh, God, Julien said to himself, not that stuff again. "I don't want to think about that, Shannon."

"Well, I don't either, really. That's the trouble with being raised the way I was. The nuns tell you these stories when you're young, and you can't forget them. And parts of the stories are always true. Things do happen to make you change. Like when you went to sleep that night. That kind of zapped me, though of course I didn't go blind."

Damn, Julien thought. He had to make her forgive him. She had to love him the way he loved her. "I'm sorry," he said. His voice was light, breathless. "You've got to forgive me."

"Sweet Julien," she said, "it's not that. Of course I forgive you. You couldn't help going to sleep." She lifted his hand, kissed the tips of his fingers. He was moved by this simple gesture. His throat tightened. He had to press his lips together to keep tears from gathering in his eyes.

Shannon said, "I wanted you that night. It's probably dumb for me to tell you that, but I can't worry about being dumb anymore. I had to make you keep away from me in the elevator and stop touching me in the living room, because if I hadn't, I couldn't have stopped myself."

Julien hadn't believed that his desire for her could increase, but now it did. He was dizzy and in pain, as if wanting her were a sickness. "Let's go to your apartment," he said. "For God's sake, let's go now."

"Sh—," she said, "listen. What I told you about not having the right underwear is true, Julien. Not having it wouldn't have kept me from making love to you, but I thought about it. When I came out of the shower, I put on an old terry cloth robe I got when I was a freshman at Emory. Then as I was drying my hair, I thought, this is terrible, I can't wear this. My underwear was just as bad. Not as old, but plain white stuff that works under my uniforms. I was afraid you wouldn't like me. I mean, I knew that you wanted me, but I thought that Justine probably had beautiful lingerie, and if you didn't notice it before, after we'd finished, you'd compare me to her and see how shabby I looked. I didn't even own a nightgown."

"No, no, no. That's crazy, Shannon."

"Well, it probably is," Shannon said, "but that's what I thought, and that's what people have to go on. I mean, what you think is what's real to you until you begin to think something else. But that's not the point. When I first came into the living room that night, I thought you were just dozing, that you'd wake up. But then I saw you wouldn't wake up unless I did something violent. I started to yell in your ear. It's hard for me to believe now, but I almost did that. I sat down beside you and gave you a couple of punches in the ribs. I took a deep breath and got ready to scream, but then I realized how stupid that was. I mean, that wouldn't have been the way to show I loved you, would it?"

"I think it would," Julien said.

"No. If I had awakened you, we'd have made love, and maybe that would have been all right. It might even have been better than my not waking you, but that's not what we did. That night, when I made you say you loved me, I was sure that I loved you, too. But when I didn't wake you, when it came to me that if I truly loved you I wouldn't wake you, something happened. I don't mean that I had been loving you and all of a sudden, I loved you more. It was that, but it was something else, too. It was a different feeling, more intense, but quieter. It took in more territory, covered everything about you and me and what we might do together for the rest of our lives. I still wanted you, but I knew that even if I wanted you more than I did, which didn't seem possible, I'd still let you sleep."

"Oh, God," Julien said, "if we love each other, why do we have to keep on sitting here?"

She smiled. It was a nice, gentle, loving smile that like everything else she did or said made his love for her deepen. "Julien, you used to make fun of me when I told you how I needed to find out who I was and what my life was about and all that. But that's why I left. After I discovered how much I loved you, I decided I had to know who I was. I knew what I used to be, God help me for that. But I needed to find out if I had changed, if I was really somebody different like I hoped I was, and I couldn't do that with you trying to get me in bed every minute."

"Okay," Julien said. "You found yourself."

120

"Well, it wasn't really that simple. What I found first was my *doppelgänger*."

"You found your *what?*"

"I took a literature course in college, Julien. That's where I learned about *doppelgängers*. Of course, I thought they only happened in books. There would be a character who would be a sort of double of the main character, a kind of alter ego, I guess. But I found my real *doppelgänger* the morning I left you sleeping on the couch. She was at the rest stop right after I had come across the Georgia line into Tennessee."

"Wait a minute," Julien said. "You were already in Tennessee. You started in Tennessee."

"Yes. That's a complicated part of the story. You see, when I left you, I was pretty upset. I was sad about having to leave you, and I was scared about what I might decide about myself. What if I found out that I was still what I used to be? What if I found out that I wasn't worth anything? That I wasn't good enough to have anybody love me? It wasn't easy, Julien. I was crying, and that made me miss my turn."

"Damn it," Julien said, "I've already told you that I love you."

"But you don't know about me."

"All right," he said. "What turn did you miss?"

"Well, I thought I'd go to St. Louis or Chicago, someplace where people don't talk the way you do—"

"Talk the way I do!" Julien said. "What the hell does that have to do with it?"

"Now, Julien," Shannon said, "there's no reason to be offended. You have quite an upper-class southern accent. I think it's cute. But remember, I was going away to find out about myself, and I didn't want to be reminded of you every time I overheard a conversation. Somehow I got on 24-East, which meant I was slanting south toward Chattanooga, but it seemed like such a nice highway, I decided to stay on it. That's how I got to Georgia."

"Well, yes. But you said—"

"That's the funny part, Julien. Before you get to Chattanooga, the highway makes a little dip down into Georgia, then comes right back to Tennessee. I stopped to use the bathroom at the welcome station, and when I came out my *doppelgänger* was waiting for me. I don't know whether she knew who I was, but I recognized her."

"Couldn't you tell me this some other time?"

"No. You have to listen now, Julien. I need to tell you what I did on my trip."

"I don't care what you did on your trip," Julien said. "You robbed a bank. You ran over a policeman. You turned left on red."

"Well, not exactly any of that, but my *doppelgänger* did misbehave."

"And they thought it was you?"

"What?"

"When your whatever it was did whatever she did, the police or somebody got confused and blamed whatever it was on you. Since she looked like you, I mean."

"Oh, no, Julien. They knew it was her all the time. In the first place, she didn't look like me. You're missing the point about the *doppelgänger*. Anyway, I was the one who called the police."

"*You* called them?"

"Yes. I felt terrible about it, but I had to. She had my car and my purse and everything. I thought if she had just left me a credit card so I could keep on eating and sleeping, I'd wait a day or two before reporting that my car had been stolen. I meant to give her a chance to get to St. Petersburg, which is where she said she was going. I thought she could leave the car on the street, and the police would find it. I was hoping she wouldn't trash it."

I'm a fool, Julien thought. I'm as big a fool as she is. He was not only listening to this nonsensical story, he was getting ready to ask a question, the answer to which would, he knew, add to his confusion. Be quiet, he told himself. Let her finish. Then maybe she'll let you take her to her apartment. But he spoke before this thought was fully formed in his brain.

"Wait a minute. How could this girl be your double and not look like you?"

"What I meant was, she reminded me of myself. Not the way I am now, but the way I was when I was her age. She was very young. She tried to pretend she was older, swaggering a little bit, standing up straight, which most tall girls don't do when they're young. When she saw me coming, she lit a cigarette, which was one of the things I used to do when I wanted people to think I was older than I was. She was wearing torn jeans, which is the way I used to dress, and even though she was puffing tobacco smoke, she smelled like pot, which I guess is the way I used to smell. But her hair and her hands and her face needed washing, and I always kept myself clean."

She looked down and rubbed the bridge of her nose. Then she said, "At least, I think I did. I was stoned and strung out a lot. I might have gone around dirty and not have known it. Anyway, the girl called me ma'am, which I think got me rattled. I never thought of myself as being that old. That was what you said to your mother when you were using your manners. I almost looked around to see who she was talking to. Then she asked me where I was going, and the funny thing was, I didn't know. After I'd got on I-24 by mistake, I hadn't thought about it anymore. I'd just tooled along and watched the sun rise. But of course, I couldn't say that. I mean how many people are driving down the Interstate at five in the morning not knowing where they're going? So I lied and said Atlanta, which was the first name that came to me, and knew when I said it that I was stuck with going there and stuck with her. She was obviously on something. As soon as she got in the car, she let the seat back and went to sleep. I had to fasten her seat belt.

"I thought that by the time I wanted to stop, she would have slept off whatever she'd been taking. I could buy her some food and give her some money, and she could get on the road again. But she kept nodding off in the motel dining room. I figured the only thing to do was take her to my room. If I left her where she was, they'd have her arrested.

"Now, Julien, here's what's funny. I had started out to go north, and I'd gone east by mistake. Now I was going south because that's the way this girl wanted to go. At first, I thought I'd stop in Atlanta. Then I thought maybe I'd better go on a little south of there, so she'd have a better chance of getting another ride. I had planned to get some sleep and start back north again. After I had to take her in as my roommate, so to speak, I thought, what the hell? I might as well drive on to Florida. Maybe that was where I had been supposed to go all the time. Then when I was asleep, she robbed me."

Julien squeezed her hand, caressed her arms, leaned far enough across the table for the backs of his fingers to brush her breast. "I'd never do that."

"Do what?"

"Steal from you."

"Julien, there's something wrong with the way you listen to me.

You keep on missing the point of what I'm saying."

"No," Julien said, "some people steal women's underwear. I read a long time ago that some of Jackie Onassis' servants stole her underwear and sold it for a lot of money."

She peered at him and shook her head. "That's weird, Julien."

"Well, you're the one who brought it up. That stuff about not having anything to wear that night."

"Listen," Shannon said. "I'm telling you something. I suppose I slept too long, because when I woke up, the girl was gone and my purse and car were gone, too. So I had to call the police, but guess what?"

"You found the girl yourself before the police could get there?"

"Oh, no. The police had already arrested her, and they were trying to find me. They'd called my apartment, but I assume you'd left by then. At least, nobody answered."

"I think that was my mistake," Julien said.

"What?"

"I should have stayed there."

"No," Shannon said, "if you had answered my phone, that would have only confused matters. Anyway, the police caught Amy— that turned out to be her name—and got my stuff back before I even knew it was missing. I thought that was pretty impressive."

"Hooray for the cops," Julien said glumly.

"Amy ran off the road, is what happened. She must have taken another hit of whatever she was on before she left the motel, because she didn't get back on the Interstate. She wandered off into a residential area and drove the car into some lady's flowerbed." Shannon thought for a moment. "I don't know. Maybe I should have paid for the lady's flowerbed."

"Paid for it?"

"Well, from what she said, it was pretty badly torn up. Amy had kept spinning the wheels trying to get out. Then the tow truck had to drive through the lady's yard, and it had been raining a lot down there."

"Shannon, look over here. My name is Julien. You've been going out with me for a long time. About two hours ago, I told you I loved you. I asked you to marry me. Do you remember that?"

"You're exaggerating, Julien."

"What?"

124

"We haven't been here two hours."

"I think it's more like two years. Shannon, give me a break, for God's sake."

"Julien, your tone of voice would have fit right in at the police station. When I got there, the flowerbed lady was yelling at the chief of police, and the chief of police was yelling at the man who drove the tow truck, and the man who drove the truck was yelling in general about how he hadn't been responsible for the rain that made the ground soft. Amy was in a chair nodding off like she'd done in the restaurant, but just as everybody paused for breath, she came to and said some words that the flowerbed lady wasn't used to hearing. I think she even shocked the police chief.

"For a while after Amy said what she said, nobody else said anything. The flowerbed lady turned gray. Her hair was already gray, but her face turned the same color. Even her lips were gray. She kept opening and closing them as if she were going to say something, but there was no sound. She even put her hand on her breast like women used to do in those melodramas."

"My God," Julien said, "what did Amy say?"

"Nothing that would have upset you. It's just that this was a little Georgia town, and she was a very old lady. Anyway, I thought she was going to have a heart attack and I'd have to do CPR, but the chief got her into a chair and started fanning her with his handkerchief. The truck driver brought her a cup of water. When it looked like the lady was going to be all right, the chief started yelling at Amy, but that was a lost cause. She was flopped back in her chair sound asleep with a silly little smile on her face as if she knew something the rest of us didn't know, and she wasn't telling.

"Now here's where luck came in, Julien. Whatever it was Amy was hitting on, she'd apparently taken the last one at the motel. The police didn't find anything on her, so they couldn't bust her for illegal possession. They knew she was drugged, but they didn't know on what, and it would have been too much trouble to get a court order to make her take a blood or a urine test. There was the flowerbed, of course. And I think the chief would have liked to book her for using bad language, but that's not much of a crime anymore."

"How about grand theft?" Julien said. "She'd ripped you off."

"Well, that was just it. The chief was ready with the warrant for me to sign, and I almost did it. I was mad, Julien. It's strange. I did a lot of stuff when I was young, some of which I may never get up enough courage to tell you about, but I never stole anything—except for my father's vodka and my mother's sleeping pills, which I figured didn't count, that being in the family. So I thought, damn it, I never ripped anybody off, and Amy shouldn't have hit on me, especially not after I'd given her a ride and bought her food she didn't eat and let her sleep in the other bed in my motel room."

Shannon paused. Then she said, "Julien, Amy wasn't just my *doppelgänger*. She was like me, all right, but the reason I couldn't send her to jail was that she looked like a friend I used to have—a girl named Mason who got killed in an automobile accident. It was because she looked like Mason that I had given her a ride in the first place. Now Amy had let her head drop forward, and she looked more like Mason than ever with her thick black hair falling over her face and her long legs stretched out in front of her."

Damn, Julien thought. Shannon sounded sad, and he didn't want her to be.

"There was a lot more yelling when I wouldn't sign the papers. Luckily, the flowerbed lady who had just about recovered from Amy's language turned gray again. While the chief was fanning her, I paid the tow-truck driver, and he helped me get Amy into the car. I think we were on the Interstate and out of the county before the chief could stop taking care of the flowerbed lady."

"So you took her to St. Petersburg?" Julien asked.

"No, I didn't really."

"Didn't what?"

"I didn't really take Amy to St. Petersburg."

"But—"

"I mean, I did take her, but that wasn't really what I was doing. It was Mason I was thinking of. I drove Amy to St. Pete because she looked so much like Mason."

Shannon was about to cry. Her face was pale and drawn with sadness. There were lines across her forehead and around her mouth. Julien was touched by the sorrow in her face, the pain she seemed to be feeling. This was love, he thought. He had learned when he was with Justine that love sometimes took you where you didn't want to go. Emotions turned suddenly, took unforeseen directions. He wasn't sure that he could do it, but he had to try to stop thinking about himself and do something to comfort her. He patted the back of her hand. He searched his mind for soothing words, but not much came to him. Finally, he said, "I'm sorry. About Mason."

"Well," Shannon said and paused, her voice uncertain. "I was with her, Julien."

"It was an accident," Julien said gently. "Nobody meant for it to happen."

"I know," Shannon said. "I know. And she was driving, which is better than if I had been. But we were drunk and stoned. If we had just done a few things differently, Mason would still be alive."

Yes, Julien thought, that's one of the reasons they call them accidents. "I'm sorry," he said again.

"Amy slept most of the way through Georgia. It was a long haul. We stopped to eat a couple of times. I drank a lot of coffee. If Amy had had any speed, I would have taken it, but she was out of everything, even pot, and she was jumpy. She fidgeted and smoked. I cracked the windows and listened to the wind. She complained a lot. She didn't like my tapes. She said once she didn't like my car. She wanted a beer, but I wouldn't buy it for her. After that, she refused to wear her seat belt, and when we stopped at a Stuckey's, she locked herself in a bathroom stall and stayed there half an hour just so I'd have to wait for her. Every time I thought, to hell with it, and was about to put her out, she looked or moved some way that reminded me of Mason."

"So you took her to St. Petersburg."

"All the way. I kept trying to decide whether to give her some money. If I did, she'd probably spend it on drugs, but she wouldn't have any way to buy food if I didn't. I hadn't decided until she got out of the car. Then when she turned away from me, she looked so much like Mason, I called her back and gave her twenty dollars. All in all, I'd been a pretty soft touch, even if I hadn't bought her beer, but she didn't like me."

"Why not?" Julien asked.

"I don't know. Maybe because I was older than she was, from what she considered another generation. Maybe I reminded her of her mother or somebody, somebody at home that she was running away from. Anyway, when I gave her the money, I said, 'Take care of yourself, Amy.' She stared at me, her rigid face framed by her dark hair. She hadn't thanked me for the ride, but I thought maybe now she was working herself up to thanking me for the money. But she wasn't. What she finally said was, 'Fuck you, too, lady,' which

Mason might have said, but not necessarily under those circumstances."

"That was terrible," Julien said. "What did you do?"

"Headed east," Shannon replied. "Back to Jacksonville, back to the scene of the crime. I hadn't meant to go there at first. But now it seemed the logical place to try to find out what kind of person I'd turned into."

# XIII

For most of Max's life, doctors had been telling him that he would feel better if he cut down on his drinking, but now he had cut down on his drinking and he felt worse. I need to drink more, he told himself, I need to make sure that I get my whiskey. Every night before he went to sleep, he tried to plan his drinking for the next day. He had never done much nipping before breakfast—this had never seemed gentlemanly to Max—and he didn't want to start now, but sometimes he thought this might be the only way he could get his proper ration. He might keep a flask under his pillow and have a snort or two as soon as he woke up. He might even put a bottle in the shower— he'd have to be sure that he didn't get it confused with the shampoo —and have a few sips while he was adjusting the faucets. But as Max knew, drinking on an empty stomach was risky. If he drank too much in the shower, he might get careless when he shaved. He might even get careless in the shower and fall, and then he'd be in a wheelchair like Bunnie, and with both of them out of action, Mrs. Smith and Mrs. Pakenham might not bring them any booze at all. Clearly, drinking before breakfast wasn't a good idea, but he needed his drinks, and Bunnie was filching them.

I'll sit somewhere else, Max told himself before he went to sleep. If he shifted to the other end of the couch, Bunnie wouldn't be able to reach his mug. If she tried to move close to him, he could stretch out his legs and block her, or if that didn't work, he could get the mug himself and hold onto it. He was pretty sure she couldn't take the mug away from him. This was a good plan, and Max could see it in action when he thought about it at night, Bunnie trying to push past, and he holding firm, his legs solid and unyielding. She'd be angry, of course. She'd demand that he let her by and probably say some things that neither Mrs. Smith nor Mrs. Pakenham would approve of. If worst came to worst, he could drink everything in his mug when he saw her coming. But as he recognized in his brighter moments, even this plan depended on his staying alert, and not staying alert was his problem in the first place.

His mind, which had been failing for a long time, was failing faster than ever. Max felt as if there were a great division in his head. He recalled the past in bright detail: he saw places that he hadn't visited in fifty years; sometimes he thought he heard his mother speaking to him. But the part of his brain that was supposed to get him through the day was no longer working. He could remember to go to the kitchen and pour a drink, but when he sat down on the couch and started to read, he forgot about it. Bunnie would drink her drink and then drink his, and for a long time, Max didn't notice what was happening. "We need a drink, Maxie," Bunnie would say, and sure enough, Max would see that this was true. He would look at his empty mug and assume that he had emptied it, but at lunchtime, he felt strangely sober.

Without his booze, his appetite declined. He lost weight that he couldn't afford to lose. He was weak and trembly in his joints. When he tried to sit down, his knees gave way and dropped him with a thump on his emaciated buttocks. He decided that he would take his whiskey neat, drink it from the shot glass and finish it off before he left the kitchen, but the force of habit overcame him. Before he realized what he was doing, he would be moving toward the living room, carrying his and Bunnie's drinks, and once more, he would forget about his after he had had a sip or two. There ought to be something that would help him remember to drink, Max thought. He decided to consult Tommy Harper.

"You look a little peaked, Max," Tommy said. "I don't believe you're taking your vitamins."

"Vitamins?" Max replied. He couldn't remember whether he was taking them or not. He didn't know whether he had any, and if he did, he couldn't imagine where he would keep them. He was sitting in an examining room, having been driven to Tommy's office by Mrs. Pakenham. He had left her to wait for him, but how could he be sure that she had stayed put? She might be listening at the door. Max leaned forward and spoke in a whisper. "Whiskey. Not vitamins. Whiskey."

"What?"

"Whiskey," Max whispered once more.

"You're going to have to speak up, Max," Tommy said in a loud voice. "For a minute, I thought you said whiskey."

"Damn it, I did," Max replied, "but you don't have to tell the world about it."

Though he was fully clothed, including coat and tie, Max was sitting on the examining table. Tommy, seated on a stool, had to look up at him.

"Well, what about whiskey?" Tommy Harper said testily. "You didn't have to come to the office to find out that I think you and Bunnie drink too much."

"Not enough," Max said.

"What?"

"Not enough," Max repeated. "I'm going downhill because of it."

Tommy peered sternly up over the wire rims of his glasses. "I haven't got time to trifle, Max."

"No, by God," Max said. "It's Bunnie. She drinks her drink and mine, too. I have trouble remembering."

"You've had trouble remembering for thirty years," Tommy Harper said. "It's not likely to get any better."

"Listen," Max said, "I can remember it at night. Then I get up in the morning, and it all goes out of my head. When I don't drink, I don't have any appetite. I don't feel good, Tommy."

"Hmm," Tommy Harper said. His stool was on wheels, and he rode it back as if he were trying to put Max in a different perspective. "You're off your feed. What else do you feel, Max?"

"I'm weak," Max replied. "And tired. Even when I sleep all right, I'm still tired in the morning."

"Take off your coat," Tommy said. "Let me listen to you."

Max stripped to his undershirt. Tommy Harper thumped and punched and used his stethoscope. He shone a light in Max's eyes, looked at his throat.

"I didn't say there was anything wrong with my mouth," Max said. "I can swallow. I just can't remember to pick up my mug before Bunnie gets it."

Tommy sat down again on his stool. "Max, did you ever think about how long those people in the Bible lasted? I'm not just talking about Methuselah. Isaac lived to be a hundred and eighty. Job reached a hundred and forty after all he'd been through. I don't think God makes people the way he used to." Tommy paused. "Of course, that is if we can believe the Scriptures, but that's out of my jurisdiction."

"They had faithful servants," Max said, thinking of Mrs. Smith and

Mrs. Pakenham. "People to bring them drinks when they needed them."

"Hah," Tommy Harper said. "Well." He fingered the shiny disk of his stethoscope. "Maybe it's the world we live in. You and I are old for our time, and you're only ninety."

It seemed to Max that Tommy was getting off the subject. "All I need is something to help me remember to take my whiskey."

"You're better off without it," Tommy said, "but let that pass. Max, we reach a certain point. Things start to go wrong. Your heart or your kidneys, your liver or your pancreas. First it's this, and then it's that. You treat one ailment, and then you've got to treat another."

"Yes, but—"

"No, wait. I need to tell you this, Max. Your heart sounds a little weak, but I don't believe that's the major problem. I think there's something else wrong, but I can't know for sure without putting you in the hospital."

Max's mind was wandering. He had spotted Tommy's medical diploma on the wall, and that had reminded him of his own college days. He was walking across the campus on a Sunday afternoon in spring, wearing white duck pants, a dark blue coat, a straw boater. The word *hospital* penetrated his reverie. "No," Max said, "I wasn't going there. Most likely I was going to visit Bunnie."

"What? Going where?"

"You said *hospital.*"

"Yes. Yes, I did," Tommy Harper replied. He unbuttoned his white coat and leaned forward. "They're not pleasant places to be, Max. They put you through a lot when they examine all your organs."

"I know," Max said. "Bunnie wasn't happy there."

"Yes. That's why I think in some cases it's better just to wait and see. Let people have what peace they can. Do you understand what I'm saying?"

"Well, it appears to me that Bunnie's doing pretty well," Max said. "She's way ahead of me when it comes to drinking my whiskey."

"Bunnie's not the one I've got in mind. It's you I'm talking about." Tommy got up and stood by Max, his hand on Max's shoulder. "Take care of yourself. Get plenty of rest. See if you can't get your appetite back without drinking."

It seemed to Max that his visit to Tommy had been a waste of time.

He had gone for advice about how to get more to drink, and Tommy
had told him he was going to die soon, which he knew already: he
had bought himself another cemetery lot in order to be prepared when
it happened. Tommy was old now, of course, and no doubt getting
weak in the head like Max, but as far as Max could remember, Tommy
had never had the right priorities. Tommy had usually come when
Max and Bunnie had invited him to their parties, but he hadn't
done anything when he got there: nursed a weak bourbon all night
and danced mostly with his own wife and left early. And drinking
wasn't the only one of life's pleasures that he advised against. When
Max had worked at the newspaper and put in some evenings at Miss
Baby's, Tommy had had the nerve to warn him not to take a disease
home to Bunnie. Max had never told Tommy—or anybody else—
that Miss Baby had been partially responsible for Max's return to the
Church. This wouldn't have mattered to Tommy in any event. He had
a scientific turn of mind that put everything in the wrong context.

Miss Baby, Max thought. He hadn't remembered her since the fifties
when Bunnie was in Rome and he was living alone at Nineveh, his
conscience haunted by all the bad things he had done to Bunnie. In
the first days after Bunnie had left, Max thought only of the proposition he had made to Susan. His shame was such that he couldn't
bear to go into the library. He mixed his drinks in the kitchen, sat in
the living room, did without books that he thought might get his mind
off how he had disgraced himself. Writing was out of the question.
Every morning he went to his study, but the paper in his typewriter
was the same shade of white as Susan's outraged face had been when
he put his hand on her thigh and said what he had said to her. Bunnie's
face had been white, too, when she found out what he had done. The
only story he could think of to write concerned a middle-aged man
making a pass at his wife's niece, which wasn't a plot he wanted to
dwell on.
  Max tried to think of what he had done as if it were fiction. If it
were just sex, the novelist's part of his mind said, it could happen to
anybody. Men make passes at women all the time, and that includes
their wives' relatives. Max had read stories of men who propositioned
their wives' sisters and their brothers' wives, not to mention their own
cousins. He had heard one particularly vulgar account of a young
man who had gone for his mother-in-law, but Max preferred not to

believe that one. Well, it wasn't just sex, Max said, trying to explain to himself his lingering sense of guilt, but as time passed and Bunnie remained in Rome, the sexual aspects of his encounter with Susan became more vivid in his imagination. He knew that he had wanted a son. He would still like to have one. But increasingly as he lived his celibate life, he remembered Susan, her legs pulled up on the couch, a loose wisp of dark hair at the base of her smooth, tanned neck. He thought of Bunnie, too, Bunnie dressing and undressing, Bunnie in garter belt and stockings, Bunnie leaning forward with her hands under her breasts getting her brassiere positioned to her satisfaction.

Finally, Max returned to the scene of his crime. He stood in front of the couch where Susan had been sitting. He touched the cushion on which she had sat. Before he went to bed that night, he looked in Bunnie's closet, felt the material of her dresses, smelled the lingering sweetness of her perfume. Max considered what he might do. In the old days, things had been easy, everybody sleeping with everybody else. People had got their feelings hurt, of course, and some of the men had had fist fights, but in the long run they had all remained friends. Max thought of the women he had had affairs with. Edith Ross was out of the country. He hoped she was with John in Italy, which would make it more difficult for John and Bunnie to get together, but wherever she was, she was too far away to help Max. Assuming that she would, Max thought, even if she were here. It seemed to Max that as women got older they lost the spirit of adventure. They were willing to go to bed with men, but they wanted relationships. What Max wanted was companionship until he could get back together with Bunnie.

Having exhausted his list of possible partners—they all seemed to be newly remarried or still married to rich men whose money they didn't want to risk losing or living somewhere else or dead or decrepit—Max thought of Miss Baby. The house was gone, of course, the whole red-light district shut down by the provost marshals in 1939 after Roosevelt had instituted the military draft and soldiers had started coming to Nashville on weekends. In his present state of deprivation, Max recollected his nights at Miss Baby's with particular fondness, though on his first visit there, he had been with a group of rowdy college students; Ruby had stuck him most painfully in the butt with a hatpin when she herded the college boys out the door. Later, he and Ruby had become good friends, and Max had had a crush on Miss Baby. Occasionally, he had dreamed about her, seeing in his sleep her white skin and black hair and the ample body that she was always about to let Max explore just as he woke up.

No one ever saw Miss Baby go upstairs with a man, but it was rumored that she had clients: bankers and insurance executives and highly placed politicians. Ralph Applegate, Max's colleague on the newspaper who wrote sob stories and would believe anything, claimed that Miss Baby had a lover, the president of a railroad from Louisville who entertained Miss Baby in his private car. Why not a yachtsman, Max asked, who came by boat? He and Miss Baby could have their fun going up and down the Cumberland River. If Miss Baby had lovers, she met them at odd hours, because her house was open seven nights a week, and she was always there, walking through the parlor from time to time, but spending most of the evening in her private sitting room talking to one of the customers. Miss Baby had a passion for conversation.

Her parlor was off the vestibule of the once-elegant town house in which she ran her business. It had wine-colored carpet and wine-colored velvet draperies, a carved marble mantelpiece and Victorian furniture. Miss Baby usually sat in a rocking chair with her full but shapely legs crossed; she would swing her foot if she thought your attention was wandering. She liked to talk to Max, because she knew from her own experience that there was more going on in town than the newspapers printed. She questioned Max about bankruptcies and embezzlements, the dissolution of partnerships and stock issues gone bad and bonds in default. At first Max thought she was interested in money, but he soon learned that with Miss Baby it was *cherchez la femme.* According to her, Adam would have stayed in the Garden of Eden if God had forgotten about creating women. "But then he made us, you see," she said to Max, "and ever since, men have been doing bad things. All this stealing and suing and going to prison is done for us. There's always a woman behind it." She wouldn't believe Max when he tried to tell her otherwise.

"Now, Max," Miss Baby would begin, "Mr. Holcomb jumped in the river, didn't he?"

"Yes," Max replied, "but he was a gambler, Miss Baby. He had lost fifty thousand dollars of the bank's money."

Miss Baby swung her foot. Max felt a quickening of desire. "Oh, no," Miss Baby said. "That's only what you wrote for the newspaper."

"Why would I write it if it weren't true?"

"That's just it," Miss Baby said. "That's what I'm trying to get at."

Max felt as if he were mesmerized by the shining toe of Miss Baby's patent-leather slipper. He longed to put his hand on the thin silk that covered her knee.

"Think about it, Max," Miss Baby said. "If it had just been the money, he would have shot himself. When you jump off the bridge in December, it's got to be love."

For a moment, the only answer Max could think of was that it didn't necessarily work that way, which was not the kind of answer you could give Miss Baby. "Listen," Max said, "if there had been a woman involved, I wouldn't have been on the story in the first place. They get Ralph Applegate to write stuff like that."

"Ralph Applegate!" Miss Baby said in disgust. "Ralph Applegate! If I go to the poorhouse, it will be because of Ralph Applegate. Darlene was so upset when she read that story about the Belle Meade girl and her East Nashville boy friend getting hit by that train, she let Ralph Applegate take her upstairs three times without paying."

"Ralph said he was going to pay later."

"Pay later!" Miss Baby said. "Pay later! Whoever heard of a charge account in a whorehouse? How am I going to repossess the merchandise if he don't pay?"

She got a cigarette and thumped the end of it on the table as vigorously as if she were pounding Ralph Applegate's head. "Those girls ought to quit reading the newspaper. I ought not to let it come into the house."

"Now, Miss Baby."

"Don't Now, Miss Baby me! I mean every word of it. Get rid of the paper or get rid of Ralph Applegate. One time I told Ruby not to allow him to come here anymore, but I let her talk me out of it. She said keeping him away would upset the girls."

After a pause, Max said, "I'll tell you what, Miss Baby. Let's go to your room."

"Max, you know—"

"If you didn't want anybody to know about it, we could stay right here." Considering the Victorian furniture, this seemed hardly feasible, but Max was desperate. "We could lock the door."

"Behave yourself, Max. I'm old enough to be your mother."

"Oh, no."

"Max," Miss Baby said, "I've got a house full of pretty girls. I wouldn't blame you if you didn't want Darlene after the way she's acted with Ralph Applegate. But why don't you take Priscilla? She looks just like me when I was young."

"Miss Baby, Priscilla's a blonde."

"Oh, Max," Miss Baby said, "that's all fake. You just haven't looked in the right places."

My God, Max thought, he would take any of them now, whatever the color of their hair or whatever they had done with Ralph Applegate. And why not? Max asked himself, surprised that he hadn't thought of this sooner. Why not? The houses were gone, but there were call girls now. There was a good chance that Miss Baby was still in business. If so, how would he find her? His memory, much better then than now, suggested that he look under "Escort Services" in the Yellow Pages. Here he found column after column advertising female escorts, male escorts (deplorable, Max thought), Oriental escorts, southern escorts, California escorts. There were blonde escorts, brunette escorts, red-headed escorts, French escorts, Strictly English escorts (oh, oh, Max thought, be careful about those). Discretion was guaranteed, transportation for the client could be provided, special costumes would be worn on request. Max could hardly believe that sex had become so complicated or that so many women had undertaken the profession. It seemed to him that unless there was a lot of cross listing, half the women in Nashville had turned hooker. How, Max wondered, had evil so far overcome this once-devout city? Disgraceful, Max thought, as he read the ads over again and felt his pulse quickening.

Abbie's girls were listed; Amanda ran a service; Angel offered her angels; but there was no Miss Baby. Max was tempted simply to telephone for a girl, but he couldn't get his mind off Miss Baby. She would be older, of course, and probably no more inclined to go to bed with him now than she had been then, but he longed to see her. Who knew how well she might have aged? Who knew what she might be inclined to allow Max to do—for old time's sake, perhaps, in token of their long friendship? It occurred to him that he might call down the list of escort services and ask to speak to her, but considering the nature of the business the services were in, whoever answered the phone might not admit that Miss Baby existed. What was her real name? Max asked himself. She'd probably have an unlisted number, but if he could remember her name, he might find her.

Though he still had pangs of guilt from time to time, Max had reestablished himself in the library. Early afternoon though it was, he had a drink to stimulate his brain, and sure enough, he recalled that her name had been in the paper every two years when the incumbent mayor had the police raid the houses as part of his campaign for re-election. Max had one more drink. He paced the floor. Though her name continued to escape him, Miss Baby's face and figure grew more vivid in his mind. The memory of her thin nose, her full lower lip, her bare arms, and the way her soft dresses draped over her hips was like an ache in Max's breast. He sighed in his exquisite pain. He poured more scotch. Then suddenly he remembered. There it was, or more properly, he thought, *Voilà*. Her name was Celeste Marivaux. She had come to Nashville from some unlikely place such as East Texas.

Max again consulted the phone book, the white pages this time, but once more he was disappointed. There were some listings for Marivaux, but no Celeste, none with the initial C. Knowing that he would have to track her down increased Max's excitement. With the face and figure of Miss Baby growing ever more desirable in his memory, Max planned his campaign. He tried to recall whom he knew at the telephone company. Booze and lusty fantasies concerning Miss Baby seemed to make his recollection work: he thought of Harry Schmidt, who did something at South Central Bell, called him, and got unsatisfactory news: there was no phone, listed or unlisted, for Celeste Marivaux. What now? Max asked himself, and reached once more into his old newspaper reporter's bag of tricks. He called the county trustee's office. There was no real estate listed in Celeste Marivaux's name. He called the records room at the police station and was told that he would have to come and check for himself: they didn't have time to search for the last known address of Celeste Marivaux. For a moment, Max couldn't think of what to do. It was too late for him to go to the police station, and it wouldn't be best in any event to arrive there with booze on his breath. He would have to wait until tomorrow to start his search again, unless he did what he had thought of doing in the first place. Why not call the escort services and ask for Miss Baby? He might get lucky.

With a fresh drink at hand, the phone book in front of him, and his glasses clamped firmly to his head, Max got down to business. He dialed and asked for Miss Baby. He dialed and asked again. He dialed once more, mixed another drink, and dialed again. He got through the *A*'s, the *B*'s, the *C*'s. He talked to a woman at Daphne's Escorts and to another at Delilah's, but Miss Baby was not to be found. It was hopeless, Max thought. He must have dialed twenty numbers already. He took a break, stretched, mixed a new drink, and went back to the phone. He was into the *L*'s and ready to give up when a woman at Leonora's said, "Well, of course, we've got Baby, honey. She's out right now, but she'll be checking in soon."

This sudden success after so many failures left Max momentarily speechless. "Miss Baby," he said finally. "Miss Baby's there?"

"Baby. Miss Baby. You call her what you want to. You got any special requests?"

"What?"

"Well, some of the gentlemen . . . but I guess you don't. Where can she find you?"

Max hadn't thought this far ahead. He knew enough not to say Nineveh. The first hotel that came to him was the Hermitage, but he didn't think that would work. He named a motel near the Vanderbilt campus.

"What name?" the woman at Leonora's asked.

Max hesitated. Miss Baby would know who he was, but there was no use to tell the entire community.

"Listen," the woman said, "here's how it works. You go to that motel and register under any name that suits you. Baby's going to call and ask for your room. You're going to tell her the room number, and she'll come knock on your door. You got that, sweetheart?"

Max thought for a moment and came up with a joke. "Ross," he said. "John Ross. But you tell Miss Baby that my real name is Max."

"Okay, Max," the woman said. "Cash. No checks. A hundred dollars an hour plus whatever extras you and Baby agree on."

The woman hung up, but Max remained at the desk; he held the telephone until the receiver began to beep. I'm really going to do this, Max thought. The notion that he was going to see Miss Baby again and do with her things that twenty years ago he had dreamed of doing filled him with a sense of awe. There was a pause in his perception of the world. Everything stood clear and still before his eyes: the books on the shelves, the bottles on the bar, the flowered upholstery on the couch where Susan had sat that fateful morning. It took time for his excitement to build. It came as a warmth inside his head and moved downward, engulfing his limbs and body. "By God!" he said.

He took a joyful turn around the room then ran upstairs to select his clothes: he wanted to wear the best he had for this reunion.

Registering at the motel was easier than Max had expected. He paid in advance, signed John Ross's name. The clerk asked for no identification. He took scotch and bourbon to his room. Did Miss Baby possibly prefer gin? He hoped not. It was too late now to do anything about it. He got ice, thought of having a drink but decided against it. He turned on the TV, but he was too excited to watch it. He went into the bathroom, saw that all was in order and appeared to be clean. He opened the draperies and watched the traffic growing lighter up and down West End Avenue. Would Miss Baby come in her own car? Would she take a taxi? He thought how lucky he was that she was working now, doing tricks. She must have had a change of fortune when the houses were put out of business. He jumped when the phone rang, then ran around the bed to answer it.

"John Ross?"

Was the voice familiar? Max couldn't tell after such a long time. His breath was coming short. He felt for a moment as if he couldn't answer.

"Hello. Is this John Ross's room?"

Max managed to speak. "Yes. But it's not John Ross. It's really Max, Miss Baby."

"All right, Max." The voice sounded not so much strange as far away. A bad connection.

"It's been a long time," Max said, fumbling, a little embarrassed, and thinking what a fool he was to be making conversation when she could be on her way to see him.

"It always seems that way," Miss Baby said. "What's your room number?"

Now, now, now, Max thought, hardly conscious of the words that were going through his mind. After Miss Baby's house was closed, he had believed he would never see her again, and now she was on her way to his room. Back at the window, Max saw a car turn onto a side street and move out of his view. Was that Miss Baby? She could come in the back entrance. Another car turned. Other cars passed. Max listened for footsteps, but of course the hall was carpeted. Where was she? he wondered. He should have asked where she was calling from. When the knock came, he was as startled as he had been by the ring of the telephone.

She'll be changed, he told himself as he moved toward the door. She's older. She's probably gained weight. He couldn't bear to think that her face might be deeply wrinkled. He paused with his hand on the knob, letting anticipation build, not wanting to rush and make the evening end too soon. He breathed deeply. His heart was pounding. There was another knock. Max opened the door. There she was. How fine she looked. He wouldn't have recognized her in the dim light of the corridor.

She was shorter than he remembered, but perhaps she looked this way because she had lost so much weight. In the old days she had been what Ralph Applegate with his penchant for fancy language had called voluptuous. Now, even though she was wearing a raincoat, it was clear that her body was as slender as a girl's. Her face was half in shadow, but the part of it he could see was smooth and thin like the rest of her, the bone structure showing nicely, the skin unlined and very white next to the hair, which remained as black as ever. But the hair was unwaved now: it was cut straight across her forehead and hung down straight over her ears. It seemed to Max that the person who stood in front of him was so different from the woman he remembered that she could not possibly be Miss Baby. But of course it had to be. Doubtless she had had a face-lift, watched her diet, done aerobics.

"You want me to come in or not, honey?"

"Oh, yes. Oh, yes. Come in. Come in." Max wondered how he could have so far forgotten his manners.

Miss Baby crossed the threshold, and Max suffered another thrust of doubt. This couldn't be Miss Baby. Whatever she might have done to her face and figure, she couldn't have taken inches off her height. The woman looked so young she made Max uncomfortable. Max started to say that he believed he had made a mistake, but when he was about to speak, the woman, who clearly was not Miss Baby, took off her raincoat. She was wearing a white blouse, a blue plaid skirt, white socks, and saddle shoes. Around her neck, she wore a small gold cross on a chain—the uniform of a student at a parochial grammar school. Was this some kind of joke? No, it wasn't a joke. Something had gone badly wrong. The woman on the phone had misunderstood him when he asked for Miss Baby. She had thought that he was asking for this woman who looked and dressed like a child.

At first, Max couldn't speak. He stared at the girl who was not really a girl. There were faint lines at the corners of her eyes, the barest beginnings of creases across her forehead. She was at least thirty, which, Max thought, should have made him feel better about being in the room with her, but it didn't. All his earlier passion had drained away. He felt old, tired, light-headed with weakness, as if he were just coming out of a debilitating sickness. He glanced at the bed and longed to lie down on it, but first he had to deal with this woman-girl.

"I'm sorry," Max said. "There's been a mistake. You're not the person I sent for."

"Did you ask for Baby?"

"I asked for Miss Baby," Max said. "I was looking for—"

"Stop looking," the girl said. "I'm here. Let's get it on, Daddy."

"You don't understand," Max said. "This isn't what I had in mind."

"Ha, ha," the girl said as if she were truly amused. "You're something else, Pop. I see all kinds, you know. Some of the men pretend they're my uncle, and some of them want to be my daddy. Keeping it in the family seems to be a big thing with men who like children. If you get off on pretending you'd never lay a hand on a little girl, it's okay with me. I'll put a move on you."

Max didn't want to believe he was hearing what he was hearing. He didn't want to believe he was in this motel room or that this woman dressed like a child was in the room with him. "Listen," he said. "I think I've made a mistake. I mean, I really . . . I didn't . . . "

"Sure, sure," the girl said. "You play it however you want to. But if I have to chase you all over the damned room, I'm going to charge you extra."

"Listen," Max said. "No. Wait, now."

The girl was moving toward him. She was reaching out to him with her slender arms. Suddenly, he was against the wall with a table on one side, a bed on the other.

The woman put her small hands on Max's shoulders. "I'm bored, Uncle Max," she said in her child's voice. "I want you to play with me."

"Oh, no," Max said. "Oh, no." He had to escape. He moved left and right, bumped against the bed, bumped against the table. He tried to push the girl away and found his hands on her barely formed breasts.

"That's it, Uncle Max," she said. "Let's play together."

Max made a desperate leap and leapt too hard. He bounced on the bed, went down on his back, and immediately the girl was on top of him.

"No, damn it!" Max said. He tried to wiggle out from under the girl, but she was too agile. Max pushed off the bed with his hands and feet. Momentarily, he thought he was free. Then he was on his back again, and the girl was straddling his chest, her skirt up exposing her childish thighs, her panties.

"Let me up," Max said. "That's all I want you to do. Let me up. I'll pay you."

"You pay to play," the girl said, "and now we're playing."

To avoid peering up the girl's dress, Max turned his head and closed his eyes. While he wasn't looking, the girl slid down and unbuckled his belt, opened his pants, yanked his zipper. All right, Max thought, this was too damned much. He had been taught never to hit a girl, but this was an emergency. He drew back his hand, but before he could swing, the girl was at his underwear, and he had to roll on his side to keep her from touching him. He went to the left, then to the right. He managed to get on his knees and buck like a horse. The girl slid off his back, but she grabbed his pants as she went. He kicked, and she pulled. His pants came off, and Max was standing by the bed without them. Could he take comfort in the fact that he still wore his coat and shirt and tie? Not much. He was thankful that he still had possession of his boxers.

Max was glad to see that for the moment he was no longer the center of the girl's attention. She was looking at her skirt. Apparently, she had ripped a seam when she jumped on top of him.

"That's all of that I'm going to do," the girl said. "You already owe me extra for my skirt. Now let's get down to business."

"Excuse me," Max said. He had meant to sound dignified, but he sounded as if he were mimicking the girl; the words came out with adolescent uncertainty. "Excuse me," he said again, half expecting to hear his voice crack. "I need my pants. I'll have to trouble you for my trousers."

"Do you want to—"

"No!" Max said. "No! I don't want to."

The girl stared at Max. After a moment, her expression changed from bewilderment to comprehension. "You poor old guy," she said. "You can't even do it anymore, can you?"

Max was offended by this calumnious reference to his manhood. Except for drinking too much, he took excellent care of himself: ate properly, swam and walked and lifted weights. If he could believe Tommy Harper, his prostate was in fine working order. Max was tempted to tell this girl about the robust state of his health, but that might induce her to start chasing him again. The girl returned his pants, he took out money and gave it to her. "Listen," he said, "all this . . . I mean, your coming up here. It was all a misunderstanding."

"I know," the girl said. "It always is."

"No," Max said. "There was a woman I knew over twenty years ago. She was . . . in your line of work. I was hoping I could find her again. She went by the name of Miss Baby."

"I know," the girl said. "There's always a reason."

Max was anxious that the girl hear what he had to say. "She ran a house. You could do that then. I had a crush on her."

"You don't have to explain anything to me," the girl said. "Men like what they like. My business is to try to make them happy." Standing in the doorway, she turned back toward Max. "Call me again if you change your mind. You can remember my name. It's Baby." Then the door closed behind her.

Max felt terrible. He needed a drink and intended to have one, but first he needed to put on his trousers. In went one leg, then the other. Hook the hook, button the button, zip the zipper. How shameful, he thought, that he had allowed himself to be depanted by a woman no bigger than a—he didn't want to think the word *child*, but there was no avoiding it. He told himself that this misunderstanding had not been his fault. He couldn't have known that the escort service would send him a woman dressed as a girl when he asked for Miss Baby. But as Tommy Harper, given the chance, would be all too glad to tell him, Max should never have become acquainted with Miss Baby in the first place. Tommy, who had probably given up sex after his last child was born, thought he had all the answers. He would see Max's life the way he saw everything else: as a chain of interconnected events, one thing leading to another. Twenty-five years ago, Tommy had advised him to stay away from Miss Baby's. Now Max's old lust for Miss Baby had returned to haunt him.

But Max knew life wasn't that simple. If Bunnie weren't in Rome, Max wouldn't be here, and Bunnie wouldn't be in Rome if Max hadn't made a pass at Susan. When he put his hand on Susan's thigh, he hadn't been thinking of Miss Baby. Still, since this too had to do with sex, Tommy would probably make a connection. Max was miserable. Old regrets possessed his mind. He thought of himself and Susan in the library, and his breath came short. He was sorry that he had slept with Edith Ross. He wished that tonight he hadn't tried to find Miss Baby. The people at the escort service, the woman who had come to his room, had thought he was perverted. Well, he wasn't perverted in any ordinary sense, but there was something wrong with the way he had been conducting his life. When he was young, living in Mississippi, day had seemed to follow day in a regular order. He had known what was expected of him, known what he could and could not do, known what was right and wrong, good and bad, decent and unthinkable. Everywhere he had turned, there had been someone to advise him, to encourage or to reprimand him: his mother and father, the sisters at his school, the priests in the confessional. Max wasn't foolish enough to believe that he could ever reprise the moral certainty of that time. His life and the world he lived in now were different. But he longed to do something to make his life more orderly.

# XIV

"You're pretty careless, Julien. Did you know that?"

"Hmm," Julien said vaguely. He was half-asleep, drowsing in his happiness, conscious only of the comforting weight of Shannon's head on his shoulder and the warmth of her breath against his cheek.

"Listen," Shannon said, "you'd better wake up and think about this. You didn't take any precautions. You didn't even ask me. I might have AIDS."

"What?"

"I said, I might have AIDS. You don't know. We're in the nineties now. You can't just go around sleeping with people and not worrying about it the way your mother and father did."

"My mother and father?" Julien said. "You've got the wrong example. They probably had to have counseling beforehand so they'd know what to do on their wedding night."

"That's not the point," Shannon said. "Back then, people could hop in and out of bed with anybody they wanted to, and the worst thing that might happen to them was something they could get over. But now . . ."

Julien pulled her closer. He wanted to hold her so tightly that her flesh would join with his. He wished there were some way that he could feel her heart beating in rhythm with his inside his breast.

"Okay," Julien said, "do you have AIDS?"

"Julien, you sound like one of those Polish jokes that nobody's supposed to tell anymore. You don't ask afterward, you ask before. It's too late afterward."

"All right."

"All *right*?" Shannon said. "It's not all right. I'm trying to teach you something."

Julien kissed her forehead. He wanted to kiss her lips, but to do that he would have to slide down in the bed, and he didn't want to move.

"Are you listening to me, Julien?" Shannon said.

"No." Julien kissed her again. "I'm thinking about the wedding."

"What wedding?"

"Our wedding," Julien said. "Maybe we ought to get married the day Max and Bunnie celebrate their sixtieth anniversary. We could invite all our guests to their party instead of having a reception. Think of all the money we could save."

"Julien, I haven't said I'd marry you. We don't know each other well enough to be talking about that. This is the first time we've slept together."

"Of course," Julien said, "we'd have to buy our own cake. Shannon, I hope you have good taste. I'd be embarrassed if you got a cake with those silly bride and groom dolls on top of it."

"Damn it, Julien." She tried to move, but Julien wouldn't let her.

"Then there's the champagne. Bunnie and Max say it gives them gas, so they probably won't have any. I don't think it would do for us to toast each other with vodka."

"Julien, I'm not going to toast you with anything except maybe on the barbecue grill. I never said I'd marry you."

"You have to," Julien said. "I've robbed you of your virtue."

"Julien, stop this. *I'm* the one who's supposed to be hassling you, remember? Where was your mind all those nights in the bar when I was giving you grief?"

"We're in bed now," Julien said. "That makes it different."

She tried to move again, but he held her, loving the strength of her body, knowing that she could escape from him if she really tried.

"I'm going to get a job," Julien said. "In spite of the fact that you kept me from getting my proper rest, I'm going to graduate. I've already had three interviews."

"Julien, will you listen to me? Have I ever said straight out that I would marry you?"

"I think I've got a lock on a job at a bank, but I don't know. If I'm going to crunch numbers, maybe I'd be better off at a brokerage house. How much money do you think I ought to ask for? You might want to quit work when you start having children."

"Quit work when I have children! Do you know how my mother spent her time when I was growing up? She was always working, she just didn't get paid for it. Off doing something for the Junior League or the Ladies of Charity or the Diocesan Board of Education or the hospital or the theater or the symphony."

"That sounds good," Julien said. "I like the theater. I like music. I'll admit I'm not much on hospitals."

"Julien, you're missing the point. As a matter of fact, you've lost the drift of the whole conversation. First, to repeat, I never said I would marry you. And second, if I ever do marry you, I might want to keep on working. I might like taking care of sick people better than staying at home."

"Well," Julien said, "with six or eight children, you'd always have one or two of them sick. You could stay home with them and have the best of both worlds."

"The best—"

"Or the worst," Julien said. "It depends on how you look at it."

"Julien," Shannon said, "I'm going to kill you."

"I know. I've already taken that into consideration. I'll work hard all day to support all those children, and then you'll make love to me all night. I'll die of fatigue. It's what I've thought was going to happen for a long time, but I didn't know it was going to be so pleasant."

"Go home," Shannon said. "Leave."

"I can't."

"Damn it, you have to. Julien, you're in my bed. This is my apartment."

"I know. That's why I can't leave. I have to explain some things to you that you don't know about life. Remember, I'm older than you are, and I haven't been confused by a Catholic education."

"I think I'll call the police," Shannon said.

"No, you need pay attention, because what we've done is a little bit out of the ordinary. You see, in the old days, a boy promised a girl he'd marry her if she would go to bed with him, but a lot of times after the girl had gone to bed with the boy, he'd refuse to marry her or maybe leave town if he'd got her pregnant."

"What am I supposed to say to that, 'Twenty-three skidoo'? No, that would be too modern. Julien, you sound like an escapee from the Twilight Zone, somebody who got zapped by a time machine and sent back to the dark ages."

"Well," Julien said, "I'll admit you didn't promise to marry me before we made love, but I asked you to marry me, so now that we've made love you have to marry me."

"You've got to do better than that," Shannon said. "If that were true, all yuppies would be married."

"Okay," Julien said, "listen to this. I love you. I love you and you love me and we're going to get married. How's that? People fall in love, get married, and live happily ever after, just like they told you in catechism class."

"Told me in *catechism class*?"

"Well, I don't know where you learned it, Shannon, but that's the way things are supposed to work. You have to admit that."

"My God," Shannon said. "How did I wind up here?"

"I seduced you," Julien replied. "It was pretty easy once you let me come into your apartment."

"Do you know what I think I ought to do?" Julien said. It was another night, and they lay in their usual resting position, her head on his shoulder.

"No," Shannon said, "I'm afraid to guess."

"Of course, you know more about this than I do, being a nurse and all, but I think maybe I'd better use reverse psychology."

"I don't want to hear the rest of it."

"You have to. You're the one I'm going to use it on. See how you like this: I'm not going to marry you, Shannon. I know now that we're sleeping together, it would be the proper thing to do, but I'm sorry, I'm just not going to do it. There's no use to argue."

"Thank God," Shannon said.

"What?"

"I said, thank God. Those are the first sensible words you've uttered since we started coming here instead of going to the bar after I get off work."

"This is not the way you're supposed to act, Shannon. You're supposed to want what you can't have even if you didn't want it before you were told you couldn't have it. Do you understand that? Even if you didn't want to marry me when I was asking you to—"

"I wonder if they miss us," Shannon said.

"Damn it, listen to me, Shannon."

"Probably not," she said. "We never drank much, and most of the time we were there, you were sulking."

"Shannon, what are you talking about?"

"The bar, of course. The one we used to go to. I think we'd better start going back there, Julien."

"Like hell," Julien said. "Maybe thirty years from now when our youngest child is old enough to stay by himself. But that doesn't mean that we won't make love when we get home. Don't think you'll be getting out of anything."

"Or herself."

"Herself?"

"Yes. Don't be a male chauvinist, Julien. If we got married, and if we had children, which at the moment seems a lot more likely, the youngest might be a girl. You see? You didn't even think of that."

"Wait a minute!"

"Well, you didn't."

"No, not that. You said that it's more likely we'll have children than get married."

"Yes."

"But I thought—"

"Julien, I pointed out to you the first time we made love that you weren't taking any precautions, and you made a joke of it. Actually, what you said wasn't funny enough to be called a joke, but you didn't take me seriously."

"For God's sake," Julien said, "you told me I ought to be careful because you might have AIDS. You didn't say anything about children."

"I didn't think I had to spell everything out for you, Julien. Most men know all about condoms."

"Shannon," Julien said, "do you mean that for the last couple of months we've just been doing it? I mean, just . . ."

"According to nature," Shannon said. Julien couldn't see her, but he knew she was smirking. "That's how all these babies you like to talk about get here."

"No."

"Of course it is. Did you think the stork brought them?"

"Damn it, that's not what I'm talking about. There's something called the Pill. You're a nurse. I thought you knew about that."

"They're a hassle, Julien. You have to remember to take them on schedule. Besides, since my druggie days, I've had an aversion to pills."

"Yes, but—"

"Julien, do you really want children, or was all that talk a bunch of bull?"

"Of course I want children, and since we seem to be about to start having them, we'd better get married."

150

"Maybe you're right. But that's not a commitment, you understand. It only means I'm leaning in that direction."

"We've got to get cranking. It takes time to plan these things."

"You know what?" Shannon said. "If we go through with this, we might do it at the bar."

"At the what?"

"The bar, Julien, where we went on all our dates. After all, who knows what's going to happen to us. Right now, I've got good sense, and I think I can keep us from making fools of ourselves. But who knows? After I've raised all those children you've been talking about, I might be as uptight as you are."

"As I am!"

"Yes, and you're just the type to get sentimental and want to spend an anniversary revisiting where we got married. I think it would be less embarrassing for both of us if all we had to do was go back to the bar."

"Shannon, will you get serious? Nobody marries in a bar."

"You don't appreciate what I do for you, Julien. You're the one who suggested that we get married when Max and Bunnie have their party so we could save money. Well, the bar already has a piano player, so we wouldn't have to hire any musicians. And you know how people at bars are. They'll be half-sloshed, and they'll buy us drinks. The bartender would probably serve us champagne on the house. All we'd have to worry about is the cake, and I think we can do without a cake. Cake's fattening, you know, and I'll look fat enough by then, anyway."

"That's the—Wait! What do you mean, you'll be fat enough by then?"

"I wonder," Shannon said, "if a bartender can perform weddings. You know, like the captain of a ship."

"Shannon, what are you saying to me?"

"Well, somebody has to perform the ceremony. That is, if I decide to go through with this business."

"Shannon."

"What?"

"Are you pregnant?"

"We really ought to marry in the bar, Julien. Then when you forgot our anniversary, it wouldn't be as bad as if we'd married in a church."

"Damn it, Shannon, tell me whether you're pregnant."

"Well, that's what I'm talking about," Shannon said. "You don't notice things, Julien. I mean, you've been coming home with me every night for two months, and it hasn't even occurred to you that sometime along the way I should have had a period."

My God, Julien thought. It was true. She should have had a period a month ago, and he had been so deep in the joy of loving her that he hadn't noticed. "Damn," he said. "I thought you were doing something about this, Shannon."

"I was," Shannon said. "I was getting myself pregnant so when I told you, you could leave town like those ancient heroes you were telling me about."

"You know I'm not leaving town. Damn it, Shannon, all I've been saying to you, almost since the first time we met, was that I love you and I want to marry you. But why in the hell did we have to do it this way? Couldn't we have gotten married first? Why does everything you do have to be different from the way other people do it?"

"I told you that, Julien, the very first time we talked."

"Shannon," Julien said, "don't start that stuff about having to live your own life. That's all right when you don't have anything to do but get up and go to class the next day. We're grown now. Talk sense. We're going to get married, and you're going to have a baby."

"Not necessarily."

"*What?*"

"No, no, I didn't mean *that*. I may not marry you. Right now, you sound like you might not want me to. But I'm going to have the baby."

"Oh, damn," Julien said, "I'm sorry." He turned on his side so he could put his other arm around her and hold his cheek next to hers. "I thought maybe after we got married we'd have a couple of years with just us. Nobody else that we'd have to take care of. Nobody to worry about if we suddenly decided to go off for the weekend. I love you, and everything's all right. But it wouldn't have hurt anything to have waited."

"Oh, I don't know, Julien. People take babies everywhere now. Of course, we'll have to wait a while before we take her scuba diving. We'll have to let her sinuses develop."

"Scuba diving, hell!" Julien said. "Shannon, don't you think you might have just mentioned this business to me. I mean, would it have been too much for you to say that you weren't on the Pill?"

"Julien, we've already talked about that. Now, listen. I'm going to have the baby. The truth is, I've been thinking about transferring to the maternity service because being pregnant makes the whole idea of babies so appealing. Now—Wait! No, damn it! Get away. Don't touch me, Julien. Get on your own side of the bed so we can have a conversation."

"I don't want to talk."

"You know something, Julien. It's curious how men get excited by everything. You don't want to have this baby. At least, you don't want to have her now. But the idea that you've made me pregnant gets you all worked up again."

"Yes," he said. He moved back toward her, reaching for her.

She pushed him away, her hands on his chest. "Julien, if you don't get away from me, I'll never speak to you again."

"All right."

"It's not all right, damn it! I'll accuse you of date rape."

"I wish we were married," Julien said.

"It wouldn't do you any good. In Tennessee you can be arrested for raping your wife. I guess I should have told you that, too, before you asked me to marry you."

"Shannon, if I didn't love you so much, I think I'd move to Brazil. I'd buy a chain saw and help cut down the rain forest, so everybody would be as frustrated with me as I am with you. Pay attention now. Do you love me?"

"Well . . . yes."

"Much?"

"Julien, if I answer that, you'll start grabbing for me again. We have to talk."

"I am talking. When do you want to get married?"

"It depends. Some women show sooner than others."

"Then the sooner the better, in case you begin to show early."

"No, just the opposite. We can't get married until people can tell I'm pregnant."

"But I thought—"

"I know it's too early, but I keep looking in the mirror. Sometimes when I put my hand on my stomach, I think it feels different, but it's probably my imagination."

"Let me see," Julien said.

"No! Julien, could you possibly behave yourself for about three more minutes?"

"Then can I feel your stomach?"

"I'll consult the baby."

"I'll put my ear up close to hear what he says."

"*He*," Shannon said, "*he*. I don't know whether it's a boy or a girl, but why couldn't you just as well say *she*?"

"I'll say anything. Let me feel of her."

"Not yet. Do you remember when I was gone? I told you that after I'd driven Amy to St. Pete I went to Jacksonville. I guess it was being around Amy, being treated like such a bitch all the time I was trying to help her, that made me think I'd go to see my mother. I told you Amy was like me when I was her age, and the way she treated me made me wonder if I'd been too harsh in judging my mother. That maybe we could make up some way. Be friends like I've been told mothers and daughters ought to be."

"I'm glad you went to see her," Julien said, "but don't you think we ought to get this marriage business settled before she finds out you're pregnant?"

"Actually, I didn't go to see her. Things didn't quite work out that way."

"Well, even so, you're going to have to tell her we're getting married. We'll have to let her know she's going to be a grandmother."

"I meant to see her, Julien. I really did. But I'd stayed up all night and driven from Nashville to St. Petersburg and from St. Petersburg to Jacksonville. During the last part of the trip I was so spaced out I was seeing things—you know, people on the road who weren't there. Once I thought I saw a squirrel on my windshield. I kept thinking how much I wanted to be back with you, but like I told you, I felt like I had to do something to make up for what I'd done to Mason."

"I remember," Julien said softly.

"And for myself, too. I didn't want you making love to the kind of person I'd been before I met you."

"It was the nuns, wasn't it?" Julien said. "After all those years, what they said was still bothering you."

"I don't know. I just remember that finally I was in Jacksonville. I don't know what time it was. All I remember is that it was daylight, and I stopped at the first motel I came to and hung the Don't Disturb sign on the door and slept. And I was going to see my mother. I swear to God I was. I got up the next day and had breakfast because she'd always told me that I ought to eat breakfast. It was one of the things we'd argued about. I washed my hair and put on a dress, and hose, and neat little shoes that I thought she'd like, and makeup. I even thought about polishing my nails, but I couldn't quite bring myself to do that, and I didn't have any nail polish anyway."

"It's exciting to think about all that," Julien said. "I wish I could have watched you dress."

"Julien, if you don't listen to our baby when she starts growing up any better than you listen to me, you're going to be a terrible father."

"I hear what's important," Julien said. "Tell me about your mother."

"I called her, but when the phone started to ring, I panicked and hung up. I couldn't think of what I'd say to her when she answered."

"But you've been talking to her. You've told me that you've been on the phone to her now and then."

"I know, but it wasn't the same. When I was in Nashville and she was in Jacksonville, there were all those miles between us. If things got bad, I could hang up. Seeing her face to face was going to be different. I kept wondering what I was going to say to her. No, it was worse than that. I couldn't decide what I would do when I got to the door. I still had a key. Should I just walk in and yell, 'Hey, Mom, it's me! I'm home,' as if she and I were the leads in a female version of *Leave It to Beaver*? This was probably what she would expect me to do. She wouldn't want me to wait on the porch for her to answer the bell. She wouldn't think that would look right to the neighbors."

Julien put his hand on her stomach, and she let it stay. Was he touching close to where the baby was? How big was a month-old, unborn baby? "So what did you do?"

"I cried. Damn it, Julien, it was the worst thing I could have done. I'd used a little eye shadow trying to look healthy. I didn't want to have to listen to her tell me that I didn't eat right and didn't sleep enough and that I ought to take care of myself. I pulled into a Kroger's parking lot and sat there with tears screwing up my eye shadow, thinking the only thing in the whole God-damned world I had to be thankful for was that I didn't use mascara."

"You could have been thankful for me."

"Yeah, right. For all I knew, you were still asleep on my couch. When I left you, it looked like you might snooze till the year 2000."

"So what did you do?"

"Well, I stopped crying and got my face cleaned up, but my eyes were red, and, oh, God, she would notice. If there's something you don't want her to see, that's the first thing she looks at. I didn't want her to know I'd been crying, but she was just as likely to think I'd been smoking pot."

"Women are supposed to cry," Julien said. "Maybe if you'd gone straight to your mother's house with your eyes still red, you could have cried some more and she could have cried. Then you could have hugged each other, and you wouldn't have had to say anything."

"You know, Julien, that's another one of your chauvinistic remarks. You stereotype women. But that's damn near what I did. I didn't think exactly that we would cry and hug each other. I just thought, I'll go and see what happens, because even if we both screw up, it won't make things between us any worse. But I didn't go there. I went to see Mason's mother instead."

"Why?"

"By accident. Like I told you, when I got to my mother's, I lost my nerve. Without admitting it to myself, I was hoping all the time she wouldn't be there. I had figured out how her car would be gone, which would mean that she was gone, too. I could go to the door and ring the bell, and when she didn't come, I could head back to Nashville and tell myself that I had done my best, it wasn't my fault that I had missed her. But as soon as I saw it, I knew the car in the driveway had to be hers. What other forty-eight-year-old woman tools around in a red Saab convertible?"

"I don't know," Julien said. "But then, my mother's fifty-something."

"I kept going. I took a swing around the neighborhood, thinking she might be gone when I came back again. But of course she wasn't. It looked like I'd hit on the one day that she wasn't going out to lunch or to some meeting or to play golf or tennis or bridge or take her turn dishing out beans in the soup kitchen."

Shannon's voice had risen. Julien suspected that she might be about to cry. "Baby," he said, "what's so bad about all this? She wasn't going to do anything awful to you. She's only your mother."

"Yes," Shannon said, "she's only my mother. I think I understand that now. But let me tell you what happened. I was thinking so hard about my mother, I didn't pay any attention to where I was going. All of a sudden, I was at Mason's house. I was there before I realized that I was even on her street, and *her* mother was at the mailbox. I had to stop."

"She recognized you?"

"Actually, she didn't. It had been more than five years since she'd seen me, but I didn't think of that until I was out of the car. I'm not sure that I would have recognized her if she hadn't been standing in front of her own house. She's older than my mother. She was about sixty when Mason was killed. She'd had wrinkles and white hair even then. Now, if you looked only at her face, you would have thought she was seventy. But she was still thin, and she held herself very straight. The way she stood was one of the things I remembered about her."

"Did you want to see her?"

"Obviously, once I was out of the car, it was too late to consider that, but I think I did. There was a moment, a few seconds really, when she couldn't place me. She looked at me with eyes that were so much like Mason's, I thought I wouldn't be able to bear it if she didn't know who I was. But of course she did know. 'Shannon,' she said. 'Oh, Shannon.' And we did what you recommended that my mother and I do. We hugged, and both of us cried a little bit."

Julien held her more closely. "It's all right, now. Think about us. Think about our baby."

"One thing, Julien. You'd better not ever go in Mrs. Kennedy's house. It would give you the willies."

"Give me the what?"

"I'm trying to talk your old-fashioned language. I mean, if we're going to get married, we ought to be able to communicate."

"Shannon, every time I think your heart's about to break, you find a new way to give me misery."

"Comic relief," she said. "Listen. Unlike my parents, the Kennedys didn't have a mixed marriage. They're both religious. Their house is full of holy pictures and icons and statues. Mrs. Kennedy even has a little shrine to the Virgin in her bedroom. The family said the Rosary together every night when Mason was growing up. One of her brothers is a priest."

"Jesus," Julien said. "In that case, why had you rather see Mrs. Kennedy than see your mother?"

"I needed to know she didn't hate me for killing Mason."

"Shannon, you haven't killed anybody." Julien lifted his head off the pillow. He wished there were enough light for him to see her face. "Mason was driving. You were with her. It wasn't your fault."

"I owed Mrs. Kennedy something, anyway," Shannon said. "Mason and I had gone out that night, and I was the one who came back alive. But we had a hard time getting around to Mason."

"Talking about her, you mean?"

"We spoke of everything but her. I asked about Mason's brothers and sisters. Mrs. Kennedy asked about my work and how I liked it, and said what a kind thing it was to take care of sick people. We sat there and sipped Cokes and spoke all these words that didn't mean anything. All the time I knew that if I turned my head, I'd see a table covered with pictures of the Kennedy children and grandchildren and right in the middle of them would be a picture of Mason. I thought that if by some accident I let myself look in that direction, I'd become so hysterical that I'd wind up back in the sanitarium."

"How was Mrs. Kennedy holding up?"

"That's just it. Whatever she'd been feeling, she must have seen what was happening to me. She put her glass down very carefully as if she didn't want to startle me with any sudden movements. She patted her lips with her napkin. Then, still slowly, she got up and got Mason's picture and sat down beside me on the couch and put her arm around me. She said, 'She was lovely, wasn't she? It's no wonder, is it, that we were so fond of her?'"

"Oh, my darling," Julien said. "That must have been tough."

"Yes, but in a different way. For a moment, I felt as if my heart had stopped. There was a sense of absolute stillness in the room. I don't mean just silence. It was as if Mrs. Kennedy and I had quit breathing, as if outside the house, birds had stopped flying and automobiles had quit moving up and down the streets. I thought, I can stand this if I can only keep this stillness for a moment. I was afraid Mrs. Kennedy was going to break it. There was the possibility that she would bring religion into it, and I knew if she said something about God, I'd be on the edge of hysterics again. But she didn't. We looked for what seemed a long time at Mason's beautiful face. Then Mrs. Kennedy patted my arm, and I got up from the couch, and she got up with me."

"Did you go back by your mother's house?"

"Of course not, Julien," Shannon said. "That's what I've been trying to explain to you, but as usual you haven't been listening. I knew then that before I tried to make peace with my mother, I needed to come back here and get pregnant."

# XV

"Stately, plump Buck Mulligan," Bunnie wrote on her yellow pad, "came from the stairhead, bearing a bowl of lather on which a mirror and a razor lay crossed." This seemed all right, Bunnie thought, a good sentence with which to begin a novel, but Bunnie had an uneasy feeling that she had heard this line before. One of the reasons her novel was going so slowly was that sometimes she quoted other writers without meaning to and sometimes she wasted a week or more before she discovered that she had become an accidental plagiarist. Now she was vaguely troubled by *stairhead*. Was that one of her words? She didn't remember having used it before, and which of her characters, the friends and acquaintances whom she had decided to put in her book, was to be named Buck Mulligan? Certainly not Max. Max had never been stately or plump in his life, and in any event, Bunnie wouldn't give Max such a name. Buck Mulligan sounded vulgar to her. Shanty Irish.

Poor Max, Bunnie thought. Far from being plump, he was getting thinner by the day. He had almost stopped eating and almost stopped drinking, too, which was a serious matter, considering that Bunnie had been drinking his drinks as well as her own and now had trouble getting Max to fix drinks for either of them. Max looked unwell to Bunnie. His hair, which had been white for years, appeared to have grown even whiter, and it stood out from his head like an unruly halo. His eyes were vague and dim and rimmed in red, and often when he got himself fully settled on the couch, he couldn't get up without help from Mrs. Smith or Mrs. Pakenham. Max's memory, which had been atrocious for years, seemed in the last three months to have deteriorated further. He could still recall, sometimes in minute detail, things that had happened fifty years ago, but dealing with the present was another matter.

"Maxie," Bunnie would say, "we need a drink." Max would agree that this was true. But by the time one of the ladies had got him on his feet, he would have forgotten why he had got off the couch in the first place. He would stand and look around, his gaze pausing on a table or a chair as if he were on a tour of the White House.

"A drink, Max," Bunnie would say. "You got up to fix us a drink."

"Oh, yes," Max would say, but as likely as not, he wouldn't move.

"In the kitchen, Max. The booze is in the kitchen."

He would start then, but he might go anywhere: down the hall, into the dining room, out the front door if he could make it before one of the women caught him. When he got to the kitchen, he might not remember what he was there for. Once he brought Bunnie an apple, and another time he appeared with a corkscrew, which was close but still not what Bunnie wanted. "No, Max," Bunnie would say, "a drink. We need a drink." Sooner or later, she would get one, sometimes strong enough to flatten a mule and other times too weak to pacify a puppy. Bunnie thought Max could do better if he would only pay attention, but he looked so frail and helpless she didn't scold him.

To tell the truth, Bunnie thought, nobody was paying attention. Julien was in love. Whatever else he might be doing—changing Bunnie's diaper or setting out for class—his mind was on Shannon, which was all right with Bunnie. Julien was old enough to settle down, and who better for him to settle down with than a nice girl like Shannon. Bunnie was pretty sure Shannon was Catholic. If they married, naturally Julien would join the Church to be in it with Shannon, and they would start having babies. Bunnie would enjoy that. She had a vision of Shannon and Julien bringing their first baby to see her and Max, a human being no bigger than a doll, snug and warm in a blanket. Would it be a boy or girl? Bunnie truly didn't care, though for a fleeting moment she thought how proud she would be if the baby were a girl and they named it after her. But except for her own, no parents in their right minds would name a child Bunnie.

Mrs. Smith and Mrs. Pakenham weren't paying attention because their minds were on the anniversary party. The invitations had been mailed, acceptances were coming in: Mrs. Pakenham checked the names on a master list and gave Bunnie a daily update on how many people were expected. Susan called the caterer long-distance and then called Bunnie and then called the caterer again. All this long-distance phoning excited Mrs. Smith and Mrs. Pakenham. "It's Mrs. Talbot on the line," Mrs. Pakenham would say, "It's Mrs. Talbot,

Mrs. Howard." They talked of shrimp and dips and cheese and carrots, little sausages to be kept warm in a chafing dish and cold tenderloin sliced thinly. Should they have salmon? Yes, Bunnie thought, if only for the sake of those who preferred white wine to real drinking.

Bunnie wanted to be sure that she had enough liquor. She used a page of her novel pad to make a list of what she needed. More than a hundred people had accepted Bunnie's invitation. Even if some of them had to cancel, that would still make a good crowd, and who knew what they might decide to drink when they got on the premises? Bunnie had always bought enough booze so that if everybody drank the same thing, she still wouldn't run out. Besides, whiskey would keep, and she and Max could use any that was left over. Cases, she thought. A case of bourbon, a case of scotch, a case of gin, a case of vodka. White wine and maybe some red. Rum? Did she and Max know anybody who drank rum? No, but get a couple of bottles anyway. Get some brandy, to be safe. But Bunnie drew the line at tequila. She didn't want a bottle containing a dead worm set out where her guests could see it.

In spite of the interruptions that planning for the party caused, Bunnie tried to keep writing. She was still undecided about which character she would call Buck Mulligan, and she wondered if she were doing this right, if other novelists had as much trouble attaching names to their characters as she was having. When she had first started thinking about her book, she had used the characters' real names. John Ross had been John Ross and Max had been Max and she had been Bunnie. She thought it would be easy to rename everybody when she started putting words on paper, but now she had come up with a name she didn't like, and she didn't know whom to give it to. Who among her characters had been plump? She and Edith Ross when they reached middle age, but even though you might call a woman Buck, Bunnie wouldn't have a woman in her novel lathering her face and shaving it. Still, she didn't want to give up what she thought was a fine opening sentence, provided, of course, she was the first one to write it. What of John Ross? she wondered. Not plump. He had never been plump. But in some of his manifestations, he had been stately.

There had been John Ross, her friend, John Ross, her lover; John Ross who was Max's drinking companion and literary adviser; John Ross the famous novelist who had abandoned Edith. He was stately,

Bunnie thought, when he was performing in public, lecturing or reading his fiction. She thought of a literary meeting in New Orleans when she had been on a panel that discussed John's fiction, and John had sat at the table with the panelists and had the last word. On the panel, besides her, there had been two men, full professors, well along in their careers, and a young woman just out of graduate school clearly determined to make her way in the world. She hadn't been beautiful: her face was too lean for Bunnie's taste. But in contrast to most of the young women whom Bunnie had seen in the hotel lobby, she was neat and clean. Her hair was long and shiny black. She wore a little lipstick and a tailored green dress and pearls. With an ease that betrayed no conscious intention, John Ross managed to sit by her. He had looked stately that day, Bunnie remembered. Always, when he set out on a new conquest, he appeared to be larger somehow; he held his chin a little higher and made occasional gestures to accompany his wonderful voice.

That afternoon, John Ross had whispered to the girl. The girl smiled. Bunnie read her prepared remarks. She tried to listen to the opening statements of the other panelists and to follow the discussion, but she couldn't keep her mind or her eyes off John and the girl. It's all right, she tried to tell herself. She knew that John Ross flirted with every woman whose path he crossed, whatever her age or physical configuration. When the panel discussion was over, he would probably get the girl's address and telephone number. He would suggest that she have her university invite him for a reading. If she did, he would go, and if she were willing, he would sleep with her. Who knew how many women he had made love to on college campuses? It was, he said, part of the compensation for people in his line of business.

Looking down the table as the discussion progressed and John and the girl continued to smile at each other, Bunnie began to suspect that it wasn't going to be all right. Damn you, she thought, don't you dare do this to me. She had agreed to be on this panel because John had insisted. He had written and then telephoned imploring her to come. She hadn't wanted to. Or rather, she had wanted to, she had wanted very much to see him again, but she had been faithful to Max since they had returned from Rome. For two years, she and Max had lived on good terms, trusting each other, neither of them having to wonder what the other was doing when they were apart. Then came the voice of John Ross, tempting her from a thousand miles away. No, no, Bunnie had said, that's over. I know, I know, John Ross had said, his voice so sincere he almost convinced her that no impure thought had ever entered his mind. He said, You're better acquainted with me and my work than anyone else who'll be there. I need you to protect me. I'm asking as a friend. She had said, I'll see. I'll talk to Max.

Of course she went. John Ross met her at the New Orleans airport. Like Rome, Bunnie thought, when she caught sight of him. But it wasn't going to be. Not this time. He kissed her lightly on the lips, stood back, then put his arms around her and kissed her again. "Why didn't you come last night?" he said. "We could have—"

"No, we couldn't."

He pulled her to the side of the concourse and waited until the other passengers were gone. "Bunnie, Bunnie, Bunnie," he said. "You don't know how I've missed you."

"That's all over. Things are different now."

"No, they're not. You want me as much as I want you. You know you do."

"No. You're still married to Edith. Since Rome, I've been faithful to Max."

"Max is in Nashville."

"Yes," Bunnie said, "and tomorrow I'm going to be there with him."

"Of course," John Ross said. "It was tonight I was thinking of."

"No," Bunnie replied, "not tonight. Not anytime."

They moved down the concourse in silence. She hoped he was angry. She knew the dimensions of his temper, the things he could say when he was crossed. She wanted him to berate her, curse her, call her names that even he would be ashamed of later—anything to help her resist the charm of his presence. He smiled, pulled her bag off the carousel, and guided her to a taxi.

She could hardly refuse to have lunch with him. He sat across from her in a booth in the hotel coffee shop and used his arsenal of extraordinary gifts to try to charm her. He asked about Max and seemed genuinely interested in hearing about the book Max was working on. He spoke of mutual friends, writers mostly, whom he saw more frequently than she and Max did. He had recently been to England and France. In London, the American cultural attaché had given a dinner in his honor. John made Bunnie remember the glittering world she had shared with him in Rome: cocktails at the embassy, parties at the American Academy, a lunch one day at a village on a mountaintop where everybody at the table except her had won a Pulitzer Prize.

They were silent for a moment. Then he said, "I need to tell you that I'm miffed at you. I didn't even know about your piece on Hardy until it came out. Why didn't you send me a copy?"

"I didn't think it was good enough."

"It's damned good," John Ross said. "It says things about Hardy that have never been said before. That's quite a feat, considering all that's been written about him."

As he spoke, he put his hand on hers in a way that seemed meant to do no more than reenforce the compliment he was paying her. He had never before praised her mind. This was a new approach for him, and God help her, it was working. She wanted to pull her hand back, but she couldn't force herself to move.

"No," she managed to say. "It's pretty dull stuff."

John Ross smiled and shook his head. "Ah, Bunnie," he said, "you've always been too modest."

The pressure of his ankle against hers made her catch her breath. She could feel her resistance dying. Take your leg away from his, she told herself. Get up. Go to your room. She felt as if she were living in a dream. She was in grave danger and trying to escape, but her muscles and nerves refused to obey her mind. Could she speak? With great difficulty she managed to say, "I have to leave now."

John Ross rose from his seat, and for an instant she believed that she was saved, that he was going to walk with her back to the hotel lobby. But he came quickly around the table and sat beside her in the booth. He put his hand on her thigh, and she found herself wishing not that he would move it, but that there was less of her thigh for his touch to delineate. "Listen," he said softly, his mouth close to her ear, "we'll be through with the panel at four. I've promised to meet some people who want to start a magazine at four-thirty. I'll get away from them as soon as I can. I'll come to your room. At six."

She shifted her position, moved away from him, then moved close again, drawn there by the warmth that was spreading through her body. She wanted to say, I'll meet you in the lobby, but it was too late now. Damn him, she thought. He was right. She wanted him as much as he wanted her. She had come down here because she wanted him. How could she have made herself think, even for a moment, that she could be alone with John Ross and remain faithful to Max? Feeling the tip of his finger touch the flesh above her stocking, she trembled. "Stop!" she whispered. "Don't do that here." She paused and glanced around the room, wondering who might have been watching them. "I'm leaving now," she said. "Don't come with me. We've made enough of a spectacle of ourselves already."

John Ross smiled. "Six. I'll be there at six."

Now the panel discussion was ending. Typically, John Ross was complimenting the participants on their insights and thanking them for their flattering interpretations of his work. How could he know? Bunnie wondered. How could he have heard what they had been saying when all the time his attention had been on the girl? She felt as if she had been betrayed in public, as if everyone present knew that John had induced her to come here and charmed her in the restaurant with the same eyes and voice and movements that he was now using on the girl. Had he put his hand on the girl's thigh? Bunnie wondered. What would have prevented his doing so? The front of the table where they sat was draped.

Damn you, she thought, damn you! She ought not to let him in when he came to her room. Better still, she ought not to be there. She could roam through the lobby and make new friends, cadge dinner from a textbook salesman or a publisher. Why not? She didn't need him. But the truth was that she did. Anger and outrage increased her desire. She wanted to kill him. She wished there were some legitimate way that women could be like black widows: make love and then kill the son of a bitch you'd made love to. Her colleagues on the panel were standing up. Belatedly she joined them. A few people congratulated her and the two male professors. A larger group had gathered around John and the girl, who remained next to him. Bunnie peered across the platform trying to catch John's eye, but he didn't look at her. He was too busy being told how good he was, how much his work was admired.

She was calmer when she got to her room. She had a drink, took a bath, sat in her slip by a window and watched the sun go down. At five-thirty, she poured another drink and wondered whether she ought to bother to put on her dress, but she had to observe the proprieties. She would dress and fix her hair, put on perfume and makeup, all to be done over again when they had finished making love. That was, Bunnie knew, one of the differences between adultery and marriage: in affairs you usually started with your clothes on. At five minutes to six, she put on her earrings. Should she have another drink? Better wait, she thought. She didn't want to have too much before John arrived. At her age, she needed to pace herself.

At six, she tuned in the local news, but her mind was not on it. Once she thought she heard a knock, but when she looked out there was no one. At six-fifteen, she turned off the television. Five minutes later, she did fix a drink and stood by the window sipping it slowly. It was dark outside now. Traffic was thinning. Well, Bunnie thought, John Ross never changes. She knew what had happened. He was still with the people who wanted to found a magazine, giving advice, being flattered. Or maybe he had left them and consented to have a drink with another group of his admirers. The anger Bunnie had felt earlier began to build again. John Ross had no right to treat her this way. She would give him five more minutes. Then she was leaving. As she was reaching for her purse, the phone rang.

"Where the hell have you been?" Bunnie said. "I was about to leave here."

There was a long pause. "Bunnie?"

"Yes, God damn it, Bunnie. Where in the hell are you?"

"I've been thinking," John Ross said.

Was he drunk? Bunnie couldn't tell. After a dozen drinks, his speech would still be precise. "Thinking what?" Bunnie said. "That it didn't make any difference how long you kept me waiting?"

"Bunnie." He paused. She could hear him breathing. Had he lighted a cigarette? "I think you're right. If you and Max have . . . well, turned over a new leaf . . ." He hesitated once more. "Hard as it is for me to say it, I believe you'd better keep on being faithful to him."

"You think that, do you?" Bunnie had meant to make her voice keen with irony, but the words came out weak and thin. "I know that's exactly what you think. I was there when you started thinking it."

"Bunnie, listen to me. We're old friends. I really do believe that you and Max are better off this way. I wish Edith and I could have brought it off. I envy you."

"Sure you do," Bunnie said, "sure you do. That's what you'll be thinking all night, isn't it? When you get in bed with that girl from the panel, you'll be thinking how lucky Max and I are."

"Please, Bunnie. I'm only agreeing with you."

She wanted to say, Damn you, don't talk to me that way. You know

I came down here because of you. I'm here because you begged me. But she held her tongue. She didn't want to make an even bigger fool of herself.

"Bunnie?" John Ross said.

"Yes, Bunnie. That's whom you're talking to. I understand how you might get confused."

"I'm sorry, Bunnie."

"Don't let it bother you," Bunnie said and hung up the phone.

She stood for a moment thinking what a scoundrel he was. Someday she was going to tell him so. But not now. The ticket now was to have a drink, forget John, forget panels that engaged in literary discussion, forget young assistant professors who had sense enough to wear pearls and smile and whisper seductively when they sat next to John Ross. Bunnie found her glass, threw out the watery remains of her old drink, and built from the beginning. She made a vodka on the rocks and drank it with dispatch. She congratulated herself. That was the ticket indeed. She felt better. She refilled and sat down by her window. After the hiatus between the end of rush hour and the beginning of the evening, traffic had built up again. This was New Orleans. Things were going on. She'd have another drink or two. Then she'd go down to the lobby. Who knew what she might find there or where else she might go? The evening was just beginning.

When Bunnie woke up, her head was throbbing as if a ball were bouncing around inside her skull. Her throat was sore, and her nose was stopped up. She felt so bad, she wanted Max to comfort her, but when she reached across the bed toward him, she felt the quilted top of a bedspread. Where am I? she wondered. What awful thing has happened? She opened one eye, closed it, and opened the other and closed it, too. She remembered now. She was in New Orleans, in a hotel room, and she had neglected to draw the draperies. Light through the window made the ball in her head take a particularly hard bounce when she cracked an eyelid. She was sick, she knew that. Whatever she had wasn't simply the beginning of a cold and a bad hangover. Surely, she had caught some exotic disease in this subtropical climate, though at the moment, the climate felt anything but subtropical to her. She was cold, shivering.

She had to open her eyes and see what was wrong. She might be broken out. She might have some kind of pox; she needed to look in the mirror. Her eyes might be bleeding, for all she knew. "Oh, oh, oh," she said, as the light nearly fractured her plague-stricken cranium. She had to get up, painful though it would be. She moved and discovered that except for her shoes, she was still fully dressed. She was lying on top of the spread, and as she raised up, she was vaguely aware of her girdle squeezing her uneasy stomach. My poor dress, she thought. It was twisted and rumpled and probably out at a seam or two, but this was no time to inspect her wardrobe. She needed to go to the bathroom. She needed water. She needed seventeen aspirin and ten cups of coffee. She started to call room service, but she didn't know about the coffee. She didn't know whether she could keep it down. A shower? Oh, God. Later, when she had more strength.

All right, now, Bunnie thought, I need to start at the beginning. The clock on the radio said 12:10, daytime, obviously, but what day? She thought back. The panel. John. The girl beside him. That was Friday, which meant this was Saturday, and that meant something was wrong, but Bunnie couldn't remember what. She forced more water down her painful throat, blinked her eyes to get her brain working. Oh, no! She was going home today. She had a plane to catch. When did it leave? Where was her ticket? Was it in her purse? She looked around, but there was no pocketbook in sight. She paced the room searching for it and almost tripped over the stockings that had fallen around her ankles when she got out of her girdle. She looked in chairs and corners. She looked under the bed. At last, she discovered it just inside the door, lying open with her compact, her lipstick, her wallet spilled on the carpet. But no ticket.

The ticket was in her suitcase, and when she read it, her heart sank: her plane left at 12:55. Phone the airport, she told herself. Tell them to hold the plane. Pack. Leave. She grabbed the phone book. Damn. She needed her glasses. But where had she put her purse? She found the purse again, got the glasses, called the number, heard the ring. "It's not on time, is it?" she said to the man who answered. "Flight 412 to Nashville is late?"

"No, ma'am," the man said. "As a matter of fact, it's boarding now."

Well, then, another flight. No, this was the last flight on Saturday. Would she like to book a seat for tomorrow?

"I don't know," Bunnie said, her voice so weak that she wasn't sure the man heard her. "I needed to go today."

But of course if she couldn't go today, she would have to go tomorrow. She called back, made her reservation. She'd have to telephone Max, but what would she tell him? Given the distance from Nineveh to the Nashville airport, he might have already left to meet her. She ought to phone him right now, but when he answered, what should she say? How about, I'm sorry, Max, I overslept? That was true, but not an explanation. Why had she overslept? Why hadn't she set the alarm? Why hadn't she left a wake-up call? Oh, dear, Max knew that John Ross was here. Max had been glum when he had seen her off. He would think the worst and have every reason to think it. How could she convince him that she hadn't been with John? She needed to tell him what she *had* been doing last night. To do that, she would have to remember and to remember, she'd have to feel better. The aspirin she had taken hadn't helped. The question of what to do pounded along with the ache in her head. Oh, dear, oh, dear, she thought. She caught sight of the vodka bottle. That was it. A hair of the dog. There was no ice, but any port in a storm. She poured a couple of fingers, added tap water. Ah, she thought, that was better. The alcohol warmed her stomach like a celebration. Another drink seemed not only desirable, but called-for.

All right. Last night. What had she done? John telephoned. She had a couple of drinks. Then she went down on the elevator and across the lobby to that nice arrangement of tables and chairs where you could order drinks and wait for something good to happen. The evening came back to her in fragmented images. Did a man she had known in graduate school try to put a move on her? She thought so. She believed that he put his arm around her as they walked across the lobby, but she was pretty sure she hadn't come back to her room or gone to anyone else's. Sometime during the evening, her old classmate left— he could have fallen into a hole for all Bunnie recalled—and she was in a bar with people she had never seen before who were almost as drunk as she was. She remembered riding in a cab. She remembered being in a restaurant. She could recall getting out money to pay her part of the bill, but she couldn't remember eating anything. After the restaurant, she remembered a glass in front of her, faces around a table, laughter. Someone had tipped over in a chair—could it have been she? Oh, God, what a spectacle she must have made of herself! How had she got back to her room? she wondered. Someone must have helped her.

Why had she come to this alien world where she didn't understand the customs or speak the language? Why was she still feeling so bad in spite of her two drinks of vodka? Maybe another drink would help. It would certainly augment the courage she needed to talk to Max, and she had put off calling him too long already.

She dialed. Max answered. He had been leaving for the airport when the phone rang. "Where are you?" Max asked.

"I missed the plane." She was able to make her voice sound weak. "I'm not feeling well, Maxie."

Max said nothing. The silence that seemed to resonate along six hundred miles of wire made her nervous. She wished she were at Nineveh. She believed that if Max could see her face, he would know she wasn't lying.

"Maxie?"

"I'm still here."

"Maxie, I swear to God I didn't do anything wrong last night. I haven't even seen John since the panel was over yesterday afternoon."

"You should have come home," Max said.

"I got drunk, Max." How nice to be telling the truth. "I saw some old friends and some new ones, too, I guess. We drank too much."

"You've got a hangover," Max said in a tone that seemed to imply that he had never had one.

"I've got something else. My throat's sore. My head's stopped up. I'll be home tomorrow."

"All right."

"Max?"

"Yes."

"I miss you," Bunnie said. "I love you."

There was another silence. "It's all right," Max said finally. "I'll meet you tomorrow."

When she hung up, she felt both better and worse. She was relieved that Max had forgiven her, but now that she had talked to him, her conscience hurt her more than ever. She wanted to get out of this room where last night, if things had gone according to the plans she had made, she would have committed adultery. She showered and dressed, had another drink, and went out into the clear afternoon, the bright November sunlight. She went down a narrow street, past bars and boutiques and antique shops. She reached a corner where some musicians played the kind of music she and Max had danced to in the twenties.

Bunnie felt shaky. I ought to eat, she told herself, but when she got inside a small restaurant, she ordered a vodka martini, drank it, and went out feeling a little stronger. I'm drunk again, she thought, but being drunk didn't make her happy. She was still angry at herself, still ashamed at what she had almost done, what she had meant to do, what she would have done if John Ross hadn't jilted her. Max would always believe that once more she had been unfaithful to him: in a thousand years, she wouldn't be able to convince him otherwise. The day was warmer than she had thought. She was perspiring when she reached Jackson Square. She went into the cathedral to get out of the sunlight. She sat down and let her eyes get used to the gloom. She studied the statues and the candles that burned beneath them. In front of her, a few men, a few other women, were scattered among the pews. Along one wall, a line of people waited their turn to enter the confessional.

How did they do it? Bunnie wondered. What did they say after the priest had blessed them? What did the priest say to them after they had confessed? Dear, dear Max, she thought. For all she knew, he might be waiting in another line—a shorter one, no doubt—in the little church at Nineveh. She had never understood all this. What she wanted was forgiveness from Max, not absolution from some voice from behind a screen. She wanted to go home and put her arms around him. She wanted to do something that would convince him that she loved him.

# XVI

"Think about it this way," Shannon said. "I had to get pregnant to avoid all the agony."

Julien knew he was supposed to say, What agony? but he didn't want to talk. He was lying with Shannon in his arms, his hand on the little mound of her stomach that was just large enough to be interesting. Tomorrow they would be married, which, Julien had to admit, was a kind of anticlimax since the baby was already on its way, but the prospect was exciting nonetheless. Not the ceremony, of course. Why in the hell Shannon had given in and let her mother talk her into getting married at the cathedral, Julien couldn't fathom. If this was what she thought of as avoiding agony, then maybe he ought, after all, to ask her what kind of agony she had in mind. But talking was trouble. He settled for slipping down in the bed and nuzzling her ear.

"Julien?"

"What?"

"Do you know why most marriages break up?"

"I'm not married," Julien said.

"Damn it, Julien, you may never be, if you don't behave yourself. Most marriages break up because people don't communicate."

"I'm not married," Julien said again. "Tell me this tomorrow night when we're on the plane. I wonder what movie they'll show. I hope we haven't seen it."

"What movie they'll show! Julien, you'll have a wife. You'll be a newlywed. You're supposed to be giddy with love. You're not supposed to be able to look at anything but me. You're not supposed to want to look at a movie."

"You'll go to sleep."

"No, I won't."

"You probably will, but even if you don't, we can't make love. It's just not possible with those seats the way they are. Not to mention all the other people."

"Hold my hand."

"I am," Julien said.

"On the plane, I mean. Kiss my fingers. Stroke my thigh."

"You'll be wearing slacks. I expect what I'll do is pet the baby."

They were quiet for a moment. Then Shannon said, "Listen, Julien. What I set out to say was that you ought to thank me for all the grief I've saved you. About the wedding, I mean. See how simple I've kept it?"

"Simple!" Julien said. "Shannon, I have to wear a morning coat, which means I'll have to wear a vest in August. Not to mention the rehearsal we had and the party afterward and whatever we'll have to do when the wedding is over."

"Julien, believe me, it's not that bad. It's worse than I wanted it to be, but it's nothing to what we'd have had to go through if I hadn't been pregnant."

"It's bad enough."

"You just don't know. Julien, my mother has a million friends, and my father has nine hundred thousand friends plus a hundred thousand people in his law firm, and if we had gotten married in Jacksonville about half of those two million people would have given parties for us. We would have been married in the cathedral there, probably by the bishop since my mother gives dough every time he asks for it. We would have had to stand in line at the club for six and a half hours, smiling and shaking hands and thanking everybody for saying what a pretty wedding it was. We'd be so exhausted from that and all the other parties we'd be zombies. And the thank-you notes! Julien, I would have made you write half of them. I swear I would. We'd have silver and china and candlesticks running out our ears with no place to put them. Not to mention the fact that as soon as we got back from our honeymoon, my mother would be on the phone to me every day asking if I were pregnant. It's better to be pregnant to begin with and save the fuss."

"Shannon, did you ever hear of a justice of the peace? A judge? We talked about that. You don't have to be in Las Vegas. You can have what they call a civil ceremony. You buy a license. You get married."

"That would have been worse. As far as my mother is concerned, we wouldn't be married. We'd be doing what she calls living in sin like we are now."

"I like the way we are now."

"Julien, do you want to get married or not?"

He nuzzled her ear again.

"Stop that," Shannon said, but she didn't move her head.

"All right," Julien said. "I want to get married. But I'm still not satisfied with all the details."

"Ho, hum," Shannon said.

"Take the honeymoon. We've only got two weeks before I have to go to work. I heard about a rich couple a long time ago who stayed on their honeymoon for three years. Think about that. With the head start we've got, we could come back from our honeymoon with three children. They'd probably write about that in the paper."

She didn't say anything. In the silence, he could hear her soft breathing. "Wake up," he said. "This is your last night to live in sin."

"Hush," she said, "this is a time to be serious, Julien."

He tried to pull her closer, but she was already as close to him as she could get. He nibbled her earlobe. He kissed her neck.

"Mrs. Kennedy called this morning," Shannon said.

"Who?"

"Mason's mother. I didn't think my mother had told anybody in Jacksonville that we were getting married, the circumstances being what they are. But somebody told Mrs. Kennedy. At least she knows."

"She'll send us a candlestick."

"Julien, listen to me. I'd meant to try to make some kind of peace with my mother when I went to Jacksonville. I thought we could meet halfway or something. But then, like I told you, I lost my nerve and wound up seeing Mrs. Kennedy. I kept remembering that Mason had had as much trouble with Mrs. Kennedy as I'd had with my mother, but Mrs. Kennedy had loved Mason no matter how much she got on Mason's nerves. I guess seeing how broken-hearted Mrs. Kennedy was and how she wanted to make me feel better, I had to admit that my mother loved me, too. So I thought, Okay, I'll let her be my mother. I'll try to be her daughter. But I can't let her live my life. That's why I got pregnant. That and to save you all the trouble that you haven't yet thanked me for."

"Shannon, I'm not sure I understand all this."

"You don't have to. But, damn, Julien, I do like being pregnant. Wouldn't it be awful if I didn't? If every night before I went to sleep, instead of saying, Hey, baby, Mama loves you, grow well, which is what I say, I had to say, Baby, I just used you to make peace with my own mother. You have to tell your baby the truth, Julien. I hope you know that. But it's all right, because every day I love this baby more."

Julien patted the little mound of her stomach. "Hello, baby," he said. "Daddy loves you, too."

What a wonderful day this was going to be, Bunnie thought. She couldn't remember a day when so many fine things had happened. She had just got Max into the kitchen to mix them a midmorning drink, but she knew she was going to have to pace herself. She didn't want to doze off and miss any of the splendid events that were going to take place. First, the wedding. She suspected that Shannon was pregnant, which was not at all what she had expected of a nice Catholic girl, but everything must be all right because Father Freeman was marrying them in the cathedral. Father Freeman had come early in the morning to bring communion to Max and Bunnie—he had learned to arrive with the sacraments before Bunnie could maneuver Max into the kitchen—and he had seemed quite happy about the wedding.

"And on your anniversary," Father Freeman had said. "I'd take that as a compliment, Bunnie."

"Yes," Bunnie replied, "and they're going to come to our party before they leave on their honeymoon."

"Honeymoon?" Max said. "I guess so. We must have had a honeymoon, didn't we, Bunnie?"

"Of course we did, Maxie," Bunnie replied. She supposed they had. They had left town, which she assumed was all that was necessary. It didn't seem to matter how far you went or where you stayed as long as you got out of the city limits.

"I had a Model-A Ford," Max said. "It was a good automobile for the time. But the roads were bad. We didn't get interstates around here until after the war, Father."

"So I understand," Father Freeman said. He was old enough to remember this himself, though he was far from being as old as Max and Bunnie.

"Somebody tied tin cans to the back bumper," Bunnie said.

"Well, it wasn't that so much as the potholes," Max replied.

"No, I mean on our wedding day."

"They fly now," Max continued. "I think they smooch in the plane after the lights are turned off."

Father Freeman got up and said he would see them at the wedding. Max shuffled beside the priest to the door. Since he was already on his feet, it had been fairly easy for Bunnie to get him to mix their first drink of the day. Now she was feeling mellow, but once more she warned herself to be careful.

Poor, darling Max, she thought. How much pain she had caused him in the last sixty years, how much pain they had caused each other: twenty-five years of mutual unfaithfulness, then thirty-five years during which too many mean things had been uttered. It would have been easier, Bunnie supposed, if they hadn't had the past with which to accuse each other, but they had endured what they had had to endure and they were still together. No, Bunnie told herself, more than just together. They loved each other. She believed that she loved Max as much as she had loved him the day they were married, but now she was helpless to do much about it.

Something ought to happen to the heart, Bunnie thought. Max was ninety and she was eighty-six. She had suffered her strokes and Max had whatever it was that was taking away his memory and his strength and giving his eyes their strange, flat look as if he were peering always into the distance. It would be wrong to say that their bodies had betrayed them. Their bodies had been weakening year by year, warning them with every new glasses prescription and root canal and pain in the head or knee or elbow that they would never again be what they used to be. Your bones told you when you could no longer swim rivers or climb hills or stay up all night with impunity. Your flesh whispered warnings of mortality, but your heart went on its youthful way whatever might happen to it physically. It never stopped believing in love. It was always ready to miss a beat, to thrill, to tremble with new or old affection. Kick up your heels in joy, the heart advised, long after you had become unable to lift your heels off the carpet.

"I love you, Maxie," Bunnie said.

At first she thought he hadn't heard her, but he had. He was hiding behind his paper—for what? To consider whether she meant what she said? To devise an answer? No. To compose himself. He had always worn his feelings on his sleeve. Lately, he had become increasingly emotional. He had to drop his paper to reach his handkerchief. When he tried to dry his eyes, his spectacles bounced onto the couch beside him.

"Oh, Maxie," Bunnie said. "Don't cry. In spite of the bad things, we've had sixty wonderful years. I wouldn't take anything for them."

"Sixty years," Max said vaguely, as if he weren't sure what had gone on for that length of time. But he was still wiping tears from his cheeks. He was taking the conversation seriously.

"Listen," Bunnie said, "we're going to have a fine time today. We're going to see Julien and Shannon get married. Then we're going to come back here and take a nap. Then all our friends are coming to help us celebrate our anniversary." She paused. Unaccountably, she was feeling somewhat emotional herself. "I thought I'd better say that I loved you before we got involved in all the excitement."

Max seemed to be studying her face. For a moment, his eyes lost their distant look and focused on hers and brightened. "Did you hear me telling you I loved you when you had your stroke? Julien was there. The first night you were in the hospital, I sat by your bed and told you that I loved you."

It was customary, Bunnie was informed when they got to the church, for people in wheelchairs to stay in them, but that meant she would have to be on the side or at the back, so Bunnie refused. With the help of an usher—or a janitor, maybe: Bunnie didn't notice what clothes he was wearing—she was shifted from her chair to the aisle seat in the third row. Max managed to raise his feet and step over her legs and sit down beside her. They were early, but Bunnie liked that. She said a prayer for Julien and Shannon and another for herself and Max. She prayed vaguely for several good causes. Then she looked at the other guests who were arriving.

There were not many of them. Understandably, the wedding was going to be small with nobody coming from out of town except a few relatives. There were Shannon's mother and father, half a dozen aunts and uncles, and two of Shannon's cousins who were going to be in the wedding. There were Susan and Henry, Julien's sister Elizabeth, who was also going to be in the wedding, and her husband Nelson, but there would be only half a dozen people to come down the aisle and maybe forty to watch them. Their little crowd would be lost in the cavernous church, but Peggy Marsh had decorated the church and planned the ceremony as if Shannon's wedding were going to be the social event of the season.

There were flowers everywhere, surrounding the altar, lining the center aisle, lying against the old communion rail, brightening the entrace to the chapel. Tall white candles reached toward the ceiling and bows of gauzy ribbon decorated the pews. There was music. Not just an organ, but strings and trumpets and clarinets and instruments that Bunnie, who could hardly turn around and stare at the choir loft, could not identify. Bunnie knew that the participants, at least, would be dressed for a proper wedding. Henry, Julien's father, had complained about having to rent a morning coat, and once she got to Nashville and met Peggy Marsh, Susan began to worry that the dress she planned to wear was not nice enough. Julien's parents seemed a little put off by Shannon's mother, a little intimidated by her, but Bunnie sympathized with her and wished she could do or say something that would make her feel better.

Peggy was hurt. Even though Bunnie was childless, it was easy for her to conjure up the dreams that Peggy must have had for Shannon. When she saw how rapidly the years were passing, how quickly Shannon was growing, she would have thought of a future filled with hope and joy, college, a wedding, grandchildren: a life lived happily ever after. She was going to get the grandchild all right, but how different this was from what she must have foreseen for Shannon. Something had happened between them, Bunnie didn't know what, but they behaved very carefully toward each other. They considered what they were going to say and spoke in overly pleasant tones. They watched their manners.

Bunnie guessed that Peggy Marsh had always watched hers. Who could imagine how beautiful she must have been twenty-five years ago? She was still stunningly handsome, prettier even now, Bunnie had to admit, than Shannon. She had had her hair made brighter, slightly more blond, than Shannon's. She had a lean face with high cheekbones, trim legs, a flat stomach. When she crossed the room on her and Richard's first visit to Bunnie and Max, she moved almost as gracefully as Shannon. She had taken both of Bunnie's hands and kissed Bunnie on the cheek. "I have to call you Bunnie," she said. "You mean so much to Shannon, I can't think of you as a stranger." She had spoken in the same way to Max, who had gathered his abstracted mind long enough to be taken with her. Oh, dear, Bunnie thought. She hoped very much that she and Shannon could resolve whatever had happened between them.

Dear God, Shannon thought, as she waited with her father at the back of the church, there was no way to keep her mother from spending money. Even though the compromise outfit that Shannon wore, half-maternity dress, half-wedding gown, had no train, there was going to be a white runner down the aisle for her to walk on, which was the least of her mother's extravagances. There were flowers everywhere, music seemed to be coming from a whole orchestra, and the woman from the bridal service, whose final duty would be to see that Shannon didn't miss her cue, had brought along an assistant. Damn, Shannon said to herself, I ought not to like this. She ought to be thinking about how many poor people could be fed with the dough that was being wasted here, but she couldn't make herself stop smiling. She listened to the cello and the violins. She sniffed the flower-scented air. She gazed at the bouquet in her hand. God help her, she loved it all. She was happy.

Now Shannon's mother was going down the aisle on the arm of one of Shannon's cousins. There went another fifteen-hundred-dollars-worth of dry goods, not to mention the shoes and the hat and the underwear. Who could guess at the value of the jewelry? She looked good, Shannon had to admit. For a woman whose only daughter had contrived to get pregnant—out of wedlock, as they said—she was bearing up magnificently. At first, when she was considering how to break the news to her mother, Shannon had thought she would go to Jacksonville, wear a dress that emphasized her swelling stomach and wait and make her mother ask her if she were pregnant. But she had decided against that. Impending motherhood had made her cautious or dulled her sense of irony or taken some of the edge off her bad temper. She had called from Nashville to say that she was coming home.

"Oh, darling," her mother said, "how wonderful! What would you like to do? Whom would you like to see? Maybe you'd like to stay for a while at the beach house."

"Yes," Shannon said, "let's go to the beach." Right then it was time for her to say what she had called to say, but at first, she couldn't make herself say it. She was conscious of her mother's voice, the sound of it through the telephone, making plans, Shannon supposed, but Shannon wasn't listening. She didn't notice when her mother's voice stopped.

"Shannon?" her mother said. "Are you still there?"

"Listen," Shannon said, "I have to tell you something."

Had she taken a deep breath? She couldn't remember exactly. There had been a pause. Then Shannon said, "I know you won't like this, but I'm pregnant."

Life should be like a movie, Shannon thought. You ought to be able to watch both sides. Cut from Shannon on the phone to Peggy Marsh on the phone. Tight shot of Peggy Marsh's face. Was her mother crying? Shannon longed to know how her mother was taking this. Was she running her hand through her hair? Was she lighting a cigarette? There was silence on the line. No sob. No intake of angry breath. Nothing.

"Did you hear what I said?" Shannon asked.

Her mother still didn't answer.

"Did you?"

"Yes."

"Well?"

"I don't know." There was another pause. "I mean is it all right? Do you love him? Do you love each other?"

"Do you mean, will he marry me?"

"No," Shannon's mother said, her voice stronger, more even than Shannon expected. "Not will he marry you. Does he love you enough . . . do you love him enough? Would you want to get married even if you weren't . . . if there weren't going to be a baby?"

"I guess so," Shannon replied. "I got pregnant on purpose."

"Oh?" her mother said.

Shannon had made up her mind not to try to explain, but she heard herself saying, "A lot of people do that now. It's not like it used to be."

"I know," her mother said. "Oh, my dear, believe me, I know. I think a good deal about it."

Now there was a fanfare of brass in the high register. The groomsmen were on their way to the altar. Shannon's father squeezed her hand and said, "I love you, baby. You're my beautiful girl."

How wonderful, Bunnie thought, how absolutely splendid that so many people had come. She missed her old friends, of course, most of them dead and not to be forgotten at an anniversary party. But their ghosts could hardly suppress the joy that Bunnie felt or the conviviality of the group around her. She and Max sat at a table and received their guests—the very old and the merely old and the middle-aged and the young. Edith and John Ross were gone; so were Vera and Simmons Carlyle and, oh, so many, many more, but the children of the old crowd had come and their children and their grandchildren and in some cases their great-grandchildren. Fleetingly, Bunnie wished that the large room were not quite so noisy. It would be better if the children were outside, but they needed to be where their parents could watch them. Some of the young people sought out each other's company, but there was much mingling among generations. As the party progressed and people had more to drink, it seemed to Bunnie that sooner or later, everyone had talked or was talking to everybody else. Sooner or later, everybody came to talk to her and Max, too, which was fine, but she would give a lot now to be mobile.

Father Freeman was at one end of the room, and Father Morrison was at the other. Bunnie had noticed that priests didn't talk much to each other when lay people were around. They probably got enough of each other's company in the course of business; when they came among their flocks, they seemed to want to be the center of attention. So much better, then, Bunnie thought, that she hadn't invited the bishop. But look, there was Adelaide's great-niece. What was her name? Adelaide, of course. She was the one to whom Adelaide had left all her money. The young Adelaide, forty by now and so far unmarried like her namesake, was deep in conversation with a scraggly professor from Vanderbilt. Bunnie couldn't remember what he called himself. God only knew what he might be saying to Adelaide; whatever it was, Bunnie hoped Adelaide wouldn't take it seriously.

But there were other, nice faculty members whom Bunnie was glad to see having a good time and glad to talk to when they came to her table. Tommy Harper had brought his wife June, whom Max had never liked. Tommy had a glass in his hand, but Bunnie doubted it contained whiskey. Julien's father and Shannon's father were laughing together and lifting their drinks. Even though they were several yards away from where she sat, Bunnie could see that they were getting on famously, touching each other on the shoulder now and then, calling each other Richard and Henry. She glanced around in search of Peggy Marsh. Look for the sparkle of diamonds, Bunnie thought, then was ashamed of being so catty. It was true that the stone in Peggy's engagement ring was as wide as a watermelon seed, but her other jewelry was in expensive good taste, understated. Ah, there she was in a green dress that set off her green eyes, those marvelous eyes that she had passed on to Shannon.

Peggy Marsh had paused to speak to the newlyweds. She took their hands, smiled at them, then to Bunnie's consternation left them immediately. She was coming to visit Max and Bunnie. That's good, Bunnie thought, and noticed that here Susan came, too. The newly created in-laws could have a confabulation.

"Oh, Bunnie," Peggy said, "I'm having a good time. You certainly know how to give a party."

"Oh, no," Bunnie replied. "Susan did all the work."

Susan said that she'd only done what Bunnie instructed her to do. There was credit enough to go round. The women smiled and nodded at each other.

Peggy took the merest sip of wine. She glanced over the room where the merrymakers were still behaving themselves but making more noise than ever. She looked at Susan and then at Bunnie. She said, "Richard and I are so fond of Julien. We've come to love him in the few days we've known him."

This seemed to make Susan uncomfortable. Bunnie wished that Susan would give Peggy more of a chance. She needed to learn not to be put off by all that wealth and grace and beauty. Perhaps she was mostly embarrassed that Julien had gotten Shannon pregnant. Say you love Shannon, Bunnie prompted Susan in her mind.

What Susan said was, "Peggy, we were in Virginia, Henry and I. We didn't know they were in love. We didn't even know that they were dating each other."

Bunnie thought she saw Peggy's eyes grow moist, but her handsome face held its composure. "I haven't known . . . for a long time," she said. "There was a lot that we didn't know about Shannon."

"Well," Bunnie said brightly. "We're a family now. We'll all know more in the future."

Max, who had been silent—had he been listening to what they were saying?—began to struggle in his chair. "I'm sorry," he said. "I need to get up. Will somebody please help me?"

Where am I? Max wondered. He knew that Bunnie was with him and that one of the women who had helped him out of his chair was Susan, but he couldn't place the room or recognize most of the people who were in it. The truth was that he couldn't see the people very well. Like the blind man in the Bible, Max thought, who said people looked like trees when Jesus first arranged for him to see again. For a moment, Max thought he might be that man, that it wasn't a story he remembered but something that was happening now. But the sight of the man in the Bible had cleared. To Max, people still looked like trees, and none of the trees resembled Jesus. No, he was somewhere else. He needed to know where, so he did the sensible thing and asked Bunnie.

"The party room, Max," Bunnie said. "We're celebrating our sixtieth anniversary in the party room at the apartment house."

Why not at Nineveh? Max wondered, but he didn't ask. He didn't want to disturb Bunnie.

"Maxie," Bunnie said, "why did you get up?"

"Was I sitting down?"

"Yes," Bunnie said, "and you ought to sit down again. I'll get somebody to help you."

Then it came to Max. His stomach was mildly uncomfortable. Embarrassing as it was, he needed to go to the bathroom. But of course, this wasn't the thing to say out loud at a party. Then suddenly, he saw there was something that he had to do even before he went to relieve himself. Across the room, clearly discernible among the walking trees, was his mother. "I have to speak to Mama," Max said, but apparently his voice was too weak to be heard above the greetings of new friends who had arrived at Bunnie's table.

Max moved. He found that for a man as unsteady on his feet as he, the crowd was an advantage. Max shuffled a step or two, stopped to avoid one of the trees that on close inspection proved to be people. He had known all along that they were. He was not surprised when they spoke to him, shook his hand, patted him on the back, told him he looked great and that they would be back for his seventieth anniversary party. One or two men asked him if he needed a drink. Seeing that his hands were empty, Max thought that he did, but saying so would be too much trouble. He shook his head. He smiled, or at least felt his lips tighten. He took two more steps, paused, and stepped again. He was almost where he wanted to be. But wait now. Where was his mother?

I've come the wrong way, Max told himself. He had got turned around when he was crossing the room. He needed to retrace his steps, but he had lost his sense of direction. He looked about, but all he could see were the faces and backs of other people. Maybe he should stand on a chair so he could see better. No, there she was, the ribbons of her black bonnetlike hat tied under her chin, her face as smooth as a girl's and whiter than Max could recall ever having seen it. He started to move toward her, but the uneasiness in his stomach turned to pain, and his head was aching fiercely. As much as he wanted to see his mother, he would have to go to the bathroom first. He wanted to tell her that he wouldn't be long, but he had lost sight of her once more, and his need to go to the bathroom was increasing.

He had trouble finding it. He had to ask, and making words come out of his mouth had become burdensome. "I'll take you, Max," a man said. Max knew the face but couldn't remember the name. Whoever he was, he was a friend, and Max was glad for the support of the man's hand around Max's arm. The man escorted Max to the door and opened it for him. Max found himself in a long, narrow room that looked more like a corridor than a toilet. But sure enough, near the far end were a commode and a lavatory. Max made his way toward them, supporting himself along the wall. Now, then, he thought. He really did need to sit down, but he was incapable of hurrying. It took him a while to unbuckle his belt, unbutton and unzip and get his underwear down. He dropped with a slightly painful slap on the seat. His buttocks were too thin to do much to soften the blow. His stomach and his head still felt bad, but he had got to the toilet, and he was sitting on it. That was the main thing: he was where he needed to be.

By God, Julien thought, it hadn't been as bad as he had feared it might be, in spite of the Bible-reading and the kneeling and all the references to God at the ceremony. Pretty soon he and Shannon were going to have to get the hell out of here, but right now, having been congratulated by seventeen hundred people with whom he had had to exchange pleasantries, he was satisfied to stand in the corner he had found for himself and contemplate his own good fortune. He had meant to be abstemious at the reception, he needed to have his wits about him for the trip, but once he had tasted the champagne, far better than anything he had drunk in France, he consumed more than he meant to. Now, he was drinking Perrier, but the champagne still glowed and tingled in his brain. The truth was, he was pleasantly tight, and his feeling of euphoria was enhanced by the knowledge that his pockets were full of money.

Peggy and Richard had bought the tickets to Paris, made reservations at a hotel, and given him and Shannon a check. To Julien's surprise, his own father had come across with a thousand bucks, and Bunnie and Max had given them money. All to the good, Julien thought. If he and Shannon had had to travel on their own resources, they wouldn't have got much farther than Murfreesboro. Maybe they could have gone on and spent a night at Monteagle now that it was the end of August and the season there was over. Paris, Julien thought. They would get there just as the Parisians were returning from their vacations and when the tourists were beginning to thin out. Tables at restaurants would be easier to get, lines at museums would be shorter. For a moment, he felt anxious. There was a little jump in his heart when it occurred to him that he would be showing Shannon places and things that he had seen for the first time with Justine.

He hoped that Justine had forgiven him. He regretted that he had lacked the courage to come right out and tell her he was leaving her. He had slipped out while she was at work, leaving behind a note that would have embarrassed the characters in a grade-B movie. "I love you," he had said. "I will always love you. But there is no future for us. For both our sakes, I need to go back home." How badly had she been hurt? he wondered. After he returned to the States, he had tried to telephone her, but her number had been changed and her new number was unlisted. He thought of writing her, but what would be the good of sending another letter? He hoped that she was happy. He hoped that she had married and was at this moment sleeping contentedly beside her husband. Perhaps they were at her condominium in Normandy. Tomorrow, which would be soon in France, they would pack for their return to Paris. As if his thinking it could make it so, he created for Justine a world full of joy in which, now and then, she thought of him without rancor.

Julien glanced at his watch. He and Shannon would have to go soon. He made his way through the crowd and stood at the table, waiting his turn to speak to Bunnie, who appeared to be enjoying herself. She must have asked several people to bring her a drink. There were three full glasses in front of her, and she was holding another, raising it to her lips. The man who had been sitting beside Bunnie told her good-bye and kissed her, managed to rise and go tottering on his way. Julien hadn't ever seen so many old people in one place. With some red ribbon and mistletoe, it would be like Christmas at the nursing home. There was already paper on the floor from the presents the guests had brought Max and Bunnie.

"Oh, Julien," Bunnie said. "It was a lovely wedding. Let's drink to it."

Julien lifted his glass of Perrier. Was that bad luck, or did the prohibition against drinking toasts only apply to tap water? "I wanted to say good-bye to you and Max. Then I've got to find Shannon. I'm afraid it's time for us to get out of here."

Bunnie leaned forward for Julien to kiss her. "I don't know where Max has gone," she said. "When you tell him good-bye, send him back over here."

Julien made a circle of the large room, passing among children whose riotous behavior made them seem more numerous than they had been when the party started. Were they drunk? Julien wondered. You couldn't tell what children might do nowadays. Julien had to pause while a little girl with a red stain on her dress chased a little boy who was trying to defend himself with a flyswatter. Behave, children, Julien said, or may have just thought it. Though he continued automatically to search for Max, his mind was already beyond the room: he and Shannon were hugging each other in the darkened airplane. He was kissing the tips of her fingers just as she had asked him to. Max wasn't at the bar. Julien kept walking, looking. He made two more circuits of the room and noticed that the crowd was beginning to thin. Damn, he thought. He needed to leave. Finally, it occurred to him to look in the men's room, and there was Max, sitting on the commode. How embarrassing, Julien thought. Max should have locked the door. He was getting more and more forgetful.

If Max didn't come out of the toilet soon, Julien would tell Bunnie where he was, but now Julien had to find Shannon. Time really was running short, and he couldn't locate her. Damn it, he thought, damn it! He could see them missing the plane, or they'd be so late getting to the airport that their luggage would be left behind. Wherever in the hell Shannon was, why wasn't she looking at the time? But here she was. He might have guessed—like Max, she had been in the bathroom.

"We've got to move," Julien said. "I've told Bunnie good-bye."

"Did you say good-bye to Max?"

Julien smiled. "Not exactly. He's in the bathroom sitting on the john. I didn't want to disturb him."

"We have to tell him good-bye."

"It's late, Shannon."

"It's all right. My father kept the limousine. The driver's already got our bags. He's waiting in front of the apartment."

Damn, Julien thought. There was nothing to do but follow Shannon.

"Oh, Bunnie," Shannon said, "I liked your party. It was just right to wind up our wedding day."

Bunnie smiled. It seemed to Julien that both Shannon and Bunnie were taking this farewell too seriously. Bunnie clung to Shannon's hand as if she were reluctant to allow Shannon to leave. Shannon was making no effort to disengage herself.

"Shannon," Julien said.

"I may phone you, Bunnie," Shannon said. "My father gave me a card that I can use to call the United States. I think I'll run up a bill for him."

"Please, baby," Julien said. He shifted his gaze. "We really have to leave now, Bunnie."

"Say good-bye to Max," Bunnie said. She peered around. "But you'll have to find him. I don't know where he is. I don't think I've seen him in an hour."

"He's in the bathroom," Julien said.

Shannon looked at her watch. "Well, it's time for him to come out now. Get him, Julien. We can wait for that. He needs to be with Bunnie."

My God, Julien thought when he caught sight of Max, I hope I never look that way. The flesh on Max's skinny legs was tinted blue. Max's elbow was resting on his knee, his chin was in his hand. He looked as if he intended to stay where he was for a while. It was as if he had decided to settle the problems of the world while he sat on the crapper. Was he all right? Julien wondered. "Are you all right, Max?"

Max didn't reply. He didn't seem to have heard. Julien moved toward him down the long, narrow room. "Come on, Max. Shannon wants to tell you good-bye. Bunnie wants to see you."

Max, as motionless as the stool on which he sat, said nothing.

He must be sick, Julien thought. He must be really sick. Julien called Max's name once more. Then he went to find Shannon.

"Where's Max?" Bunnie said. She and Shannon were still in conversation.

"He'll be along," Julien said. "Would you excuse Shannon for a minute, Bunnie?"

Only a few people now remained in the room. Almost everybody had had sense enough to leave except him and Shannon. The plane was going to take off without them, and how in the hell were they going to get another reservation? He was tempted to grab Shannon's hand and pull her out the door. Whatever happened to Max would be somebody else's business.

"Damn, damn, damn!" Julien said under his breath. "Listen," he said to Shannon. "We've got to let somebody else take care of Max. If we don't get out of here right now, we're not going to make it."

"What?"

"Damn it, we're going to miss the plane."

"No. What do you mean, take care of Max?"

"I'll tell you on the way to the airport. We have to run, Shannon."

"Where is he?"

"He's still in the gents. I think he's been there for an hour. Now, for God's sake, come on."

She was too quick for him. He would have caught her, picked her up, and carried her out the door, but she was three steps away before he reached for her. She was on her way to the men's room. When she got there, she didn't hesitate. She opened the door and went smoothly through, her gracefulness undiminished by her pregnancy. Julien felt a thrill watching her, but he was annoyed with her too. She shouldn't go barging in on Max like that. Even if she was a nurse, she ought to respect people's privacy.

Julien looked at his watch and cursed. There was no way to make the plane. They had missed it and probably missed their trip, too. He was disappointed, and he was angry with Shannon. He had wanted with all his heart to return to Paris.

"Damn it, Shannon!" he said. She was back now, having come quickly through the door and closed it behind her.

"I've got to go back to the bathroom. I might be needed for something." She looked around quickly. "Send Father Freeman to the bathroom. Send your mother to the table to be with Bunnie."

"Wait a minute," Julien said, "if Max is sick, hadn't we better get him back to the apartment? Let's find Dr. Harper."

"I think Dr. Harper's already left. Where's your mother?"

"Talking to yours. They're probably arguing about what to name our baby."

"Take them to Bunnie. Get Father Freeman."

"I can take Max to his room. We can pull up his pants, and I can deposit him in his bedroom." Maybe the plane would be late, Julien thought. Maybe the traffic would be thin. Maybe the limo man would drive like a maniac.

Shannon put her hand on Julien's shoulder and spoke close to his ear. "Max is dead, Julien."

"On the john!" Julien said. "That's ridiculous, Shannon. Falling in the shower is one thing, but dying when you just sat down to—"

"It's not all that rare, Julien. He probably had a stroke."

"Yes, but on the damned commode." It didn't seem right to Julien.

"Move now," Shannon said. "Send in the priest. I don't think it's too late for him to anoint Max. At least he can bless him. Then Father Freeman can tell Bunnie that Max is dead, and our mothers will be there to put their arms around her."

"But Dr. Harper . . ."

"We'll call Dr. Harper. We'll have to call a lot of people. The best thing to do is to get Bunnie and our mothers back to the apartment. Then Father Freeman can tell Bunnie. Dr. Harper will probably want to look at her."

Poor old Max, Julien thought. What a terrible way to die. How undignified. It didn't seem fair that you should live for ninety years minding your manners, acting like a gentleman, which Max had always done, and then die with your pants down and your ass exposed to the view of anybody who happened to wander into the bathroom. People ought to be allowed to choose where they wanted to die. There ought to be a form to fill out in advance of the occasion. Maybe Father Freeman could make dying in the john sound reasonable when he broke the news to Bunnie.

Ah, Bunnie thought, I must have been dreaming. Long and disjointed as the memory of it was, it must have been a dream, because here she was in her own bed at Nineveh. Beyond her open window, a mockingbird sang; there was a patch of sunlight on the familiar wallpaper. She had seen into her own future and not liked it much: she had been old and sick and living somewhere else, and Max had died and they had brought him to Nineveh for burial. "Oh, no," she said, her voice not as loud as the song of the distant bird. It hadn't been a dream. Her lungs tightened until she thought she couldn't breathe. She would cry if she could, but no tears came. She lay panting. She swallowed hard. Max would want her to pull herself together.

How long ago was it that Susan and Peggy had rolled her from the party room to her apartment? How long since Father Freeman had explained to her that Max was dead. She thought at first that he was telling her only that Max was very sick. He had used the word *stroke,* and she knew about that. She had had her own stroke that had plunged her into darkness and left her maimed in mind and body, but she was still alive: she could talk and eat and drink and think if the subject she set her mind to wasn't too complicated. She asked where Max was, demanded to see him. Father Freeman saw that she didn't understand.

"Bunnie," he said, "it's worse than just being sick. He passed away, Bunnie. Max is not with us any longer."

What then? What had she felt when this news had plunged into her heart? Grief so intense that pain flashed through her head and her throat made moaning sounds without her intending to make them. But not for long. Tommy Harper had insisted that she take a pill. She took it and went to sleep, and for the next day—two? three? how long had it been?—she had swallowed pills when she was told to and swallowed drinks when she could get them and dozed often and lived in a world that never quite came into focus. Now she recalled that in spite of pills and booze, she had been sufficiently at herself to cause difficulty.

Susan had insisted that the funeral be in the cathedral. Most of Bunnie's and Max's friends lived in Nashville, and if most of the people who had come to the party came to Max's funeral, the little church at Nineveh wouldn't hold them. Bunnie had agreed, but she had insisted that the wake be at Nineveh, which meant a good deal of traveling for what remained of poor Max. They had brought him from Nashville and put his casket in the living room. Bunnie had thought of putting it in the library, close to the windows with Max's head toward the bar, but Susan wouldn't hear of that, and Bunnie got the idea that Peggy also thought poorly of such a notion.

Dear Peggy, Bunnie thought, dear Shannon. Susan was sweet and faithful and willing, but she didn't know what a Catholic funeral required. On the night before the burial, Susan helped Bunnie dress and wheeled her into the living room, but of all the family, only Shannon and Peggy knew the Rosary. They sat one on each side of her and said the Our Fathers and Hail Marys with such assurance that Bunnie could allow herself to doze, knowing that the proper responses would be made. It was the same at the mass, the same at the burial. Bunnie could let the pills she had taken and the booze she had drunk work to her mind's contentment. Peggy and Shannon knew the drill.

Now, Shannon was with her. Had there been a knock, had Bunnie said, Come in? Shannon couldn't have changed much in a day or two, but she seemed to Bunnie to have become rather pretty. Her not-quite-blond hair was thick and glistening. Her eyes appeared to be greener than usual. She was wearing lipstick. If Bunnie hadn't noticed the strained relationship between her and her mother, she would think that Peggy had taken Shannon in hand. Shannon was dressed to go somewhere. Bunnie remembered. She and Julien had delayed their honeymoon until after Max's funeral. There had been some trouble about their getting another reservation.

"Are you all right, Bunnie?" Shannon said. "Would you like for Julien and me not to go?"

Truly, Bunnie thought, she would. She had always loved Julien. In many ways, Julien had been like a son to her. Now she had become almost as fond of Shannon, who seemed always to know the best thing to say or do. Right this minute, Bunnie longed for Shannon to lift her up and hold her in her arms.

Shannon did. She put pillows behind Bunnie's back, sat on the side of the bed, and put her arm around Bunnie's shoulder. "We don't have to go," Shannon said. "We can stay here with you, if you want us. Maybe we could all stay here at Nineveh for a while."

Bunnie couldn't say that was not what she wanted. There wasn't anything in the world that she had rather do. If she tried to lie, she would give herself away. The only thing Bunnie could think of was to blame poor Susan. "Susan wouldn't stand for it," Bunnie said. "She and Tommy Harper think I ought to be in the city. Maybe we can stay here sometime after you and Julien come home."

"Oh, Bunnie," Shannon said, "I don't want to leave you."

Bunnie was on the verge of tears. She had to say something, and she knew that when she did, her voice would break. The only thing to do was what she wanted to do anyway. She spoke of Max. "He looked nice, didn't he? So trim and neat and dapper. He reminded me of himself."

"A good thing, too," Shannon said. "It wouldn't have done if he had reminded you of somebody else."

Bunnie felt herself smile. "I mean, I could see all of him there. I know that to everybody else he was just an old man lying in a casket, but I could see him when he was young, too. I could see him through all the years we were together."

Shannon hugged her. She leaned her fragrant young head against Bunnie's slightly aching skull.

"We'll stay if you want us to."

"No," Bunnie said, "write me a postcard. Send me a picture of the Champs-Elysées."

"I'll try," Shannon said. "Knowing Julien, he'll probably want to send one with naked women on it."

"How's Bunnie?" Peggy asked. She was sitting in the library, smoking a cigarette, looking at a book of poetry. She and Susan were going to drive Shannon and Julien to the airport, but apparently Julien and his mother weren't ready. "How's Bunnie feeling?"

Why, Shannon wondered, was she irritated that her mother should ask this perfectly sensible question? She had to press her lips together to keep from saying, Fine. Great. She and Max were only married for sixty years. She hadn't really had time to grow fond of him.

"Well," Shannon said, "well." She couldn't think of anything else to say, and she was about to cry anyway. One thing she surely didn't want to do was to cry in front of her mother.

"Baby," Peggy Marsh said, "are you all right?"

"Fine," Shannon said. She found a chair across the room from Peggy, but Peggy came and stood beside her.

Shannon didn't know why she should feel so sad, except, of course, that once again she was thinking of Mason. She was ashamed that it had taken Max's death to bring Mason back into her mind. From the time she had discovered she was pregnant until the funeral, she had not thought much about Mason, and this seemed wrong since she was alive and happy and Mason was dead. Being with Bunnie this morning, seeing once more how much pain bereavement caused, had filled her heart with sorrow. Come on, Julien, she wanted to say, take me away from here. She knew she was being foolish. The only way he could make her feel better would be somehow to take her away from herself. He would be taking the same old Shannon to Paris.

"What would happen . . . ?" Peggy said. "I mean, would it be too awful if I hugged you?"

Shannon shook her head. Peggy knelt beside her. Shannon caught the smell of tobacco again, just as she remembered it when Peggy told her Mason was dead. She wanted to move away, but she didn't. She endured the soft weight of her mother's arm around her shoulders, the touch of her mother's hand on her arm.

"Darling," Peggy said, "Max's dying is one of the few things that make sense in life. Of course it's hard for Bunnie to give him up, but he had lived for ninety years. He'd done a lot of things. And he didn't linger and suffer. It's what all of us ought to wish for."

And what Mason didn't get, Shannon thought.

As if she had been reading Shannon's mind, Peggy said, "The tragedy is when it happens to someone like Mason."

Now there was nothing she could do but cry. Peggy pulled her close, Shannon's head on Peggy's shoulder, Shannon's tears dampening Peggy's dress.

"I'm sorry," Peggy said. "I'm so sorry that you lost Mason. I've wanted to tell you that for all these years, but I couldn't find a way to do it." Peggy's voice trembled. For a moment she stopped speaking. Then she said, "I didn't know what to do, Shannon. You seemed so unhappy. I didn't want to say anything that would make you more miserable than you were."

Oh, God, Shannon thought, I didn't need this. She wanted to get out from under her mother's arm, but to do so might hurt her mother's feelings. There was too much pain between them already. But again as if she knew what Shannon was thinking, Peggy rose and went to get her purse. Naturally, she was well supplied with tissues. She was always prepared for any minor emergency.

"Here, baby," Peggy said.

Shannon was thankful that Peggy hadn't held a tissue under her nose and told her to blow. For a moment, there was silence while she and her mother tried to repair their faces.

Then Peggy said, "Sweetheart, you've thought enough about death. Think about life. Think about the baby you're going to have. I'm glad you're pregnant, Shannon. I really am." Peggy managed a smile. "I'll admit that I thought your timing was a little off, but I've always been glad that you're going to have a baby."

Of course she was right, Shannon thought. Life was the only thing you could think about, or at least do anything about. But damn it, it wasn't that easy. The very fact that you couldn't do anything about death gave it its power to haunt you. Still, Peggy was right about the baby. Shannon had to be happy about that. She felt of her stomach, which she did about a million times every day, and thought of how much she loved her baby.

"All right?" Peggy said.

Shannon nodded, but the shift of her head was so slight Peggy may not have seen it. What she meant was that she would try. Loving Julien had helped. She had come a long way already. She gave her brief nod again. Then she said, "Listen, if you want to live to be as old as Max, you'd better quit smoking."

"Julien," Shannon said, "do you know what I did before we left?"

Julien was having a glass of champagne. Shannon's father, who seemed able to do anything, had managed to get them new tickets to Paris, this time in business class, and Julien intended to make the most of it. "Let me see," he said. "You carried a gun through the metal detector. You mugged a stewardess."

"Damn it, Julien, I'm your wife. You're supposed to take me seriously."

"All right," Julien said. "Seriously, you bought a magazine. You went to the ladies' room."

"Well, yes, I go a lot now that I'm pregnant. But that's not what I was talking about. I kissed my mother."

"Well, I kissed mine, too. And yours, as a matter of fact. There was a lot of kissing going on at the airport."

"Julien, what's happened to me?"

"Well," Julien said, "you got married. You went to a funeral. You've been to church twice in the last three days. That's enough to put a strain on anybody."

"No, listen. First, I liked the wedding, but I could have gotten over that if Max hadn't died. I mean, it took something out of me, Julien. It softened me up somehow."

Julien put his arm around her. "I like you soft. I like you soft and cuddly. So far, I like you pregnant."

"Well, it was really my mother who did it. She told me not to grieve over Max." Shannon paused. "She told me not to grieve over Mason. She told me to think about life. She said she was glad that I'm pregnant."

"That's good," Julien said. "People in families need to get along with each other."

194

"I don't know," Shannon said. "I think it's all over with me. Julien, do you realize that if I don't toughen up again, we'll probably wind up going to see her and Daddy in Jacksonville. They'll make us go to dinner at the country club. Daddy will probably try to make you take up golf. It's a terrible way to live, Julien."

"My parents are pretty bad, too," Julien said, "but we won't go to see them very often." He thought for a moment. "What do you think will happen to me when I go to work for the bank, Shannon? They might want me to play golf, too. I might even like it. I might turn out to be a nerd. Have you thought about that? I hope I didn't make a mistake going to business school."

"Oh, dear God," Shannon said and sighed. "That's awful to think about. Maybe we can work it out as long as you don't get religion."

The stewardess brought Julien more champagne. The lights went out, the movie started.

"Don't do that," Shannon said, trying to keep her voice low.

"You told me to stroke your thigh."

"That's not my thigh, Julien, and you know it."

"Isn't it nice?" Julien said. "I like you in slacks. I'm just beginning to discover the advantages of maternity clothes."

"Damn it, Julien, I won't be able to go to sleep. If you don't stop, I'm going to kill you."

"I know," Julien said. "I'm looking forward to it."